# GOLD EARRINGS

*To Joyce Shockley*
*In Him,*
*Diane E. Tatum*

# GOLD EARRINGS

A NOVEL

## DIANE E. TATUM

Tate Publishing & *Enterprises*

*Gold Earrings*
Copyright © 2011 by Diane E. Tatum. All rights reserved.

No part of this publication may be reproduced, stored in a retrieval system or transmitted in any way by any means, electronic, mechanical, photocopy, recording or otherwise without the prior permission of the author except as provided by USA copyright law.

Scripture quotations marked "NIV" are taken from the *Holy Bible, New International Version* ®, Copyright © 1973, 1978, 1984 by International Bible Society. Used by permission of Zondervan Publishing House. All rights reserved.

This novel is a work of fiction. Names, descriptions, entities, and incidents included in the story are products of the author's imagination. Any resemblance to actual persons, events, and entities is entirely coincidental.

The opinions expressed by the author are not necessarily those of Tate Publishing, LLC.

Published by Tate Publishing & Enterprises, LLC
127 E. Trade Center Terrace | Mustang, Oklahoma 73064 USA
1.888.361.9473 | www.tatepublishing.com

Tate Publishing is committed to excellence in the publishing industry. The company reflects the philosophy established by the founders, based on Psalm 68:11,
*"The Lord gave the word and great was the company of those who published it."*

Book design copyright © 2011 by Tate Publishing, LLC. All rights reserved.
*Cover design by Kristen Verser*
*Interior design by Sarah Kirchen*

Published in the United States of America

ISBN: 978-1-61777-574-1
1. Fiction / Christian / Historical
2. Fiction / Christian / Romance
11.06.13

This novel is dedicated to my family and
friends, who believed that publication
of this novel would occur:

To my husband, Ken, who loves me and
encouraged me to make writing my day job.

To my sons and their wives, Dan and Becca, Brad
and Julie, for their unconditional love and support.

To my mom and dad, who invested
in this book and in me.

To my high school friends who read
the short story way back then.

The LORD does not look at the things man looks at. Man looks at the outward appearance but the LORD looks at the heart.

1 Samuel 16:7 (NIV)

# TABLE OF CONTENTS

THE SETUP. . . . . . . . . . . . . . . . . . . . . . . 11

ARRIVAL IN ST. JOE. . . . . . . . . . . . . . . . . 19

GETTING TO KNOW YOU. . . . . . . . . . . . . . 29

THE CHAPLAIN AND THE CAPTAIN . . . . . . . 39

SUNDAY NIGHTMARE. . . . . . . . . . . . . . . . .49

QUILTING BEE . . . . . . . . . . . . . . . . . . . . . 59

TORNADO. . . . . . . . . . . . . . . . . . . . . . . . 69

REPAIRS. . . . . . . . . . . . . . . . . . . . . . . . . 81

BOX SUPPER NIGHT . . . . . . . . . . . . . . . . . 95

FOURTH OF JULY FAIR. . . . . . . . . . . . . . . 107

MYSTERIOUS SUSPECT . . . . . . . . . . . . . . . 121

HOPE CHEST SHOWER . . . . . . . . . . . . . . . 131

FASHION CONSULTANT TO ST. JOE . . . . . . . . 141

EDWARD'S SUGGESTIONS . . . . . . . . . . . . . 151

THE BARN RAISING . . . . . . . . . . . . . . . . 161

THE NIGHTMARE RETURNS . . . . . . . . . . . . 173

MEASLES . . . . . . . . . . . . . . . . . . . . . . 181

ANGEL OF MERCY . . . . . . . . . . . . . . . . . 193

FAREWELL . . . . . . . . . . . . . . . . . . . . . 205

GOING AWAY . . . . . . . . . . . . . . . . . . . 217

RESIGNATION . . . . . . . . . . . . . . . . . . . 225

WEDDING DAY . . . . . . . . . . . . . . . . . . . 239

BIBLIOGRAPHY . . . . . . . . . . . . . . . . . . . 249

# THE SETUP

Dr. Graves sank into the leather-upholstered desk chair. The early spring air was brisk on his stroll home from the Harvard Divinity School campus after a long and tiring day. Arguing theology with young, adamant, closed-minded divinity students became more and more exhausting these days. Pastoring seemed easy in comparison. Though pastoring hours were longer, at least one knew what good or ill had been accomplished at the end of each day. Teaching young theologians was much riskier. Who knew what each student might do in a church setting or on the mission field? Dr. Graves prayed that he not be held accountable for their brashness and arrogance after leaving school.

Dr. Graves pulled from his pocket the two letters the postmaster had handed him on his stroll home. He placed them side by side on the desk. One return address hailed from north Boston. The feminine hand proclaimed that the writer was his goddaughter, Angelina. He smiled at the thought of her.

"A lovely young lady," he said to the flickering gas lamps on the wall. The second return address was St. Joseph, Missouri. The big, bold hand announced regards from "The Reverend Jonathan Thomson of First Church, St. Joseph."

"Jonathan was always quite formal." He chuckled to himself. Jonathan had been one of his favorite students, a serious young man who had graduated just one term ago. "Another very stubborn, brilliant theology student."

"Which to open first?" he said.

Angelina won out as always. She was very special to him. From the time Madalaine Mercy had brought her to him for consecration and asked him to be her godfather, Angelina had held a piece of his heart. Angelina had been the daughter he had never had. This was one chance when Dr. Benjamin Graves had been able to affect one life to the good. Without a named father, raised in her mother's house of ill-repute, Angelina had turned into a butterfly. She was a beautiful, young Christian lady; a tall dark-haired angel on Earth. How he loved her, despite her family tree and circumstances of birth!

As Angelina's legal guardian, Dr. Graves also handled her growing trust funds, one set up by her mother and one set up by an Italian sea captain who claimed to be her father. It bothered him sometimes, handling the money Madalaine provided for the fund from her brothel. He rationalized that the money would go to a worthwhile cause when put into Angelina's hands on her eighteenth birthday in two weeks. The sea captain at least made his money honestly.

He turned the envelope over and broke the wax seal. The pages crackled as he opened the sheets to read.

> Dear Dr. Ben:
> As I'm sure you are aware, my eighteenth birthday will arrive in just over two weeks. As you know, I am no longer living at Mama's due to the unfortunate incident of more than a year ago. I hope to move to a place where no one would know of my past and could accept me as myself and not as Madalaine Mercy's daughter. Could you pray on the matter of a place where I could go?

Mama told me yesterday of a trust fund she had set up long ago with you as the guardian. I know you have safely and wisely invested the money. I plan to come to your home on Tuesday, the twenty-first, to arrange the transfer of the funds to my own account at Mr. Anderson's Bank of Boston.

Business aside, I want to thank you for your love during these eighteen years. Most of all I thank you for the religious training you provided, which led to my salvation in Jesus Christ. I trust that as I venture into a new world that He will guide me and provide for me a place where I can find human love and a proper home.

I look forward to seeing you on Tuesday. Give my love to Aunt Agatha as well.

Love in Christ,

Angelina

Dr. Graves looked at the April calendar on the wall. He marked the dates on the calendar. Angelina's birthday was on the twenty-eighth. Her visit would take place on the twenty-first. She surely knew how to handle money. The funds could be transferred easily on her birthday once the paperwork was complete. Today was the fourteenth. Only a week would pass before her visit. He'd have a week to pray and consider his advice to her. Perhaps New York City or Philadelphia would be good choices. She would have liked Richmond or Charleston if it hadn't been for that foolish war. Reconstruction was not yet much of a success in the South after all. The LORD would know the best plan. Dr. Graves knew to leave it up to Him.

Carefully setting Angelina's letter aside for Agatha to read later, he slit open Jonathan Thomson's letter. His powerful pen strokes jumped from the pages.

> Dear Dr. Graves,
>
> I wanted to let you know what the Lord has made of me so far. As you know, First Church, St. Joseph, has called me to their gospel ministry. I serve a faithful congregation of townsfolk, ranchers, and farmers.
>
> Unfortunately, sin abounds here on this western edge of civilization, with all those who pass through town heading west. I continue to hold the light of Christ high in this ever-growing part of the country.

Dr. Graves frowned and shook his head. Yes, Jonathan was a brilliant theologian, but had he not grasped the perspective of the entire Scripture? Could he still see the love of God for these sinners? What kind of theology saw only the responsibility of showing sinners God's purity without also showing them His love for them? Dr. Graves sighed deeply. It was just this kind of thing he feared day after day in the classroom. He continued to read:

> I am anticipating the bonds of matrimony after a proper and suitable courtship. The woman in question is a Miss Alice Bardsley. She is pretty, after a fashion. She is companionable enough and persistant in her affections. Her father is influential in St. Joe, and, therefore, a marriage to her could bring some of the stragglers into the church through the family's influence. She seems to have a few vices, gossip, and flirtatiousness among them. Marriage would do much to tame her in these areas.

Dr. Graves stood bolt upright, the chair crashing to the floor.

"What!" he bellowed. "What kind of a marriage is that?"

"Ben!" A female voice shouted from the other side of the closed study door. "Are you all right, dear?"

Dr. Graves strode to the study door quickly and opened it. He found his small, gray-haired wife there.

"I'm fine, Agatha," assured Dr. Graves. "I've merely had some astounding news from one of my former students."

He looked down at this gentle woman who had been his wife for these twenty-five years. Her brow furrowed in worry. His smile at her brought a smile to her lips, and they kissed.

"Dinner will be served shortly, Ben," she finally replied, when it became obvious that he would tell her no more. It had been this way when he was a pastor. She knew not to ask any more questions.

"I've had a note from Angelina as well," he told her with anticipation of her delight. "She sends her love to you too. She'll be here a week hence to transact some business related to her eighteenth birthday. We must celebrate with her while she is here."

"How lovely, dear," replied Mrs. Graves with enthusiasm.

"Not nearly as lovely as you are to me, my love," Dr. Graves replied affectionately. "I'll be to the table shortly."

He watched her go with a twinkle in his eye. *No, God did not intend us to merely have a companion and correct her vices,* he thought. *What utter nonsense!*

He closed the door, righted the chair, and picked up the letter from Jonathan he had tossed to the floor in his outrage. He completed reading the lines swiftly so as not the be late to his dinner date with his dear wife.

> And so, Dr. Graves, that is how it fares so far. I attempt to seek out the sinners and share with them the fear of God and hell so necessary to their salvation, and I hope to have found a suitable helpmate for my ministry in St. Joe. If you have suggestions, I am open to your insights into the ministry of a pastor. If you are ever in the Midwest, please feel free to stop in and see me.

I am ever so grateful for the instruction you gave me as my mentor and look forward to being of assistance to you in any way humanly possible.
Your humble servant,
Reverend Jonathan Thomson

*How alone that young man has been,* he thought. *Going to sea at fourteen after his parents' death and coming to divinity school after injury during that confounded war. He was then the oldest in a class of young college and divinity students. If only he had someone special to love and care for him,* Dr. Graves pondered. *Marriage to someone special would make him a better pastor too.*

The germ of thought fermented in the mind of Dr. Benjamin Graves at that moment. The inspiration grew. But would it be ethical?

"Ben!" Agatha called from the downstairs foyer. "Dinner's on!"

Taking another look at the two letters on his desk, he consigned the idea to after-dinner reflection and went downstairs to the meal.

---

Following dinner, Dr. Graves returned to the study. He quickly reread each of the letters.

*Could it be a coincidence that they arrived on the same day?* he reflected. *No, I don't believe in coincidence; only God incidents.*

Dr. Graves strode to the window and looked out at the lights of Boston in the distance. He pictured Angelina hard at work on the accounts at Martino's General Store. In his mind's eye, he saw her twinkling sapphire eyes and her long midnight hair as she used the brilliant mind God had given her.

He blinked and imagined the West he'd read about in the news. He pictured the tall, blond man he knew Jonathan to be, serving in the wilderness, alone.

*Then could it be the providence of God that has placed the lives of these two young people into my hands? Surely God does work in mysterious ways when He answers prayer,* he reminded himself. *I have often prayed for these two young people.*

With that thought, Dr. Graves crossed the room to the desk and prayed silently for a moment in the leather chair. Finally, he pulled two sheets of stationery, the ink bottle, and a pen from the top drawer of the desk and began to compose two letters.

# ARRIVAL IN ST. JOE

Early sunlight glimmers peeked through the parsonage window, awakening the Reverend Jonathan Thomson as it did every morning.

"Thank you, Lord, for another day to serve you," he prayed with cheerfulness.

The pastor of First Church, St. Joseph, Missouri, rose from his bed. He stretched and bent to relieve the creaks and stiffness of yet another night of compacting his too-tall frame on the too-short brass bed. Satisfied that his joints all operated properly, he arranged the covers in precise movements. Retrieving a dropped sock from the floor, he frowned at his own lapse in orderliness.

His large hands dipped into the water in the washstand bowl. The sunburn he'd received the day before welcomed the cool splash. The smell of shaving soap heralded another day as he peered into the shaving mirror he had received as a graduation gift from Dr. Graves, his mentor at Harvard.

"Remember, Jonathan, the importance of looking yourself in the mirror each and every day," Dr. Graves had said on its presentation. "The best advice I can give you now is to test yourself each morning. If you can no longer look yourself in the mirror, you need to get right with another person, with God, or, more than likely, with both."

Each morning Jonathan remembered Dr. Graves's words. Jonathan carefully avoided the need to test the mirror by reconciling all his relationships before nightfall. This morning was no different, as he used his straight razor to meticulously shave his ruddy face.

Jonathan winced as he pulled on the crisply pressed, white linen shirt over his broad sunburned back. The collar scratched the tender skin on the back of his neck. Frowning, he loosened the collar and tied his tie loosely.

"I knew I shouldn't have removed my shirt while up on the Greenes's roof yesterday," he said aloud to the man in the shaving mirror. "Thank you, LORD, for giving me strength to actively participate in these kinds of projects."

He remembered many other younger divinity students who would have watched from the shade of the nearest tree and recalled the gratitude of the new farmer for the community's help in completing his young family's home.

He took another look in the mirror, combing back the tousled, golden hair.

"Yes, definitely time to visit Henry before Miss Mercy arrives today," he announced to the mirror before storing it carefully in its soft pouch.

He picked up the list from the dresser and quickly added "Barber" to the list of jobs to complete.

"Job and living quarters for Miss Mercy, check," read Jonathan aloud. "Better check with Mr. Crabtree anyway to be sure he hasn't changed his mind about that bookkeeping job at the store and the living arrangements." He added "Crabtree's" to the growing list.

"Greet the train at three thirty this afternoon. Ask Jedadiah to carry Miss Mercy's things to Crabtree's. Show Miss Mercy the town. Dinner at the Bardsleys' with Miss Mercy at seven tomorrow evening."

He quickly scribbled "Visit with Todd Valentine concerning his mother's illness" and "Check roses for aphids."

Pulling his coat from the rack, he caught sight of the tintype of Alice Bardsley. Her petite face, with its mocking smile, stared back at him. How right Dr. Graves had been about Alice, even all the way from Boston. Hot blood rushed to his already red face when he thought of Dr. Graves's chastisement.

"Never marry any woman in the hopes of changing her, Jonathan," the note had read. "Only marry the woman the Lord provides. You'll know her as soon as the Lord introduces you to her. Before she is the pastor's wife for the community, she must first be your wife. Don't forget to love her."

Thoughts of marrying Alice ended after Dr. Graves's note had arrived. He reached for the tintype and turned it facedown in the top drawer. That same note had told of Dr. Graves's ward, Angelina Mercy, and her plan to relocate to St. Joe. Dr. Graves had solemnly charged him with caring for her in his stead. Jonathan gladly agreed.

He pulled his jacket on, removed imaginary lint from the sleeve, and set out to the rose garden in the churchyard. After inspecting the roses for insects and blight, he strode off to his quiet place beside the river to commune with the Lord and read Scripture.

The sun was higher in the sky by the time Jonathan had returned to town, following his quiet time and his visit with Todd and his mother.

"'Morning, preacher," muttered the crusty Mr. Crabtree. "Your young lady bookkeeper due in today?"

*Skepticism was second nature to Mr. Crabtree*, noted Jonathan. "Yes, sir, Mr. Crabtree. Are your room and job still available for Miss Mercy?"

"For a trial basis, they are," he reminded Jonathan of the terms of their agreement. "Like an apple and a *Gazette*, Preacher?"

Jonathan pulled coins from his pocket and purchased the apple and the daily paper, his usual fare.

"She'll be here this afternoon."

The bell announced his exit.

"Check." He marked his list.

"Good morning, Pastor," said Henry from behind the barber's chair. "Time for another trim?"

"Yes, sir, Henry." Jonathan removed his coat and carefully hung it on a hook near the door. "Just needs a little off around the edges."

"No one in town cares as much about the look of their hair as you do, Pastor. You're good for business, but you never let me shave you. You know, it wouldn't cost you any more."

"Henry, a man ought to be able to look in the mirror and do some jobs for himself. I'm just not handy with scissors, though." Jonathan laughed, as he thought about Dr. Graves's advice again. "The Lord's servant represents Him. The way I look may affect the way His people view God."

"Well, I never saw a preacher with muscles like a farmhand before," replied Henry. "But it's easier to picture the power of the Almighty that way."

They both laughed as Henry began the trim.

"Remind me of this lady you're babysitting for that professor of yours," commented Henry.

"She's his ward, and she's coming here to start a new life for herself," replied Jonathan. "I'm not babysitting, Henry. You know a woman has no place in the West without a suitable escort. I'm merely protector and provider until she's settled in."

"What's her name again?"

"Angelina Mercy. She arrives today on the three thirty train."

By three twenty-five, Jonathan had arrived at the train station. He glanced at his pocket watch and looked at the eastern horizon.

"You don't really expect the train to be on time, do you, Preacher?" called a voice from the opposite end of the platform.

"Jedadiah Johnson," called Jonathan. "I knew I could count on you to remember Miss Mercy's arrival. Thanks for your strong back."

"Preacher, you could've hauled that trunk to Crabtree's yourself if you'd worn work clothes instead of fancy preaching duds. I'd be happy to escort Miss Mercy around town for you. Any new woman in St. Joe is interesting to me."

"No, Jed, that pleasure's all mine. Guess we'll have a wait until she's here."

"That's right," confirmed the depot master. "The train is late again. Hope there's been no outlaw trouble."

Jonathan settled his tall frame onto the bench next to Jedadiah. Under the shade from the blistering June sun, they shared the *Gazette* as they waited companionably for the train.

"Three thirty-five!" Angelina snapped the watch closed. "I hope Reverend Thomson isn't annoyed at the train being late."

She smoothed the black, curling tendrils back into place from her damp face. A glance out the dusty window revealed no major change in the landscape since Hannibal that morning. Small towns and stops at Monroe City, Brookfield, and Chillicothe broke up the early grain fields of green. Her gold earrings sparkled in the summer sunlight and danced to the rhythm of the bumpy ride. She rearranged her dusty skirts.

"Excuse me," she said to the older lady beside her. "I'm terribly tired of this train, aren't you?"

The lady only grunted an answer. Angelina fell back into her own thoughts. She pulled her bag closer to her and examined the contents once more.

First, she drew out her most recent letter from Dr. Ben.

"Reverend Jonathan Thomson of St. Joe Church has agreed to find employment and lodging for you in St. Joseph, Missouri. As a former student of mine, I think you'll find him admirable and of good character. You can trust him, Angelina. He shares your love for the sea. Before divinity school, he spent a term in the Union Navy. He's not your average young pastor."

*Dr. Ben's word was as good as gospel*, she thought.

Second, she drew out a letter from the reverend himself.

"Dr. Graves informed me of your bookkeeping and retailing experience," wrote Rev. Thomson. "I have procured a trial position for you at Crabtree's General Store. His back room is available to you as long as you hold the job. I'll be on the platform when the train arrives unless the LORD's work pulls me away. If I cannot be there, count on Jedadiah Johnson to meet you. Nevertheless, I'll be at your service as long as you need assistance in becoming acclimated to St. Joe."

*How efficient*, thought Angelina. *I wonder how I'll know either one of them when I see them.*

Third, she pulled her bank books from the bag and examined the sizable balances and letter of credit from the Bank of Boston.

*For emergency use only,* she reminded herself. *I'll make it on my own without Mama's tainted money or Captain Michael's generosity.*

Fourth, she pulled her well-worn Bible from the bag.

Lord, *help me to begin a new life without the encumbrances of Mama's past,* she prayed. *Help me find Christian friends, protection from the nightmares of the past, and love from a good Christian man. Let this be my place. Help me find a way to serve You there.*

She began to read the familiar pages to pass the time. So involved was she that when the engineer blew a long series of whistles to announce their arrival in St. Joseph, she started. From the window she could see the beginnings of a town.

*It certainly doesn't rival Chicago,* thought Angelina ruefully.

Chicago reminded her of Boston with its lakefront activity and many shops and businesses. People bustled about in Chicago. It seemed like home. St. Joe looked like a boomtown in the wilderness by comparison.

The train screeched into the station at four thirty, according to Angelina's timepiece.

A whole hour late. She sighed. Reverend Thomson had probably left by now.

The older lady struggled to be first from the coach, blocking her view of the depot.

"Good afternoon," a deep voice said as the lady received help down the steps.

The lady grunted to the man who slowly came into view. Angelina caught her breath at his height, obvious strength, impeccable dress, and sheer beauty.

*I'll have to find out who this man is soon,* she noted, as she waited her turn to disembark.

The man frowned slightly.

"Are these all your passengers, sir?" he asked the conductor.

"No, sir," answered Angelina.

Her long legs felt wobbly after sitting for so long. She missed the first step, and her bag tumbled to the platform as she fell. The handsome man caught her and placed her gently onto the platform.

His strong arms and gentle touch sent a shock through her all the way to her toes.

"Let me help you, ma'am," replied the man as he gathered the contents of her bag that had spilled.

As he stood and handed her the bag, she noticed he was still taller than she. That wasn't true with most men. She looked up into his deep blue eyes, questioning.

"Reverend Thomson, ma'am," Jonathan answered the unspoken question of the lovely woman. "You must be Angelina Mercy."

"Yes, Reverend," stammered Angelina. "I am."

She took the offered bag with embarrassment. He looked at her and grinned a lopsided smile.

"Call me Jonathan," he said. "I'm sure Dr. Graves wouldn't mind."

"Good afternoon, ma'am," called a young man's voice. "I'm Jedadiah Johnson. I'll take your trunk to Crabtree's in my wagon."

Angelina saw that the voice belonged to a good-looking man with a deep rancher's tan. His Stetson perched cockily on his dark hair. She looked him straight in the eye, noting that he was as tall as she and perhaps a year or so older.

"Miss Mercy," said Jonathan, "Jedadiah Johnson. Jed, meet Angelina Mercy of Boston."

"Pleased to meet you, ma'am." He swept his Stetson from its perch as he took her hand and kissed it graciously. "If I can show you any of St. Joe, just let me know." He grinned at Jonathan.

"Thank you, Jedadiah," she replied with a laugh. "I will certainly call on you." Her smile lit up the prairie as her gold earrings danced in the bright afternoon sun. "Please call me Angelina."

"What kind of name is that?" asked Jedadiah playfully. "Sounds foreign."

"My mother is Italian," she replied. "It means 'little angel.'"

"Has she seen you lately?" said Jedadiah with a laugh. "I'm six foot tall and you're nearly as tall as me. The angel part, though, I can figure."

Jonathan tensed, waiting for her reaction to Jed's rudeness. He relaxed when she laughed with Jed.

"Miss Mercy," called the baggage man, "is this your trunk?"

"Yes, sir," she called back. "Please release it into Mr. Johnson's care." She turned back to Jedadiah and said, "Thank you for your refreshing honesty and your willingness to haul my belongings. Let me know if I can ever help you with something."

"Preacher," Jedadiah said with exaggeration, "I'm in love. Keep all other comers away as you show her the town. I'll haul her trunk anywhere, even to the Johnson ranch, if she'll let me."

"She's my responsibility first, Jed," Jonathan replied playfully. Taking her arm in his, he said, "Let me show you north St. Joseph, Angelina, and buy you dinner at our best hotel."

---

By the time they had eaten dinner and arrived at Crabtree's General Store, Angelina had no idea who anyone was or what their names were. Finally, she saw someone she recognized lounging on Crabtree's porch.

"Thank you again, Jedadiah, for bringing my trunk here," she said.

"Lovely lady," replied the man on the porch, "I'd do anything for you. Just tell me your name, and I'll tell you mine."

Confused, she gripped Jonathan's arm a little tighter.

"Jonathan, isn't this Jedadiah?" she asked quietly.

"Angelina, meet Joshua Johnson," Jonathan said. "Joshua, Angelina Mercy."

Joshua stood and bowed flamboyantly. "At your service. No doubt you've already met my brother. Yes, we're twins. He's older and more responsible; I'm younger and incorrigible. People have no trouble telling us apart."

Angelina sighed. "Jonathan, I think I've met too many people for one day. They're beginning to look alike."

The threesome entered Crabtree's, laughing.

# GETTING TO KNOW YOU

Laughter ended abruptly as the threesome came face to face with a grisly-looking man.

"Mr. Crabtree," greeted Jonathan. He extended his hand. The older man took it grudgingly, for the shortest time possible.

"Is this my employee you've finally brought by?" he inquired gruffly. "Jedadiah brought her trunk by hours ago, unlike this loiterer on my stoop." He gestured toward Joshua with disgust.

"I told you I was the incorrigible one," whispered Joshua in Angelina's ear.

She giggled despite herself. "Angelina Mercy, sir," she introduced herself to cover her slip and extended her hand.

"The job is temporary. I hope the pastor explained that to you. I refuse to hire anyone without a trial period. You can use the room behind the store as long as I employ you. The room has its own cookstove and an entrance onto the alley in back. I require bookkeeping as well as clerking from time to time. Inventory is required by tomorrow night. You can start work in the morning. The store opens at nine and closes at six. Be up and dressed in time to unlock the door. Mrs. Crabtree and I live upstairs if you require anything more."

Angelina's mouth gaped open as Mr. Crabtree marched to the stairway behind the counter and ascended the stairs.

"Oh, and one more thing. Keep a strict curfew. You should always be in the store by nine in the evening. I frown on sleepy employees."

"And on everyone else, it seems," was her curt reply after he left. "Or is it just me?"

"No, ma'am," assured Joshua Johnson. "He always frowns on me. But he loves my brother Jed. Jed sometimes makes deliveries for him for credit on the Johnson account."

"I hope this works out, Angelina," Jonathan said. "Let me know if you need anything." He showed her the door to her room. "Sleep well and spend tomorrow settling in. I'll pick you up at six thirty for dinner at the Bardsleys' tomorrow evening."

"Thank you, Jonathan, for all your help." She smiled a dazzling smile. Her gold earrings caught the lamp glow, adding sparkle to her sapphire eyes.

Jonathan's heart skipped a beat as he kissed her hand and turned to go.

Angelina awakened early, excited by the new day ahead. She opened her trunk and sorted through the clothing and belongings. She placed cotton nightgowns and lingerie in the second drawer of the nightstand beside the bed. She slipped her worn Bible into the top drawer with her combs and brushes. The rest of her clothing hung in the wardrobe on the far wall. Folded fabric and lace that her mother and Captain Michael sent with her she placed at the bottom of the trunk. She withdrew the letters and bankbooks from her traveling bag and slipped them into a hidden pocket of the trunk. Locking the clasp, she slipped the key onto a silver chain that hung around her neck.

Satisfied with her housekeeping, she sat back onto the bed and brushed her midnight hair with the silver brush until it glowed. With swift, adept movements, she twisted and twirled her silken, long hair into a high French-braided twist and fastened it with a comb. She then withdrew the Bible to spend time with the Lord on this first day in St. Joe.

"Lord, continue to bless me. Help me to make the right impression on the townspeople I meet today. Make me into your servant. Thank you for Jonathan and the Johnson twins."

Angelina entered the store through the inner door from her room. She inhaled the familiar general store aroma of cinnamon and lemon mingled with lamp oil and wheel grease. Brightly colored candy waited for children in clean, clear jars. Flour, sugar, crackers, and pickles stood in huge barrels on the floor. A cheese wheel sat on the counter. Jerky hung from the ceiling. Vibrant bolts of fabric lined one wall. Lace, ribbon, and other notions decorated the shelf below the fabric.

The store looked and smelled like Martino's in Boston. It felt like home.

At nine o'clock sharp, she unlocked Crabtree's front door.

Curious women immediately confronted her as they rushed into the store.

"Hello, I'm Angelina Mercy," she said. "How can I help you?"

She heard Mr. Crabtree creak down the stairs. At least she wasn't alone.

"Hi, I'm Mrs. Johnson, Jed and Josh's mother." The short, portly woman looked nothing like her tall, handsome twin sons.

"Jedadiah said I must meet you. He's smitten with you already. To hear Josh and him speak, you're an angel from heaven. I see what they mean. I'd like a spool of thread and a needle."

Angelina blushed and realized she had no idea where anything was. "What color thread do you need, Mrs. Johnson?"

"Oh, any color will do. I mean, white, please."

Mr. Crabtree showed her the needlework supplies, and Angelina sold her a spool of white thread and a plated needle.

The next woman refused Mr. Crabtree's help until Mrs. Johnson had finished.

"Hello, I'm Mrs. Jones. My husband's the sheriff. I need an onion."

The plain-faced woman blushed at her small purchase as Angelina rang it up.

And so it went all day. It seemed that every woman in St. Joseph needed the smallest of purchases today. Each introduced herself and took a good look at St. Joe's newest resident.

By noon, inventory had barely begun. Jonathan Thomson entered the store.

"Mr. Crabtree, have you saved me a *Gazette*?" he asked. "Angelina, how is it going?"

Mr. Crabtree pulled the daily paper from under the counter.

"Fine, Jonathan, but the tiny purchases every woman in town needs today are driving me to distraction!"

"Everyone wants a look at you, Angelina. Even though St. Joe is growing, it's still like a small town in many ways. Everyone knows everything."

The bell rang again as a petite blonde entered the store and slipped her hand in the crook of Jonathan's arm.

"Jonathan, dear, how fortunate I ran into you. I can't wait to see you this evening. Perhaps your ward will hit it off with dear Edward, and we'll have the evening to ourselves."

Jonathan pulled away from her grasp and turned, blushing, to face Angelina.

"Angelina, meet Alice Bardsley. Alice, Angelina Mercy."

"Pleased to finally meet you. Jonathan's told us so much about you. I look forward to dining with you this evening. Come, Jonathan, let's walk together and see where that takes us."

"Alice," he whispered, "Please stop making these scenes. We have nothing to talk about except your walk with Christ."

"Oh, I'm so sorry, Jonathan," she said. "I keep forgetting it's our little secret. Ta-ta." With a slight wave, Alice whisked out of the store.

"She's so exasperating," commented a female voice.

A not-too-plump, brown-haired girl stood behind Jonathan. She flicked her brown braid over her shoulder, her brown eyes flashing.

"Always, Sarah, always," replied Jonathan with a sigh. "I need to go now, Angelina, but I'll be back at six thirty."

*Gazette* in hand, he exited the store. Sarah grinned at Angelina.

"What a handsome guy, huh? I'm Sarah Jones."

"Let me think, your mother was in here earlier for an onion, right?"

"A stupid purchase. Mom raises onions in her garden. Probably has a million of them in the cellar. Everyone in town is determined to find out for themselves whether Alice was right or not."

"Alice? Right about me? She barely even looked at me."

The pretty, rounded girl gave her a look of disbelief.

"Listen, Angie, don't be naive. She'll get you then. She's been saying the worst things about you for months. Ever since Jonathan let us know you were coming, she's been spreading interesting stories about you. Don't ever let your guard down around her."

"Why would she do that when she doesn't even know me?"

Gold Earrings | 33

"She's afraid you'll take Jonathan," Sarah stated firmly. "They courted for a while until Jonathan called it off. I think he finally got wise about her. She's a gossip and immoral."

"Sarah!"

"It's true. Mary Taylor caught her with Joshua Johnson one day in the groves on the bluff. I don't know what they do in Boston, but here that's called fornication. Immoral. But you sure caught her off guard. She's been telling anyone who'll listen that you're short, fat, and ugly or that you're pregnant and disgraced. Gossip. Pure and simple. One look at you proves her dead wrong, though. You're about as un-short, un-fat, and un-ugly as they come. And there's no way you could be pregnant with that figure. What I'd give for those curves."

Angelina blushed. "Sarah Jones, is there anything you won't say to a stranger?"

"No. I think we'll hit it off well, as long as you stay away from Edward Bardsley, Alice's brother."

"Why, Sarah?" asked Angelina.

"The Bardsleys have lots of money. I aim to turn Edward's head and marry me some of it. So we'll be great friends if you stay away from him."

"Miss Mercy, a little more work and a little less gossip, if you please," called Mr. Crabtree from the hardware section.

"Friends," said Angelina. "I don't think I'll even notice Edward tonight."

"Good," confirmed Sarah. "Jonathan needs a tall, beautiful Christian woman."

They giggled as Sarah left.

Six thirty came sooner than she had expected, with the inventory still incomplete. She dressed in her best royal blue dress, recombed her hair in a formal fashion, and chose a hat to wear with it. While she waited for Jonathan to arrive, she continued to count the endless piece goods, notions, and accessories. Mr. Crabtree worked in the grocery items.

The bell rang as Jonathan entered the store in his finest black suit and waistcoat.

"Don't be late, Miss Mercy. I'll depend on you to finish if I'm not done by nine," cautioned Mr. Crabtree.

"Yes, sir," she replied as she took Jonathan's extended elbow.

The Bardsley home was the newest and finest mansion in St. Joe. Never had Angelina seen such elegance. Alice possessed Jonathan from the moment they arrived. Alice sat next to her father, Charles Edward Bardsley II. He puffed at his cigar as he waited for the servants to serve dinner. His broad face seemed set in a permanent sneer. His spreading midsection betrayed the wealth of his position, as did the handsome suit that girded it. Kate Bardsley, his wife, sat at the opposite end of the table to direct the service. She sat straight and composed, with her dress and hair in perfect order. Her face was soft and beautiful, warm and friendly. Jonathan sat between Kate Bardsley and Alice. Angelina sat across the table from Alice with Edward Bardsley at her side. Edward Bardsley dressed distinctly and perfectly. His hair was jet black. His dark eyes seemed to have no color at all.

*Do I know this man? Why does he frighten me so?* thought Angelina, when introduced to Edward.

"You are indeed charming," said Edward over the soup course. "You're not at all what I expected. Give me permission to call on you in the future."

"Oh, Edward," said Alice. "She's a career woman. She'll have no time for frivolous entertainments with any man. Tell me, Angelina, where did you get such unusual earrings?"

Gold earrings caught the candlelight of the formal candelabra as she looked to Jonathan for help. Jonathan's heart caught in his throat.

"Yes," he encouraged. "Please do tell us about them."

"My mother pierced my ears when I was an infant and placed small gold rings in them. As I grew, she replaced them with increasingly larger hoops. On my thirteenth birthday, she gifted me with these golden rings. A jeweler welded them at the seam to create a seamless ring. They've never been removed since."

"That sounds like a gypsy custom," said Edward suspiciously.

"My mother is Italian, not a gypsy. It is a family custom."

"They are beautiful, Angelina," replied Mrs. Bardsley. "They suit you well. They give an exotic look to your natural beauty."

Alice fumed at the end of the table.

"Jonathan, tell us the story again about your term in the Union Navy. You know, when the Confederates sank your ship, the *Congress*, and so many men died. Weren't you injured?"

"Yes, Alice," Jonathan wearily replied. "I've told this story too many times, Alice. Your parents are no doubt tired of it."

"I never tire of hearing how our men in gray defeated a Union ship in Hampton Roads," declared Mr. Bardsley. "Politics and reconstruction make odd bedfellows, aye Jonathan? Having a Harvard-educated Union officer for a pastor gives me an advantage with the Radical Republicans in Jeff City."

"Wasn't it the *Merrimac* that blew your ship out of the water, Jon?" Alice persisted.

"Alice, the ship was the *Merrimac* when it belonged to the Union. When captured and ironclad, they renamed her the *Virginia*. Yes, I escaped with my life to Newport News. Others weren't so fortunate."

Jonathan looked across the table at his guest. Her eyes riveted to his in horror and awe. Suddenly, he was not ashamed of the story anymore, knowing that she was a Yankee like himself.

"The *Congress* fought valiantly before striking her colors, Angelina. She was towed to the shoals off Newport News and continued to fire upon the ironclad monster until the fire and carnage on board was too much. She exploded after a mighty fight. The Union should be proud of her effort."

"I think dessert would be best served without bloodshed, Reverend," pointed out Edward. He yawned to show his sudden boredom with the story and with the Union pastor. He had watched with disgust the interest Angelina and Jonathan had in each other. *If only he knew what I know about her*, he thought. *That can wait for another day, however.*

After dessert the group retired to the parlor for coffee. Edward opened the desk drawer and drew out a finely crafted gun case.

"Jonathan, as a former navy man, tell me your opinion on my latest acquisition."

Jonathan joined Edward at the desk. Edward opened the case to display a small, double-barreled pistol.

"It's a Remington forty-one caliber, double-barreled derringer."

"It's a nice piece, Edward," Jonathan said, inspecting the pistol. "Two shots instead of one is a nice feature. They're not known for accuracy at long range, however."

"Maybe not, Jonathan. If I intend to shoot anyone, however, it will be at a close distance, I can assure you," Edward replied darkly. "See how easily it can be concealed?" He slipped the derringer into his pocket. "Deadly at close range," he said with a cold smile.

"With a rifled forty-one, I'm sure you could blow a good-size hole in whatever you shot," Jonathan agreed grimly.

---

As time came to depart, Edward caught Angelina's elbow at the bottom of the stairwell.

"We've met before. Don't you remember?"

His voice frightened her, and his grip on her elbow tightened as she shook her head.

"You may not remember now, but it would be in your best interest that we meet again soon."

"Are you ready, Angelina?" Jonathan's blond head poked around the corner of the foyer. He noticed Edward release his grip on Angelina's arm and Angelina's frightened look.

"Yes, Jonathan, I need to be in soon to help Mr. Crabtree with the inventory."

"I'll call on you soon, with your permission," said Edward. His dark undertone threatened her, though.

"I need to get settled in first, Edward," Angelina replied as sweetly as possible. "You'll need to give me a little time."

Jonathan relaxed as Angelina took his arm, and they headed out into the dusk.

# THE CHAPLAIN AND THE CAPTAIN

"Tell me about the Bardsleys, Jonathan."

Moonlight lit their path as Jonathan walked Angelina home from the Bardsleys'.

"Well, they're the most prominent citizens in town. Mr. Bardsley owns the mortgage on most of the farms around St. Joe," answered Jonathan cautiously.

"I gather you're nearly engaged to Alice," questioned Angelina, squinting to catch his reaction in the silvery light.

"That was true at one time. Dr. Graves advised me to reconsider my intentions toward her."

"What does that mean?" asked Angelina incredulously. "Either you love her, or you don't!"

"It's not that simple," replied Jonathan quietly.

"Explain it to me, if you can."

"Most frontier churches don't pay a full-time minister. Most preachers serve as lay ministers. Even though St. Joe is quickly changing from a frontier town to an urban center, congregations still resent the burden of a preacher's salary." He hesitated.

"Go on," she encouraged.

"Charles Bardsley mounted the effort to bring a seminary trained minister to First Church. Edward was part of the search committee that approached me at Harvard. The Bardsleys contribute the money to pay my salary."

"Where does Alice fit in?"

"I thought perhaps she'd make a good pastor's wife here. With her father's influence …"

"And money," interjected Angelina.

"Yes, and his money, I felt I could attract the townspeople to the church who had never come before. I planned to bring people to the LORD through his influence."

"That's poppycock!" exclaimed Angelina. "Oh, I'm so sorry."

"No, don't be sorry," replied Jonathan. "Dr. Graves said the same thing. In fact he said more than that. He thought I should give it some time and marry only for love."

Angelina smiled. "Dr. Graves is a wise man. I wonder if he planned to do a little matchmaking on the side too."

Jonathan grinned back at her sheepishly and ran his large hand through his blonde hair. "I had the same feeling when you fell off the train yesterday afternoon. Would that be such a horrible thing?"

Angelina laughed and pulled her hat from her head, setting free the mass of black curls into the starlight and bluff breeze. The moonlight glimmered on her gold earrings. "Yes, Dr. Graves is a very wise man, indeed. Why did you leave the navy to enter divinity school?"

"Actually, what Alice failed to tell of the story was that God called me to the ministry when I was fourteen years old during a tent meeting. That same year my parents died when the house burned on their farm outside of Concord, Massachusetts."

"What happened to you then?"

"I was bitter. Why would God do this to me? So I sold the farm and banked the proceeds for seminary—at a later time. Like Jonah, I signed aboard a merchant ship and went to sea."

"Did you know Captain Michael de Angelo?"

"Yes, I was his cabin boy on my first voyage. Later I served as his first mate on the *Madalaine*. Why?"

"He's a close friend," she replied cautiously. *He may even be my father*, she thought.

"Anyway, I returned to Boston as the war was breaking out and tried to sign up with the navy," he continued. "But I was too tall. They tried to convince me to try the marines, but I refused to shoot young boys."

Angelina winced at his tone of derision.

"When the recruiting officer found out about my sea experience, he asked me to sign on as chaplain on the *USS Congress* just to get me on board to help the commanding officers handle a green crew. You heard the rest tonight. So you see, I'm a modern day Jonah."

"A Jonah?" she questioned as they strolled closer to Crabtree's.

"I ran away from God. As the *Virginia* destroyed the *Congress* and people died all around me, I knew how Jonah felt in the midst of the raging storm before he pleaded with them to throw him overboard." Jonathan choked back the overwhelming emotion he felt as he relived the scene. "As I watched the *Congress* explode from the camp at Newport News, I knew I had no more excuses. Injured and discharged, I finally returned to Boston to answer His call."

The lights at Crabtree's were out when they walked companionably up to the front door. He caught her hands as she turned to go in.

"Angelina, I hope you'll let me call on you frequently. And not just as your surrogate guardian."

"Jonathan, that would be wonderful," Angelina said quietly.

Gently, Jonathan bent and kissed her hand.

"I'll check on you tomorrow, Angel. Good night."

It had been such a beautiful walk home. After Jonathan left her, the river compelled her to come and sit on its loess bluffs. Below her, the water lapped the banks. Moonlight reflected on the moving surface like a million lanterns shining the way for unseen travelers. A soft breeze stirred the silent night. On the other side of the wide Missouri River lay the Kansas territory. Beyond that shore was the Western frontier. Visions of Indians, horses, cattle drives, and pioneers filled her imagination. Twenty years ago, gold drew courageous people across this river into that vast unsettled land beyond Missouri. Tonight, the wide Missouri and Angelina were alone.

Angelina sighed and longed for the busyness of Boston harbor. She missed the tall-masted ships, the bustling sailors, and the unloading of cargo from around the world. The waters of the Atlantic called to her to contemplate the Lord's grandeur. Tonight she came into His presence in prayer as well.

Questions flooded her mind. She smiled as she thought of her tall, blond guardian. She felt the stirrings of a kindred spirit with this servant of the Lord.

"What possible relationship with the Reverend Jonathan Thomson do you have planned for me, Lord?" she prayed. "Is being a pastor's wife what You want for me?"

She laughed at the thought. *What a sense of humor God must have to plan a marriage between the daughter of a bordello madame and a minister!*

"What about the Bardsleys? What kind of people are they? Why does Alice hate me so? Am I her rival? What of Edward? Why does he make me feel so frightened? Is their power so overwhelming to cause people to give up everything to do their bidding? What will they require of me? Of Jonathan?" Angelina shuddered, though the June evening was warm.

Night birds answered her petitions. She felt the LORD's peace descend on her. No matter what happened, she knew she was where God wanted her.

Angelina quietly shut the store door, catching the bell before it rang to wake up Mr. Crabtree. She knew just how late it was and hated for anyone else to also know how late she had stayed out after Jonathan had walked her home from dinner at the Bardsleys'.

As she turned around, Mr. Crabtree appeared, arms crossed across his nightshirt.

"So you've finally come in from your rabble rousing, have you?" he accused. "Didn't I tell you earlier there was work to do prior to opening in the morning?"

"Yes, sir, I'm sorry sir."

The clock chimed twelve thirty.

"Well, you'll just have to stay up and do the work anyway," he stated. "I need you to inventory the rock candy jar tonight. A new shipment is due in tomorrow on the train, and I need an accurate count of each piece prior to dumping the new batch in."

Angelina couldn't believe her ears. Count every piece of rock candy in that five gallon jar! Surely he was kidding! Why couldn't it wait until tomorrow or Monday?

"Yes, sir, Mr. Crabtree," she replied, hoping he'd soften and tell her to go on to bed.

"See to it you get every piece too!" he answered sharply as he turned to go. "That should teach you to wander about unescorted at any hour of the night!"

"Yes, sir, Mr. Crabtree."

As Angelina began to count the pieces of rock candy in the big glass jar, she muttered, "What a crab!"

It's been a long time since dinner, her stomach reminded her. *It's been a long time since I've had fresh crab too,* she thought hungrily.

The last time she'd had crab had been with Captain Michael de Angelo the previous summer. In the shadow of his clipper, the *Madalaine*, they pulled in crab pots set the day before and rowed to a protected cove. There on the cool beach, they boiled their catch. In the setting sun, they cracked the shells and pulled out the succulent meat, tossing the scraps to the ever-present seagulls swooping down from overhead.

"How is our catch tonight, Angelina?" questioned Captain de Angelo.

"Delicious, as always, Captain Michael," replied Angelina congenially.

Captain Michael, as she'd always called him, was her mother's lover and dearest friend. They'd grown up together in Italy. He sailed his merchant ship into Boston frequently to be near Madalaine Mercy. Tall and dark, he was a dashing sea captain. When in Boston, he always spent time with Angelina. They might take a midnight row in his captain's dinghy. Or he might welcome her aboard the *Madalaine* for dinner and stories of the sea. Yes, of all the men in her life, Captain Michael was her favorite. His visits were too brief and far between.

As they enjoyed the last rays of daylight, Angelina gazed into his dark eyes, framed by his bushy, black eyebrows, mustache, and beard.

"You're awfully quiet tonight, Captain Michael," ventured Angelina.

"You're right, Angelina," he replied merrily. "Much too quiet with so much to say, my little angel."

She tossed back her hair and smoothed the tangles back away from the wind and settled back against some driftwood. She waited expectantly for him to begin another adventure story or a tattling story of her mother's youth.

"Soon you will be eighteen years old. Soon you will have a home of your own and a husband. What does your mother tell you about your father, Angelina?" he asked.

She looked into the fire as the darkness grew complete. She shuddered involuntarily against the cool ocean breeze and pulled her shawl around her.

"Come, come, little one," he encouraged. "Surely you have been curious, my love."

"Mama says she doesn't know. He could have been one of many men," she stammered, embarrassed.

"And who are these men, these candidates for paternity?"

"Well, Mr. Martino, the store owner where I live and work for one," she suggested. "But I don't think it's him."

"Why not?"

"Well, he's very nice. And he did take me in when that trouble happened at Mama's house. But all his children have brown eyes. All of Mama's family has brown eyes too. My eyes are blue," she stated matter-of-factly, as though by the light of the fire the captain could miss the stunning brilliance of her sapphire eyes.

"Who else then?"

"Mr. Anderson, the banker," she supplied.

"What of him?"

"Well," she began, "he's very nice to me, and he taught me how to handle money, and he allowed me to work as a teller whenever he was short of employees in his bank. But he's not my father."

"Why not him?"

"He's too short. I'm very tall. Mama's not as tall as I am, and Mr. Anderson is shorter than us both!" She giggled at the sight they would make as a family.

"Who else?"

Angelina was glad the dark hid her deep blush. She trusted Captain Michael with her very life. Could she trust him with the rest of her musings?

"Angelina," the captain prodded. He rubbed her back. At forty, his strength was as great as a younger man. His great tenderness toward her surpassed his strength.

Her earrings flashed as she turned from the fire to face him. "Are you my father, Captain Michael?" she finally blurted out.

"I don't know, Angelina, but it's possible. I was in port at the time you were conceived. And I have always loved your mother like no one else could," replied the Captain.

He sighed and took both of her hands in his.

"Little angel," he began, "I have loved you as my own since your birth. I have offered marriage, a home, a life together to Maddie. She has refused me time and again because I refuse to give up the sea. And she refuses to give up her business dealings. Fits and snatches are all I have had of you, because Maddie and I are the most stubborn people alive!"

"But Captain Michael," puzzled Angelina, "what of my eyes? Yours too are dark!"

Michael took her face in his weather-worn hands and kissed her forehead gently.

"Angelina, my mother's eyes were as blue as the sea on a calm, fair day, and her skin was the color of the puffy clouds that blew in that same sky. Her mother was the same and her mother before that." He hushed her gasp. "You see, I have no doubt that you are my child."

Angelina threw her arms around his neck and held him close.

"Are you disappointed that your father is not a learned man or a success at business? Is a poor Italian sea merchant an acceptable man to you?"

"Oh, Captain Michael … Papa … I couldn't be more pleased."

---

As she roused from her reverie, she realized she'd only counted half the jar and the hour was very late. Yet the captain was as real to her here as he'd been at the beach almost a year ago. She could very nearly smell the salt ocean breeze and the spicy sea captain smell of him. As she always did, she missed him now.

*He always said I could have any man I wanted. Can I have Jonathan?* She mused that even fathers are wrong sometimes.

# SUNDAY NIGHTMARE

The room was so dark Angelina could barely see. What had awakened her?

The door creaked, she recalled. Surely it was someone else's door.

The floor squeaked, and she heard footsteps nearby. A dark figure appeared beside her bed. She suppressed the urge to scream, in hopes the stranger would leave, thinking she was asleep.

"So, you are the virgin princess of Madalaine's Palace I've heard so much about," the low dark voice said. "They thought they could keep you away from me, did they? None of those 'ladies' interest me as much as the one I can't have."

Angelina held her breath, hoping he'd leave, hoping he didn't mean what she thought he meant. Surely he didn't mean to …

His hands grabbed her shoulders in the dark and jerked her from the bed. With a free hand, he turned up the gas lamp. She looked into his face but couldn't see it for the brightness of the sudden light.

"There, I like to see the women with whom I have carnal relations. My, aren't you a beauty? No wonder they're saving you. Mama will get a pretty penny for you when you're mature."

Angelina seemed frozen at his touch. She couldn't scream or answer him.

*What do I do now, Lord?* she prayed silently.

The man grabbed her nightgown in his hands and tore it open down the front. He reached for her ample breasts.

It was then that she screamed and ran from her bed.

Lights lit up and down the hall as she ran down it with the man behind her. The weight of her gold earrings pulled at her earlobes as they bounced along in the darkness.

She felt him grab her long black hair and pull her off her feet. Nearly naked, she felt his hot breath on her neck as he picked her up in his arms and carried her into a spare bedroom. He threw her on the barren bed and ripped her nightgown the rest of the way off. With one hand he held her down as he undressed with the other. When her breath returned, she began screaming, knowing someone would hear her.

"Mama!" she shrieked, as the beautiful woman entered the room with her robe and gown flying.

"Get away from my daughter, you evil man!" the woman demanded, as she leveled the shotgun at the man's head. "I do know how to use this piece, and I will if I have to. Release her now!"

As he removed his hand from her chest, she rolled off the bed to the floor to recover the remnants of her gown. The man left quickly, cursing as he went. Angelina sat on the floor, clutching her knees, screaming, and crying.

"Wake up, Angelina!" a voice demanded. "Please wake up, dear. It's only a dream."

Angelina tried to rouse herself from the recurring nightmare. As she fought off sleep, she heard someone screaming. The voice was hers.

"Angelina, dear," pleaded the feminine voice. "Please stop screaming. Sheriff Jones will be here soon if you don't stop. It's only a dream, dear."

Angelina opened her eyes and closed her mouth, swallowing hard to soothe her raw throat. She looked into the face of Mrs. Crabtree, whom she had met only briefly the previous day. Behind her stood a worried looking Mr. Crabtree.

"She'll be okay now, Martha," he said. He turned and left swiftly.

"Dear Angelina, you frightened us so. Ebenezer thought we were being robbed."

"No, ma'am," Angelina replied weakly. "I'm so sorry to wake you."

"Call me Mrs. C. Everyone else does. Let me make you some tea."

Mrs. C. set the teakettle to boil on Angelina's small stove in the far corner. She pulled two teacups from the cupboard and procured the necessary tea and sugar.

"Do you take cream, Angelina?"

"No, Mrs. C.," she replied, as Mrs. C. poured the steaming water into the cups.

"Now tell me about this awful nightmare you were having. Surely the Bardsleys treated you better than that last night."

Angelina noticed the brightening sky out the alley window. Dawn was not far away now. She'd not been asleep more than a few hours.

"Mrs. C., I need to tell you something about myself. But I need you not to tell anyone else until I've had a chance to tell them myself."

"Of course, Angelina. What is it?"

"The nightmare reoccurs whenever I'm overtired." She paused. "I was nearly raped in my mother's house." Angelina stirred her tea, avoiding Mrs. C.'s stunned gaze. "You see, my mother runs a brothel in North Boston."

Angelina confided in Mrs. C. the story of her life as the daughter of Boston's famous Madame, Madalaine Mercy. She told her the dream in vivid detail.

"Didn't they ever catch the man who did this horrible thing to you, Angelina?"

"No, Mrs. C.," Angelina explained. "His face is a blank in my dream. I can never remember what he looks like. All I know is he was dark-featured and dark-haired and very frightening."

Angelina shuddered at the remembrance, though the room was already warm and humid from the June Missouri sun. She sipped her tepid tea.

"If you'd like me to go, I'll find another job and home. I found another home one and a half years ago too."

"Nonsense," Mrs. C. replied. "You need someone to care for you. Stay as long as you like. Ebenezer would never tell you, but you are the best employee he's ever had."

"How can he tell? I've only worked here one day."

"Believe me, we can tell," she said. "You're conscientious and personable with the customers. The books balance on your first try. Inventory was accurate. You stayed up much too late finishing it. I'm sure that's what brought on the nightmare."

*I wonder*, thought Angelina recalling the fear she'd felt when Edward had held her elbow so tightly. *I hope that's all it is.*

"My goodness, look at the time," said Mrs. C. as Angelina's clock chimed. "Crabtree's is closed on Sundays, in accordance with the Blue Laws. We've breakfast and dressing to finish before worship. The reverend is such a good preacher and a compassionate man despite his harsh bluster and determined passion for winning souls to the Lord. He's lonely though. Maybe you can change all that, Angelina. On beautiful days we leave a little earlier and walk to the church house. Are you up to that, or should we take the buggy?"

"Walking would be fine, Mrs. C.," Angelina replied.

After Mrs. C. returned upstairs, Angelina chose a pale pink outfit from the wardrobe. She laced the corset, though its use was chiefly to support her well-endowed bosom rather than to restrict her torso. The overdress was solid pink; the underdress was a pale pink and white stripe. She tied up the low bustle in the back. Her skirt didn't trail, however, in the latest fashion, because of her height. She braided her hair with pink velvet ribbon and wrapped it in a low chignon to de-emphasize her height. She chose a round, pink hat with cascading pink velvet ribbons. Finally, she chose black patent leather slippers. She never wore the fashionable high-heeled boots. They made her that much taller than all the men.

*Of course, with Jonathan that wouldn't matter*, she thought with a thrill.

---

"Don't you look the pale, porcelain doll, Angelina," Mrs. C. complimented her as they stepped out into the street in front of Crabtree's. "You're so very lovely. I'm sure your mama is so proud of you."

"Thank you, Mrs. C." Angelina blushed the color of her overdress at the sincere compliment.

Old structures from earlier days in St. Joe lined the narrow streets. Stone-trimmed turrets and dormer windows accented the buildings that housed the retail district. Second floors bulged out over the street from most of the shops.

"Angelina, this street was part of old St. Joe. Old Joseph Robidoux founded his fur trading post here back in twenty-six. He founded the town in forty-three. This was his home, the oldest house in town," Mrs. C. pointed out the brick building. "He died this past year."

Mrs. C. pointed out a gray brick structure across the corner. "Old Robidoux built this house for his daughter, Sylvanie."

"Will I meet her this morning?" asked Angelina.

"Oh no, the Robidoux family attends the Catholic church. They're French-Canadian."

As they walked toward the bluffs along the Missouri River, a tall steeple appeared in the blue morning sky. The bell in the belfry reflected the rays of the sun from the east. Mrs. C. gestured to the white-frame church with the copper-plated roof.

"So, here we are, Angelina, First Church St. Joe."

The church overlooked the shining river. A profusion of roses bordered the white picket fence around the small white house beside the church.

"Who lives there? I've never seen such beautiful roses!" exclaimed Angelina.

"Why, Angelina," Mrs. C. replied, "that's the parsonage. Reverend Jonathan lives there. He keeps the roses."

"He's a surprising man."

Mrs. C. eyed her suspiciously and smiled.

A strong hand grasped Angelina's shoulder. She jerked and whirled around with a cry. She looked up into a bronzed face with a mass of controlled blond hair.

"Jonathan!" she exclaimed breathlessly. "You frightened me!"

"I'm so sorry," apologized Jonathan. "I didn't mean any harm."

"Nightmares last night," explained Mr. Crabtree. "Came in too late last night."

Jonathan's quizzical look at Angelina caused her to avoid his eyes.

"I'll make sure she's in earlier next time she's out with me," he promised. "Forgive me, sir."

The Johnson twins sauntered up to the group around Angelina.

"Good morning, lovely lady." Jedadiah tipped his Stetson as Joshua kissed Angelina's hand.

"I still can't tell you apart," Angelina admitted.

"Never mind," replied one twin. "Just remember that the handsome one is Joshua."

Jedadiah laughed and answered, "Thank you, Brother. That's the closest thing to a compliment I've had in a long time from you."

Each twin took an arm, ushered her into the church, and found her a vacant seat.

"Ah, Angelina, how lovely you look this morning. Pink becomes you almost as well as the sapphire gown you wore last evening."

The deep voice behind her made her shudder. Could it be?

She turned around in the pew and looked into the face of Edward Bardsley. Angelina nodded and turned away from his lurid gaze.

Sarah, sitting between Sheriff and Mrs. Jones, turned and winked at Angelina from the second row as the service began. Mr. and Mrs. Crabtree occupied the rest of the row.

In the third row were David and Phoebe Greene with their toddler. To Angelina's surprise, Phoebe looked sure to deliver another child during the service. In Boston, a pregnant woman stayed home when she began to show. Henry Miller, the barber, and his wife completed the third row.

The fourth row reverberated with activity. Mary and Philip Taylor spent most of the service tending to the needs of their five small children. Jedadiah had told her their names, but the only one she recalled was the oldest boy, Ethan. He looked to be only eight or nine years old.

The Bardsleys sat behind her. Edward seemed to breathe down the back of her neck the whole time. Alice looked like a peacock, dressed in a confusion of ribbons, tassels, feathers, and lace in the latest fashion.

Angelina noticed that only she and Alice wore fashionable dress. The other ladies, while neat and clean, dressed simply in a single full skirt with over-bodice. Their skirts had no crinoline or bustle. Angelina made a mental note to wear her two good outfits at special formal occasions only. Her work dresses and skirts would suit this Sunday crowd better.

The difference between the Johnson twins became apparent during the service. Jedadiah sang all the hymns in a loud, clear tenor. He opened his Bible and listened studiously during the sermon. She noticed Jedadiah's hands were roughened and scarred. Joshua's hands, however, were smooth and tender. During the hymns he flirted with every woman in sight. Mrs. Johnson sat beside Joshua and poked him occasionally to rouse him during the sermon.

As Jonathan preached, Angelina viewed him more closely. He tousled his blond hair, perfect at the beginning of the sermon, by habitually running his hands through it. His bronze face grimaced in pain at man's sin, gloried in God's provision of salvation, and glowered at Satan's attempts to destroy mankind. His broad shoulders filled the pulpit with power. His blue eyes flashed with enthusiasm as he pleaded with the congregation to repent from their sins and allow Jesus to be Lord in their lives.

Before she knew it, the service had ended. She was chagrined to note that she couldn't recall a single specific word of Jonathan's sermon. The people of St. Joe had captivated her entire attention.

"Angie!" called Sarah as she stood to leave. "What a beautiful dress! So much more dignified than that contraption Alice wears and calls fashion."

"Sarah, it's the Lord's day. Surely you have some compassion for the woman," rebuked Angelina.

"Didn't you go to dinner there last night?" asked Sarah. "Does she deserve any compassion?"

Angelina giggled. "I guess not."

"I want to invite you over after lunch, Angie. All the ladies are coming for the afternoon to quilt. Say you'll come."

"Of course I'll come, Sarah." *She won't take no for an answer anyway*, Angelina noted.

"Hello, Angelina. We'll talk later about where you went after I took you home," teased Jonathan as he greeted her at the door.

"Merely to the bluffs to think and pray, Pastor," Angelina replied. She felt the strength in his roughened hand as he took her hand.

"Are you free to take a buggy ride through the rest of St. Joseph with me this afternoon?" asked Jonathan.

"I'm sorry, Jonathan. Sarah's invited me to quilt this afternoon."

"Then I'll pick you up at five at the Jones's, okay?"

"Fine, Pastor."

"I'll keep you company while the women gossip, Pastor," Jedadiah said from behind Angelina. "I've got to bring Mama to town anyway."

# QUILTING BEE

"What's bothering you, Pastor?"

Jedadiah walked into the small stable behind the parsonage after delivering his mother at the Joneses'.

"Why do you ask?" A shirtless Jonathan pumped two iron cannonballs in his hands as he spoke. Sweat glistened on his broad chest. Scars from war ridged his back.

"You only torture yourself with that shot when something's eating at you," Jedadiah replied. "Where did you get those things anyway?"

"A friend salvaged them from the remains of the *Congress* for me."

"Why would you want them, Jon? I'd think the last thing you'd want would be reminders of the war."

"When I began serving as an officer, I no longer did the work that kept my muscles taut and strong. I used two cannonballs to keep in shape on the ship in case I needed to haul lines or load cannons someday in the absence of available crew. I refused to be a weak, useless chaplain. I still keep that resolve as pastor."

"So what problem drives you to them on a Sunday afternoon? Come on, Jon, even a pastor's got to talk to someone besides God."

"Have you ever been in love, Jed?"

Jedadiah stripped off his Sunday shirt and hung it on the nail beside the buggy whip. He picked up the grooming brush and played with it.

"How would I know, Jon? I'm not married either. You're the one who contemplated marrying the town dragon lady."

"Contemplating marriage is no proof of being in love." Jonathan faced him and asked, "Seriously, Jed, have you ever been in love?"

Jedadiah thought a long time before he answered.

"Yes, Jon. But she only has eyes for Edward Bardsley's money," he replied quietly.

"Sarah? You're in love with Sarah?" Jonathan asked. "This must be the best kept secret in town, Jed. You're my best friend, and I had no idea!"

Jedadiah laughed his easy laugh. He began grooming Jonathan's horse. "Being in love hurts, Jon. But it's also the best feeling in the world when I see her, when she laughs, when she speaks to me. She thinks I'm safe, secure, and stable—like I'm her brother. I don't know how to make her think differently. Maybe I should pick another girl." Jedadiah looked sideways at Jonathan. "Like maybe Angelina Mercy."

Jonathan nearly dropped the shot.

"So that's it, Jon. Angelina's the one, isn't she?"

"I'm not sure," replied Jonathan shakily. "She has my attention, though."

"Yours and half the town's too, Jon." Jedadiah smiled. "As long as you keep her, she's yours. But if you ever let her go, she's mine, friend."

"She makes me homesick, Jed. For the first time in my life, I miss Massachusetts, Boston Harbor, and the sea breeze. But when I'm with her, it's like I'm home again."

"Ooh, boy, Jon," teased Jedadiah. "You've got it bad."

"It's funny, though." Jonathan laid down the shot, ignoring Jed's jibes. "I knew she'd remind me of Dr. Graves, being his goddaughter. Something about her also reminds me of Captain de Angelo."

"She doesn't look a thing like a sea captain to me, Jon. Seriously, you'd better declare yourself soon, before you have to stand in line. Make this decision with your heart, Jon. Love isn't supposed to be logical or organized. When it comes, you'd best grab it."

---

Angelina heard Alice's voice as soon as she entered the Joneses' home.

"I tell you, Sarah, she's not normal. She's too pretty to be Christian. I warrant there's something we don't know about her."

"Like what, Alice?" asked Sarah's voice. "She seems just fine to me."

"She works, Sarah. She's educated. She doesn't have time to sew, but she has fabulous clothing. Where does she get the money? Perhaps she has a side job, selling something besides notions at Crabtree's."

"If that was true, Alice, she'd be a professional as opposed to an amateur, like you," Sarah's voice retorted as Angelina entered the parlor. "Angie, come sit by me."

Alice fell silent.

"What a beautiful quilt, Sarah. Is it yours?" Angelina sat next to Sarah. Many of the women she'd met at church surrounded the frame. "What do you call the design?"

"Why, Angelina," Sarah said in surprise. "It's a double wedding ring quilt for my hope chest. Haven't you ever seen one before?"

"No, Sarah. What's a hope chest?"

A buzz of whispers began around the frame.

"Not normal, I say." Alice's voice transcended the buzz.

"A hope chest is usually made of cedar and is filled by a young woman as she grows up with embroidered linens, quilts, blankets, and household goods in hope for the day she will be married," answered Mrs. C. "Didn't your mama give you one?"

"No, Mrs. C. She didn't start one for me. It sounds like a lovely idea." Angelina remembered a large cedar chest in Mama's room and wondered if that had been her mother's.

"I guess she wouldn't think of such a thing, with her business and all," replied Mrs. C. sympathetically. Then she gasped and covered her mouth with her hand.

"What business would that be, Angelina dear?" asked Alice.

Angelina looked at the expectant faces awaiting her reply. What was there to do but tell the truth?

"Prostitution, Alice. My mother runs a bordello."

"Well, I never." Alice jumped from her chair and grabbed Mrs. Bardsley's arm. "Come along, Mother."

"I don't think so, dear. That would be so rude. You may go, if you must, though."

Alice sat back down in a huff, while Angelina fell to silently quilting the multicolored patchwork design of the quilt in the frame. The other women followed her lead and stitched in silence. Sarah began a quiet giggle. The giggle erupted into hearty laughter. Her laugh was so infectious that all the women joined in.

"Angie," Sarah said as she laughed, "I guess a double wedding ring quilt would be out of place in a brothel after all."

"I would think so, Sarah," Angelina replied with a grin.

Mrs. C. sat on the other side of Angelina. She whispered, "I'm so sorry to spill your secret, Angelina."

"It's okay, Mrs. C. It was bound to come out sooner or later." Angelina impulsively hugged the older woman.

"Mama, look at these stitches Angie's done," called Sarah.

The women gathered around Angelina to admire her handwork.

"How did you learn to quilt so fine?" asked Mrs. Jones.

"A bordello needs quilts and linens for beds too, like any other home," replied Angelina. She was unsure what surprised them about that.

"Tell us what it's like, Angie," asked Sarah. "What's it like to grow up in a house of ill-repute?"

"Do tell us, Angelina," pleaded Mrs. Bardsley. "I've always wondered about the inside of those places."

"Mother!" Alice cried. She stormed out of the house.

Angelina looked at the smiling faces around her and knew she was in the company of friends.

"Well, during the day, Madalaine's Palace is much like a women's hotel or boarding house with a large, elegant parlor. Some of the ladies clean, some cook, and some sew just like a big family. Each of those ladies mothered me and taught me basic homemaking skills. They always dressed in the latest fashions, sewing most of their own clothes by hand. The fabric was expensive and elegant. It came from all over the world. They were the most beautiful and well-dressed women in Boston."

"How wonderful!" Sarah exclaimed.

"Sarah, we're talking about prostitutes," reminded Mrs. Jones sternly. "Please continue, Angelina."

"One of the ladies, Rainelle, taught me to quilt. She pieced the most elaborate designs I've ever seen. She had a finer hand than I'll ever hope to have. Her creations graced all our beds at Madalaine's. She gave me the quilt that I have on my bed at Crabtree's."

"It's beautiful too," Mrs. C. assured the group.

"But wasn't she a prostitute?" asked Mary Taylor cautiously.

"Of course, she was," answered Angelina. "As were they all. They were also very lonely women. Most of them ran away from bad homes, abusive husbands, or poverty. Madalaine's was a place of safety."

"Safety? A brothel?" asked Mrs. Johnson.

"Madalaine's Palace is the best house in Boston. Mama cares for her girls. She makes sure they are well-fed, well-clothed, and well-treated. She requires medical exams and treatment, if necessary, for all her girls to protect them from the diseases the men bring into the house. Mama never allows any of the gentlemen more than two drinks in her parlor. No drunks will ever maul her girls. Gentlemen are required to dress in their best attire, as though they were attending the opera or the theater."

"What an unusual life!" exclaimed Sarah.

"During the day, Madalaine's was a normal household. In the evenings, though, the ladies dressed in their beautiful ball gowns, crinolines, corsets, and gloves. Excitement ran high each evening as the doors to Madalaine's opened. Each night seemed like an elegant ball. I used to sit on the stairs until I fell asleep. I'd watch the ladies talk and dance with the men while William played the piano."

"Who is William?" asked Sarah.

"William protected the ladies in Madalaine's Palace. Occasionally William escorted a man from the parlor if he became rude. He would also carry me to bed before the ladies took the men to their rooms at the close of the evening."

"But what place did you have in this home as a young girl?" asked Mrs. Bardsley. "It must have been awkward."

"Not at first, Mrs. Bardsley. You see, I had no idea what went on after the party. As I got older, I heard the soft whispers and giggles behind the other girls' doors. It seemed beautiful and romantic. I never thought anything of it until I was thirteen."

Angelina thought back to her childhood, before the incident in her nightmare, as she stitched.

"What a wonderful birthday," she said, as she pranced before the dresser mirror in her new corset. "Thank you, Mama, for the earrings, the corset, and the gown."

"You're welcome, bambina," whispered Madalaine, as she watched her tall, young daughter become a woman before her very eyes.

"My corset makes me look ever so much more grown up. It emphasizes my décolleté," she remarked, proud of her emphasized chest and vocabulary. The new gold earrings in her ears flashed in the lamp light. "Mama, can I come down to the party tonight to make my debut and find a beau? I could wear my new blue ball gown."

"Never!" roared Madalaine to her daughter's astonishment. "You will never join Rainelle and the others in the parlor at night."

"I don't understand, Mama," Angelina replied with tear-filled, sapphire eyes. "Don't you think I'm pretty enough?"

"Come here, bambina. You are the prettiest of them all, darling," Madalaine spoke gently. "Don't you know what happens at the end of each party we give in the parlor?"

"No, Mama. I always find myself in bed in the morning," she replied.

Madalaine told her then the details of the profession. Angelina's eyes grew wide in disbelief and horror. Dr. Graves had carefully instructed her in the Ten Commandments. Adultery was definitely one of those "Thou shalt nots." She knew many of the men who came to Madalaine's. She also knew their wives and children. How ugly those parties seemed to her now!

"Angelina, keep yourself pure. Do not fall into the trap of prostitution. These ladies work here because they have no place else to go. They come here to survive. I help them by making it safer than being on the streets. Guard your virginity with your life until you marry the man who will love you and be faithful to you. It's a precious gift for a special man," Madalaine concluded.

"But, Mama," pleaded Angelina, "what you're doing is wrong. It's against God's laws. It's sin that Jesus died for. Why do you do it?"

"Angelina, some things a woman does to survive. Sometimes she does it to preserve her stubborn pride. The man whom I love would take us both away from here if I'd only ask him to do so."

"Captain Michael?"

"Yes, Michael. But I can't ask him to do it when I can't be sure who your father is. I know the church frowns on my source of income too. That is why I asked Dr. Graves to be your godfather and teach you a better life."

"Are you okay?" asked Mrs. Bardsley.

A tear had slipped down Angelina's cheek and splashed among the colorful blocks

Mrs. Bardsley reached for and held Angelina tightly. "There, there, Angelina. You're among friends here. We can tell you're an innocent victim of your mother's business. We'll care for you."

"I wonder where Alice has gone. You don't suppose she'd try to tell Pastor Thomson about Angie, do you?" asked Sarah. "I can tell already that he's smitten with you, Angie. It would destroy any man to hear about this from Alice. You'd better tell him yourself on the way home."

"He's a good man," assured Mrs. Johnson. "He'll understand if you tell him first. If he doesn't, Jedadiah or Joshua would have no trouble being faithful and loving to you. I'd certainly accept you as my daughter-in-law."

Time passed quickly as the women stitched and talked. The quilt neared completion as a rap at the door announced Jonathan and Jedadiah's arrival.

"Pastor, how is Mrs. Valentine?" asked Kate Bardsley.

"Fading, I'm afraid, Kate," he answered. "I go and read to her as I can, but she barely knows I'm there. Todd would appreciate any help you might give."

The ladies shook their heads sadly and agreed to go to the Valentines' soon.

"Buggy ride begins immediately, Angelina. I need to be back for service at seven," Jonathan told her.

Angelina hurriedly said her good-byes to keep him from waiting long.

Jonathan drove the buggy all over town, pointing out the sights. First, they drove to south St. Joe to see the stockyards and slaughterhouses. He showed her the house where Lincoln stayed during a visit to St. Joe in '59. As they headed back north, Jonathan pointed out the old Patee Hotel.

"Angelina, this hotel was once the finest west of St. Louis. Then it was the office for the Pony Express for the short time it ran."

"I bet it was lovely."

"Not as lovely as you, Angelina," Jonathan replied cautiously.

"There's something you need to know about me, Jonathan."

"I think I've already guessed at it, Angelina. It has to do with Captain de Angelo, doesn't it?"

She nodded.

"Just before I left Captain de Angelo's service to join the navy, I remember seeing him bring a very young girl on board for dinner one night. She had long black ringlets, blowing in the sea breeze. As they rowed closer to the ship, I saw her brilliant blue eyes and flashing gold hoop earrings. She was perhaps nine or ten. I helped her aboard when the captain handed her up to me. I heard her childish laugh in the captain's quarters and saw her leave with him. I never remember seeing any other woman aboard the *Madalaine*. I'd forgotten that memory until you fell into my arms at the depot Friday. You are the same girl, aren't you?"

"Yes, Jonathan, I probably am. I can't believe we met nearly ten years ago. I really don't remember." *How I wish I did*, she thought.

"How do you know Captain de Angelo so well?" asked Jonathan.

"He's probably my father, Jonathan."

"That would make your mother Madalaine Mercy, wouldn't it?"

"Yes, Jonathan."

Jonathan drove the rest of the way to Crabtree's in silence. The only sounds were the clatter of the horse's shoes on the stone street and the click of the buggy wheels.

Jonathan stopped the buggy in front of Crabtrees'. He turned to face her.

"I can tell by the Spirit within you that you have had nothing to do with your mother's profession. I know Dr. Graves also. He is a good teacher and mentor. We have much in common despite your past. Angelina, I'd like permission to court you, with the intention of discovering whether God has brought us together for the purpose of matrimony."

"Are you sure, Jonathan? Or is this like Alice?"

"No, Angelina, this is nothing like Alice. This decision I'm making with my heart and soul and not with my head. Will you grant me permission to call on you, Angelina?"

"Nothing would make me happier, Jonathan."

He jumped from the buggy and lifted her down to the street. She looked up into his glowing eyes. They kissed a sweet, brief kiss.

"Thank you," he whispered. "You've made me a happier man today, my angel."

Angelina watched Jonathan drive away in complete joy at the way the LORD worked in her life. Angelina's sleep that night was interrupted only by dreams of a tall, muscular, blonde sailor lifting her aboard the *Madalaine*.

# TORNADO

Wednesday dawned bright and warm like the two previous days. Angelina awoke to sunlight and chirping birds in the alley outside her open window. A vase containing two roses stood proudly on the sill. Jonathan had brought the pink rose on Monday and the yellow rose on Tuesday when he came for his *Gazette*. Each morning he'd been waiting on the porch for her to open the door. She smiled thinking about him being there again this morning. After she had dressed, she went upstairs to breakfast with the Crabtrees.

Mr. Crabtree yawned loudly as she entered their cozy kitchen.

"Ebenezer," Martha chastised, "please control your yawns in front of our guest."

"Martha, if I got to bed a little earlier, I'd not be yawning. With the pastor here so late courting last night, I barely got any sleep. Besides, Angelina is not our guest. She's our employee."

"Angelina is our guest and family as long as she is in our home," replied Mrs. C., winking at Angelina. "Besides, you've been saying ever since Rev. Thomson arrived that he needed a wife."

"I didn't say I cared to chaperone the courting process, Martha."

"Don't be a grump, Ebenezer. Eat your oatmeal."

"Good morning, Mr. and Mrs. Crabtree," greeted Angelina. She had learned that Mr. Crabtree was always a grump, as Mrs.

C. called him, but that down inside he was a compassionate man. He just never intended anyone to discover that fact.

"At least he won't be over this evening," Mr. Crabtree continued.

"Why not?" Angelina cried in alarm.

"It's Wednesday, dear. There's prayer meeting at the church tonight," Mrs. C. said.

Angelina and Mrs. C. chatted amiably, sipping their tea and eating their biscuits.

"The time, Miss Mercy. I should think you'd want to open on time to sell the pastor his *Gazette*."

Mr. Crabtree sipped his coffee as he watched her react.

"Yes, sir." Angelina finished the last of her tea with a gulp and ran from the table, down the stairs, and across the store to open the front door. She thought she heard a deep chuckle behind her accompanying Mrs. C.'s giggle.

"Good morning, Angel," said Jonathan, as the door swung open. He held out a deep red rose. "Add this to your arrangement."

"Pastor, you'll have no more roses to decorate your fence if you bring them all over here one at a time," Mr. Crabtree noted as he descended the stairs.

"What good are they on the fence when they can bring such pleasure in the giving, Mr. Crabtree?" he replied.

"Thank you, Jonathan. They are all so beautiful. Excuse me while I place this one with the others." Angelina hurried to put the bloom in water and get back before Jonathan left to begin his busy day.

When she returned, she noticed a dark stranger had entered the store in her absence. She moved quickly to where Jonathan waited for her on the other side of the store.

"Mr. Howard, how can I help you?" asked Mr. Crabtree.

"Gun shells and jerky. Some of those potatoes too, sir," the man replied.

"Jonathan, who is that man?" she asked quietly. "He reminds me of a sketch I saw at the depot of Jesse James."

"He's Mr. Howard, Angel. He comes through town now and again on business. He often stops by for worship when he's here on a Sunday. I hope someday he can be reached by the gospel. Besides, dear, if he was Jesse James, it wouldn't matter to anyone in town."

"What do you mean, not matter? I read about the Liberty bank robbery a couple of years ago all the way in Boston. He's robbed several banks since then and murdered many people. Why wouldn't it matter? He should be put behind bars if he's Jesse James."

"James is a hero of sorts in these parts, like a modern-day Robin Hood. Southern sympathy runs high here, just like Charles Bardsley. Quantrill's Guerrillas, with Jesse and his brother Frank, are Confederate heroes here. They killed and vandalized in the name of the South during the war. Even if people recognized him, no one would turn him in. You and I are among the very few Yankees in these parts. This young man is known as Mr. Howard here, Angelina."

His purchase complete, Mr. Howard walked over to Jonathan and spoke, "'Morning, Reverend. Got yourself a sweetie, I see. She's a beauty, for sure."

"Angelina Mercy, meet Mr. Howard."

Angelina eyed him suspiciously. "Mr. Howard."

"Pleased to meet you, ma'am. Hope I'll be seeing more of you, especially attached to the reverend." He tipped his hat and left.

"Do you think he's Jesse James?" she asked Jonathan.

"I don't know, Angel. He's never bothered St. Joe if he is."

Angelina sighed and said, "What do you have planned today, Jonathan?"

"I'll ride out to the Valentine farm this morning and read Scripture to Mrs. Valentine. She's very frail. Her son, Todd, thinks she won't last the summer."

"How sad. "

"Then I have some sermon study and preparation to accomplish at church and, later, a call at the Bardsleys'. They're probably scandalized by our relationship."

"What business is it of theirs, Jonathan?" Angelina asked angrily.

"They pay me, remember?" Jonathan headed for the door with Angelina in tow.

"That's not a good enough reason in my book."

"Is that jealousy speaking? You know Alice means nothing to me."

"I just wish you weren't a puppet for them to manipulate with their money."

"Did I ever tell you I let them manipulate me?" Jonathan asked in surprise. "I usually get my own way somehow." He grinned his boyish grin. "I need to go now. Don't work too hard. I'd hate for you to miss prayer service at church tonight."

Jonathan stepped out onto the porch, pulling Angelina out with him.

"Wouldn't miss it, Pastor." She smiled a dazzling smile, as bright sunlight caught in her gold hoop earrings.

The urge to embrace her and kiss her fully seized him.

*That would not be proper*, he reminded himself. *Is love like this?*

He settled for a brief kiss on her cheek and left for the Valentine ranch.

Angelina sat down at the work desk with the books after seeing him off. She recorded transactions and adjusted inventory counts from Tuesday's business. With the books complete, she counted money to take a deposit to the bank.

*What if Mr. Howard is Jesse James?* she wondered. *Would my money be safe in any bank in town?*

On Monday, she had deposited her money orders in the same bank Mr. Crabtree used. Thankfully it was a different bank from Mr. Bardsley's. She wanted no one, much less the Bardsleys, to know the balance of those accounts.

"My darling Angelina." The deep voice startled her from her reverie. "Say it isn't so."

"Edward, you frightened me!" she exclaimed.

His rakish smile chilled her to the bone.

"Tell me you are not being courted by that dull Yankee reverend. The grapevine says you've hardly been apart since you arrived. Your family background hardly makes you a good choice for the pastor's wife, you know." He added darkly, "Besides, I want first claims on your affections, Angelina. I thought I made that clear Saturday night."

"Edward, I am unable to accept your attentions at this time," Angelina replied stiffly.

"I believe God holds us responsible only for our own sins, Edward, not those of our parents," Mrs. C. voiced from the stairs. "Angelina, I require your help upstairs immediately."

"I'm on my way, Mrs. C. Excuse me, Edward."

He gripped her elbow tightly. "You'll not always have someone to rescue you from me, Angelina," he whispered. "Someday it will be just you and me, my darling Angelina."

Angelina jerked her arm away from his grasp and locked the money back in the safe. She hurried away from him to Mrs. C.'s parlor, where she and Jonathan had played whist with the Crabtrees the previous evening. Mrs. C. sat on the deep red velvet settee.

"What can I help you with, Mrs. C.?"

"Sit down, Angelina."

"What's wrong? Have you had bad news?"

"Edward Bardsley is bad news. Don't listen to a word that man says. He and his father believe they can control everyone with their money and influence."

"Thanks for the rescue, Mrs. C. Edward frightens me for some reason. Don't worry; I don't trust him at all!"

"Miss Mercy, Miss Jones is inquiring after you. I still need that cash in the bank as well," called Mr. Crabtree from below.

"Thanks, Mrs. C.," she said warmly.

"Don't forget what I said." Mrs. C. hugged her and sent her back down to the store.

As Angelina descended the stairs, she remembered fondly watching the parties at Madalaine's from the staircase. She sat down on the stairs and pulled her long legs under her skirt and observed the scene below. Sarah, with her golden brown hair pulled up in the chenille net Angelina had given her, was talking animatedly with Edward, who seemed uninterested but polite.

*Sarah*, she thought, *why is his money so important? Find someone else, my friend.*

The ringing bell drew her attention to the opening door. Jedadiah strode purposely into the store. He had to be Jedadiah, because Joshua would have sauntered in lazily. Angelina smiled at Jedadiah's presence and watched with great interest the play of emotions across his face.

When he saw Sarah, his face lit up. As he noticed her attention to Edward, however, his warm face turned to a scowl. Quickly he checked his expression and hid behind his everyday friendly face to greet them both.

"He's in love with Sarah," she said in a whisper. "Poor Jedadiah! He loves her, and she's after Edward's money. There must be some way to get them together." *They both deserve happiness with each other.*

Standing up from her hiding place, she greeted her friends after Edward left.

"Sarah! Jedadiah! How are you today? What can I do for you?"

"So there you are, Angie. If I hadn't seen Jonathan headed out of town earlier, I would have sworn you were out with him. Take a break and let's picnic at the bluffs. I'm dying to know if the gossip is true," Sarah breathlessly said. "Did you see Edward? I think I had his attention. Perhaps he'll escort me to the fair on the Fourth of July."

"If he doesn't, Sarah, I'd be glad to do it." Jedadiah's face showed the hurt he felt.

Angelina hurt with him. *Why doesn't she see his love when I can?*

"Jedadiah, come with us on the picnic," invited Angelina. "Would that be agreeable, Sarah?"

"Well, I suppose," hesitated Sarah, "but I only packed enough chicken for us."

"Not a problem. Sarah, let's take some of these apples too. What do you say, Jed?"

"I'd be delighted, Angie," responded Jedadiah with enthusiasm. "I'll purchase Mama's things and join you on the bluffs later."

"Good, that will give us time to go to the bank and talk on the way, Sarah. Will that be okay, Mr. Crabtree?"

"Don't be gone more than an hour, Miss Mercy."

"Let's go, Sarah. The clock is ticking. See you soon, Jed."

Angelina winked at Jedadiah behind Sarah's back. Pure joy shone from his face.

In the street, Angelina grabbed Sarah's elbow.

"Sarah, that man is in love with you. Can't you see it?"

"Jedadiah Johnson? In love with me? Impossible. We grew up together. He's like a brother to me. He's also tied down to that silly ranch and his mother. There's nothing mysterious about Jed. Edward is dark, mysterious, and wealthy."

"Edward scares the wits out of me," replied Angelina firmly. "He reminds me of someone threatening and evil. Think about Jedadiah instead, Sarah. At least Jed is trustworthy."

With the banking completed, the two ladies headed for the bluffs.

"Tell me about Jonathan, Angie. Is it true he's formally courting you?"

Angelina filled her in on the details. She assured her worried friend that she had kept no secrets from him.

"So we're courting until one of us decides this is or is not what God wants for us both," Angelina concluded.

"Why do you want Jonathan? I'll grant you he's handsome, in a rugged sort of way, and strong and honorable, but ..." Sarah held up three fingers and ticked off the reasons to choose another mate, "one, he'll never have any money for all that schooling he took; two being married to a minister is like being married to the congregation—no privacy at all; three, he's so much older than you, Angie. Jedadiah would be a better catch."

"How old would you say he is, Sarah?"

"Oh, at least twenty-five to thirty, Angie. He's probably ten years older than you are!"

"Who's ten years older than Angie?" asked Jedadiah, as he appeared behind them. "Jon? So he declared himself, did he? I thought he'd plan and organize it to death first. I thought I still had time to call on you myself."

"Don't you think Jonathan is too old for Angie? You're much closer to her age than the pastor."

"I'm much closer to your age than Edward too, Sarah."

Sarah laughed nervously as she caught a glimpse of Jedadiah's fondness for her. "But I'm not too fond of cattle since the day we played in the bull pasture, Jedadiah Johnson."

"Angie, we were maybe ten years old when we held a picnic under the shade of the bull's favorite tree. With our red tablecloth, I played bullfighter while Sarah climbed the tree as fast as she could. I followed her up, and then we waited for my father to come and rescue us from the tree." Jedadiah laughed.

The three of them ate, sharing childhood stories. Sarah tried to ignore all the indications of Jedadiah's burning love for her. Jedadiah played at being in love with Angelina instead. Angelina became thoroughly frustrated with them both by the end of lunch.

With disappointment, they noticed the sky had darkened while they ate. Jedadiah demonstrated his bullfighting skills with the picnic cloth as he helped Sarah fold it. The wind began to whip the cloth violently. Angelina looked up and saw the clouds racing the sky. Its color had changed from brilliant blue just an hour ago to menacing green.

"Jed! Why is the sky green?" she asked.

Jedadiah scanned the horizon with a worried look. "Ladies, let me take you back to Crabtree's in the wagon. It looks like prime twister weather."

"What's a twister?" asked Angelina in alarm.

"He means a tornado, a cyclone. We need to find shelter fast, Angie," confirmed Sarah. "They blow across the plains and in along the river frequently."

Angelina found it hard to control her skirts in the wind blowing from the river as she helped gather the remaining picnic items. Jedadiah finally lifted her up into the wagon next to Sarah and called to the horses to move. The horses refused to budge and neighed their fear to their owner.

"There it is," called Jedadiah over the roar of the wind.

Along the horizon, a huge funnel cloud zigged and zagged across the town. Debris blew up in its path. The horrible sounds of destruction rose above the roar.

In what seemed like one motion, Jedadiah jumped from the wagon and pulled it into the trees. He pulled the frightened women from the wagon and instructed them to lie down on the ground. Satisfied the horses were tied tightly, he flung himself on top of the women to cover them from the flying debris.

Angelina looked up in time to see the twister raise a part of copper-plated church roof and then slam the steeple and metal back down in a heap on the small, white church building.

"Jonathan!" she cried into the roaring wind. Jedadiah's weight held her firmly in place and prevented her from running through the wind to the church.

Jedadiah's voice shouted in her ear, "Pray he was still out calling, Angie. The Lord will care for him. There's nothing you can do for him now but save yourself and pray."

They watched the twister jump the river twice and then dissipate as torrents of rain began to fall. Jedadiah stood and helped the women up from their safe place.

"Come on, Angie. Let's find Jonathan."

Sarah and Jedadiah helped a physically and emotionally crushed Angelina into the wagon. Jedadiah swiftly hugged and kissed them both as he swung up onto the buckboard. The horses cooperated and raced down the bluff to the church house.

What they found when they arrived was devastation. The windows lay shattered on the ground outside the church. Pieces of roof lay crumpled over the pews and pulpit. The rain poured through holes in the destroyed roof and drenched the sanctuary.

"Jonathan!" called Jedadiah.

Sarah poked through the wreckage, looking for him.

"Sarah, be careful you don't turn something over on you," Jedadiah said. "Look in the study. I'll go next door to the house."

Jedadiah marveled at how the parsonage roses gleamed in the murky storm. The little white house sat untouched by destruction.

At the church, Angelina and Sarah pulled together to open the jammed door to the study. They heard a moan from under the desk.

"Jonathan!" called Angelina in fright. "Are you okay, Jonathan?"

A bedraggled figure emerged from under the desk. Blood from a gash in his scalp matted his blonde hair.

"Angel," he said groggily. "Thank God you're okay."

They clung together while she wept. Sarah found a rag and held it up to him for his bleeding head.

"He's not at the house," called Jedadiah as he entered the study. Relief washed over his face as he spied his friend.

"Jon, are you okay?"

Jonathan grinned as he held Angelina. "I've got quite a headache, but I'm going to be just fine. I don't think we'll be having prayer services here tonight, though."

Jed grinned back as Sarah launched herself into his arms in frightful, thankful tears.

"Thank you, Jed, for saving us," she exclaimed through her tears. "I'm so glad you came on our picnic."

# REPAIRS

"Are you hurt, Angelina? We were so worried."

Mrs. C. rushed to hold her as Jedadiah escorted Angelina into Crabtree's.

The tinkle of the bell on the door made Angelina's head hurt.

"Thank God, Jed! Thank God you're both okay! What of Sarah?"

Angelina looked down at her sodden dress. Blood stained the sleeve from nursing Jonathan's gash. Her hands shook as she pulled the remaining hairpins from her wet hair. She looked around at the shattered glass on the store floor.

"I'm fine, Mrs. C. Jedadiah took very good care of Sarah and me on the bluffs. Other than broken glass, how are things here?"

"Other than the glass, we are fine. Where are you bleeding, dear?"

"Not me," she stammered, "Jonathan. The church is devastated."

The room reeled before her eyes as she fought to stand up. Then all went black.

Jedadiah caught her as she fell and carried her to her bed.

"Angelina, it's okay. Wake up. You're in your own room."

Angelina opened her eyes and saw the roses Jonathan had brought, all three, in the same vase that had sat on the sill that morning. She turned her head to the sound of Mrs. C.'s voice.

"That's better. Have some cool water, Angelina. You'll feel better soon."

Angelina reached for her pounding head and found a cool, wet rag there. She sat up slowly and sipped the water Mrs. C. offered her.

"Why don't you change into dry clothes and comb out your hair? That would help you feel better."

"Jonathan?" she asked when she finally found her voice again.

"Ebenezer's gone to the church house with some of the other men. We've closed the store for the rest of the day. The ladies' auxiliary intends to meet at the parsonage for prayer and discussion this evening. Stay here and get some rest."

"No! I need to help too. When are you leaving, Mrs. C.?"

"As soon as you feel up to it, if you're that determined."

"Mrs. C., why isn't the vase broken? It's on the window sill still. The wind should have blown it down."

"That's the way of a twister, Angelina. It hops and skips along with no regard for any property. Some places it destroys; others it misses completely."

"Like the parsonage," Angelina remarked. "The roses, the fence, and the house were all untouched."

"Thank God for that. He'll only need to help us repair the church then."

Angelina washed in the warm water Mrs. C. brought her. She rinsed out her long hair. Then she brushed out the tangles the wind had twisted into her wavy, black mane. She tied it up in a loose ponytail reaching down to her waist with a blue velvet ribbon. She slipped into a navy-striped skirt and navy blouse. Dry clothes felt warm and comforting.

She opened the inner door to the store. Mrs. C. swept glass into the trash container as she watched.

"Are you ready, then?" Mrs. C. asked at her entrance. "You look like you feel much better too." Mrs. C. smiled.

Gold earrings flashed in the lamp light as Angelina smiled back.

The men had boarded up the broken windows, making the store dark. Angelina stepped onto the porch into the sun that shone after the rain while Mrs. C. retrieved her things. The sound of boards being hammered onto other broken windows caused her head to pound that much harder. Her feet, beneath the long striped skirt, longed to run the few blocks to the church to be sure of Jonathan's wholeness. Instead she paced the length of the porch until Mrs. C. appeared. Together they walked to the church to survey the damage.

"Hey, Gold Earrings! You okay?" shouted a Johnson twin from the rooftop. "Jed told me about your close call."

Blue stripes twirled in the sun as she turned to face the voice. Gold earrings and hair swung out from the centrifuge she created as she spun around. Angelina's smile came easier now.

"I'm better. Thank you, Joshua!" she called back.

Jedadiah caught her as she became dizzy and tripped over some debris during her spin.

"Angie! Don't stumble over something."

The bell from the steeple sat at her feet. White-washed splinters lay all about the church grounds.

"I don't think I took time to thank you for saving my life, Jed." Angelina hugged him tightly and kissed him affectionately on the cheek. "I owe you a double favor now—one for bringing my trunk from the station and two for saving my life. I'm not sure I can ever repay you, sir."

"If you can turn Sarah's head toward me for long enough that I can have a chance with her, that will be plenty. Thank you for giving me an opportunity today." He bowed, gallantly sweeping his Stetson to the ground.

Angelina affected a deep curtsy to whistles and catcalls from the men on the roof. She blew them a kiss.

"Don't give all your kisses away, Angel. Save some for me." The quiet, tender voice behind her belonged to Jonathan.

Her heart skipped a beat as he took her hands in his. His shirt was damp and dirty. With his sleeves rolled up past his elbows, muscles bulged beneath the upper sleeve, showing the strength of the sailor he had once been. Damp and tangled hair with a crudely wrapped bandage around his head gave him the look of a pirate.

"Thank God you're all right," Jonathan repeated, his heart in his throat. "Jedadiah is a good man, my best friend in all the world. Preserving your life is the greatest gift he has ever given me."

"Are you all right, Jonathan?" She touched the bandage and smoothed tangles from his hair.

"Yes, Angel, but the Lord's house is not." He pulled her hand from his head to his lips.

"She needs better kissing than that, Reverend," called Joshua from the roof. "I'll volunteer for that job if you can't handle it."

"In your dreams, Josh!" With that, he pulled her closer and kissed her soundly.

The men pulling the tent canvas over the ragged hole in the copper roof cheered, whistled, and laughed.

"Disgraceful, Jonathan. Have you no sensibilities when this … this … person is around? Has she bewitched you into slovenly behavior with her? I, for one, am shocked." The voice was Alice's. "I never allowed you to kiss me like that when we courted. I understood your need to be respected in town. Apparently, Angelina does not."

Alice stormed off to the parsonage, where the other women congregated. Jonathan blushed a deep scarlet and released Angelina. Even his ears burned from the rush of blood to his face.

"I'm sorry to compromise you in front of the town, Angelina. I guess I got a little carried away. It'll never happen again."

"Don't say that, Jonathan," she whispered, catching his roughened hands in her smooth delicate hands.

Her earrings danced in the final rays of the setting sun. She released his hands and felt the warmth of her own cheeks and smiled.

*Never have I felt this way before*, she thought. *Perhaps I do love him!*

She could barely contain her desire to skip to the parsonage. Alice's cold stare checked her excited step. She remembered Edward's words from earlier in the day about her background.

*I guess I've already violated rule number one*, she thought with consternation. *Sarah was right about having a lack of privacy.*

In a state of confusion, Jonathan watched her go.

*Have I violated your code,* Lord, *to feel such a rush of excitement whenever I touch her?* he prayed.

He felt torn between catching her up in his arms and running away to a private place for another kiss or never seeing her again for fear of not being able to control his passion for her.

*Is this excitement, love, or lust,* Lord*? Help me know if she's the one,* Lord, he prayed as he watched the progress on the roof. *Don't let me be fooled by a counterfeit infatuation.*

Jonathan hoisted the bell from the church yard and carried it back to the parsonage stable for safe-keeping. The men on the roof fastened the canvas down as best they could and came down to help clean broken glass and wood splinters from the interior of the church.

Meanwhile, the ladies' auxiliary met in the parsonage parlor. The neat, clean orderliness of the room impressed Angelina. She longed to peek into the other rooms to discover a little more about her Jonathan.

*My Jonathan?* she thought with a shock. She smiled, hoping that was somehow true.

"What shall we do?" worried Nell Johnson. "We'll need money now to fix the roof. If my Jeremiah was alive, he'd mortgage the ranch again to put money into the roof. As it is, Jedadiah's barely able to pay the first mortgage and the taxes due."

"Ebenezer has a little saved to open a new store in Kansas City. It's his dream. I can't ask him to sacrifice his dream now after so many years," Martha Crabtree added.

"The Greenes have little money. With a child due any day and a new barn to build later this summer, they'll need all they have and more," remarked Kate Bardsley.

"The Taylors have more mouths to feed than cash," commented Sue Jones. "The sheriff and I have a little nest egg we could borrow from. But it's not enough to replace that expensive copper roof Charles Bardsley insisted on."

Kate Bardsley winced at Sue Jones's sharp remark.

"Any money in the treasury, Sue?" asked Nell Johnson.

"Only two dollars," she answered.

"Father refuses to pay the church another penny while Jonathan refuses to court me," Alice announced.

"Alice, I don't believe that's what he said," Kate Bardsley rebuked her daughter. "What Charles said was that he wanted his money used responsibly, 'not to court the illegitimate daughter of a bordello madame'." She blushed. "I'm sorry, Angelina. That is what he said, though."

The women grew silent. Angelina squirmed, feeling this problem was somehow her fault. Would it help if she broke off their courtship? She thought about the money she had deposited in the bank on Monday from her trust funds.

*That money might be useful after all,* she thought. *But no one must know that it came from me.*

"We need to have a box supper," Sarah announced in the uncomfortable silence.

"A great idea!" exclaimed Kate Bardsley. "When shall it take place?"

Saturday, they all agreed, was the night. Now they only needed to get the men to agree to their proposal.

While they waited for the men, the ladies prayed and shared Scripture. They praised God for no serious injuries. They asked Him to provide the funds necessary to repair the church house.

Anger and embarrassment at Alice and her family had silenced Angelina throughout the entire meeting. She felt like an outsider to the proceedings.

"Angelina," ventured Kate, "do you have a favorite scripture to share to help us through this trying time?"

Eager faces awaited her answer. Alice looked smug, as though she believed Angelina scripturally illiterate.

"Yes, Mrs. Bardsley, I do. Romans 8:28 is my favorite verse. 'All things work together for good to those who love God and are called according to his purpose.' God, who has called us here at this time, can bring good out of bad to those who love Him. Christians shouldn't fear bad things. They should look for the miracle God will bring out of the tragedy."

"Amen, Angie," Jedadiah responded.

He and the other tired and dirty men traipsed into the parlor.

"Angelina is right," Jonathan affirmed. "God can fix the roof and replace the steeple, no matter how impossible that may seem tonight. I'll get an estimate on the cost tomorrow. We'll talk about money later."

Sue Jones nudged her husband.

"Oh, Pastor," the sheriff said, "the women want to help raise funds by holding a box supper on Saturday."

"That would be fine, ladies. We'll look forward to it."

The townsfolk left the meeting talking excitedly about the social event planned for Saturday.

"What is a box supper, Sarah?" Angelina asked as they left the parsonage.

"Oh, Angie, it's so much fun. All the women prepare a meal for two and box it up. They decorate the boxes to make them attractive. Then the boxes are auctioned off to the highest bidder. The buyer then gets the opportunity to eat supper with the lady who prepared the meal."

"How does the buyer know who prepared the box?"

"Well," Sarah began, "they're not supposed to know. The trick is to decorate the box in a special way so your beau can recognize it and bid for it."

"What if he guesses wrong?"

"That's part of the fun—the surprise at the end of the auction!"

Satisfied with that knowledge, Angelina looked around for Jonathan. She just glimpsed him heading into the church with Mr. Bardsley. She climbed into the Crabtrees' buggy and rode home with them without the pleasure of telling Jonathan good night.

Charles Bardsley joined Jonathan in his dismantled office.

"Charles," Jonathan began, "you see the situation here. I hate to come to you again for money. I know you built the church from your own funds originally. The congregation is truly thankful to you for your generosity. Can you help us again?"

"Jonathan, we never got to have our meeting this afternoon due to the storm. I have some distressing news for you, I'm afraid."

"What's that, Charles?" Jonathan asked.

"I will no longer contribute to this church while you are courting Miss Mercy."

"Excuse me? I must have heard you incorrectly."

"I'm sorry, Jonathan. I'm disappointed in your choice of women. I thought sure you'd recognize the opportunity you had in courting Alice. I guess you're not as smart as I thought you were, son." Charles Bardsley lit his cigar from the flame of the oil lamp on Jonathan's desk.

"Let me understand you better, Bardsley. You're saying that if I married Alice, I'd be well-paid and the church would prosper. If I choose any other girl, I'll be without a job and the church will fail. That sounds like blackmail."

"Hardly, Reverend. You can stay as long as you like as pastor. You'll just not be seeing any of my money. Can the congregation support you? I think not." Bardsley blew a puff of smoke into Jonathan's face. "All I want is to see my Alice happy."

"Alice would never be happy in a marriage to a man who doesn't love her and who can be bought," Jonathan answered angrily. "And neither would I."

"Pastor, don't be so emotional and righteous. Who said anything about love? Marry Alice and keep Angelina on the side as your mistress. The best people do it these days."

"God forbids it, Bardsley. Any marriage vows I make will be strictly enforced."

"Don't play high and mighty with me, Reverend. May I remind you that your sweetheart is a whore's daughter? Oh yes, it's all over town now. How do you think God looks on her?"

"Angelina is a fine Christian woman. Do not attempt to ruin her reputation with the filth of your lies, Bardsley."

Those people remaining in the street heard the harsh voices.

"I will give you one concession, Reverend. I'll happily finance the rebuilding of the roof and steeple. At interest, of course."

"No, thank you, Bardsley. Most of the townsfolk are floundering in your handsome deals now. I'll not put the church under slavery to you and your money!"

"Always a Yankee, Jonathan. I thought sure we could cure you after a year or so." Bardsley stubbed out his cigar on Jonathan's desktop. "A stubborn, high and mighty, holier- than-thou Yankee."

"Get out of my church! Get off the LORD's property, Bardsley!" Jonathan's face shone red with anger. He slammed his fist into the desk, hard enough to make all the books and papers jump.

"I'll make sure you regret this, Reverend." Charles Bardsley coolly strode from the study.

Jonathan spent the rest of the night on his knees on the damp sanctuary wood floor. Surely the LORD knew what he should do.

Thursday morning dawned too early for Jonathan. He cut himself shaving, unable to look himself directly in the mirror. His night of prayer convinced him of only one conclusion: God's work came first. Did he have to sacrifice Angelina for that work? No answer seemed forthcoming on that point.

At the shattered office in the church, he reconstructed the shelves and began replacing the scattered books. With revulsion he threw one of the books across the room. Its title read, *Ministerial Ethics*.

Finally, he made his decision. He also began a list of references and qualifications for his new résumé.

Thursday morning passed uneventfully for Angelina. Jonathan did not come for his *Gazette* and did not bring a parsonage rose.

"I'm sure he has much to concern him this morning, Angelina," comforted Mrs. C.

"I'm sure you're right," Angelina replied.

Deep inside she knew something had gone horribly wrong. She suspected the Bardsleys were at the bottom of it.

At lunch she went to the bank and made a sizable withdrawal from Mama's trust fund account, just in case the church needed it. She swore Mr. Harris, the bank president, to secrecy and reiterated the need for her privacy in these financial matters. In her room, she hid the cash in the locked trunk.

A timid knock interrupted her as she locked Crabtree's front door at six that evening.

"Jonathan," she said softly as she swung the door wide open.

"Good evening, Angelina. Can we talk?"

"Of course. Let me get my bonnet," she said. "Meet me at the outer door in the alley."

She locked the door hurriedly and rushed to get her bonnet. She swept her hair up loosely and tied the bonnet with a black velvet bow. She found him leaning against the brick wall in the alley waiting for her.

"Jonathan, you look so serious. Is your head worse?"

"No, Angelina, my head is fine. It's still the church that is not so fine. Could we take a stroll while we talk?"

"Of course." Angelina didn't like the tone he used or his lack of enthusiasm.

They walked in silence without touching.

"What is so dreadfully wrong, Jonathan?" she finally asked.

"I'm not sure how to put this, Angelina. I need to break off our formal courtship arrangement. It's not that I feel any less strongly toward you. I'm just feeling a great deal of pressure from my demands at the church right now and need to be released from our formal commitment."

Angelina nearly choked on the tears she tried to hold back. She remained silent, for fear of breaking down publicly.

When she did not answer, he continued, "Please try to understand. I enjoy your company very much. You make me feel different than I've ever felt before in my whole life. Now is just a bad time. Please allow me to call on you informally. If another man wants to court you though, feel free to consent, since I have forfeited my rights to your attention."

Hot tears silently coursed down her cheeks.

*How glad I wore this large bonnet to hide away in,* she thought. *Now if only the ground could open up and swallow me alive, I would be satisfied.*

"Please say something, Angelina," he pleaded. "I know this hurts you. Whether you believe it or not, it hurts me dreadfully. I see no other choice for now, short of resigning as pastor and moving elsewhere. I can't ask you to come with me now if I did that, so please give me this time. I don't believe God is done with me yet in St. Joe, and I feel we still have a chance at a future together."

Angelina summoned all her strength and said, "I release you, Pastor. Forgive me for compromising your position."

Jonathan stepped in front of her and grabbed her shoulders firmly.

"No! Understand what I mean! Just give me time to help the church fix this nightmare. Hold on to your dreams, Angel. Help me do the right thing by us both."

He looked down into her sapphire eyes and saw the tears welling up and over onto her porcelain skin. "I didn't want to hurt you, Angel."

"I'd like to return to Crabtree's now. Here's this morning's *Gazette*. You forgot it today."

They walked the few blocks back in silence. Jonathan hurt worse than he'd ever hurt in his life. The wounds on his back from the *Virginia*'s grapeshot and shrapnel hadn't hurt as badly as his heart hurt now. At Angelina's alley door, he took her trembling hand and kissed it gently.

"Don't give up on me, Angel. Allow me to court you informally. May I call on you without a commitment?"

"If that is what you desire, Pastor. I really do understand. Please go on to the Bardsleys'. I'm sure they are awaiting your arrival."

Jonathan's face flushed a brilliant red. *How did she know? What can I do about it? Am I selling my soul to the devil for the sake of the church's existence?*

Angelina stretched up on her toes and kissed him gently on the cheek. "Please go and settle this soon. You may call on me as you wish."

"Will you wait for me?" he asked.

"No commitments, Jonathan, so you'll be free to do what you need to do." She smiled through her tears. Her earrings reflected the sun's last rays. "Just come back to me when it's complete, if you can."

He hugged her close and kissed her tenderly.

"I'll do my best, Angel."

He left her reluctantly. His next stop on this evening's rounds was the Bardsley residence.

"Good evening, Kate. Is Charles at home?"

"Of course, Pastor. I'm so pleased with Angelina. You both make such a handsome, Christian couple. I wish you all the best."

Jonathan nearly choked on his reply. "I'm sorry, Kate, but we have broken off our courtship for the time being. It's too demanding with my load of church responsibilities. Perhaps at another time we can … pursue a formal courtship."

Kate pursed her lips. She knew Charles and Alice had had a hand in this development. Yet what could she do to change it?

"Charles!" she called, "Pastor Thomson's here to see you." To Jonathan, she stated, "I don't know why you've broken your courtship with Angelina. I don't think I want to know. Please don't give up on the relationship due to pressure from—"

"Ah, Pastor. I didn't expect to see you so soon," crowed Charles Bardsley. "How can I help you? I expect you've taken care of that little problem we discussed last night?"

"For now, Bardsley, I have. The LORD's responsibilities come first. Let's talk money."

Mr. Bardsley ushered him into the study.

"I'm not sitting down because I don't intend to stay long. The roof repair will cost about five hundred dollars. The steeple will cost another five hundred dollars. The way I see it, the ladies may raise some of the cost to repair the roof. I'll consider borrowing the remainder from Bardsley Trust after Sunday's offering. The steeple can wait until another time. We can worship without it, if necessary."

"Jonathan, relax. I only want what's best for you, the church, and Alice. Give Alice another chance too."

"No, sir. I will never love Alice, and I will never marry unless the woman is God's choice for me. Alice is not that woman. However, in accordance with your wishes, I have broken my formal commitment to Angelina Mercy, for the time being."

"Fair enough, Jonathan. I like a fair compromise. Like a brandy, son?"

"No, sir. I've compromised enough of my principles today. I prefer not to celebrate that fact. Good evening, Bardsley."

# BOX SUPPER NIGHT

"Is there something else I can get you, Pastor?"

When Angelina unlocked Crabtree's front door Friday morning, Jonathan awaited her. He bought the *Gazette* but remained quiet and distant during the transaction. As he turned to go, he looked back.

"Yes, Angelina. Don't call me 'Pastor' anymore unless we're in public. And I have a desire for Yankee pot roast and Boston baked beans. Perhaps the box supper would be an excellent time to prepare such a meal. It would be a great relief from fried chicken." He smiled conspiratorially at her. "Wear ribbons like the ones that decorate your box, so I'll know which one to bid on."

For the first time since the previous evening, Angelina smiled.

During lunch break, she procured the roast from the butcher and vegetables and accompaniments to produce a genuine Yankee meal. She ran into Sarah returning to Crabtree's.

"What have you got?" asked Sarah.

"Roast for the box supper," answered Angelina innocently.

"Aren't you devastated? I heard Jonathan broke off your courtship. Alice has the news all over town that Jonathan intends to court her instead."

"I wonder that Jonathan needs a *Gazette*. Alice is faster and more entertaining than any newspaper," Angelina quipped. "Yes, he called off our formal courtship. But I'm not letting him go quite that easily."

"Good girl, Angie. I bet old man Bardsley has something to do with all this."

"I really don't know, Sarah," she replied truthfully. "But I've not lost to Alice yet. So what are you fixing Jed for the box supper?"

"Edward, Angie. Not Jed. Really, Angie, I wish you'd help me instead of Jedadiah. He's a lovely man, but Edward is the catch I'm fishing for."

"Not on your life, Sarah. Jedadiah is perfect for you, and he loves you." Angelina tossed her a knowing look. "What could be better than that?"

"Money helps, Angie."

Sarah hugged her friend and went on with the rest of her own shopping.

Angelina arranged with Mrs. C. to use her more ample kitchen facilities during the day on Saturday so everything would be ready.

"Angelina, why wasn't Jonathan here last evening? And why was he so stilted this morning? Has something happened?" asked Mrs. C.

"Jonathan has suspended our courtship for the time being, Mrs. C.," she replied evenly. "The LORD's work comes first."

"So Alice does have reason to crow, does she?" answered Mrs. C. angrily. "I thought that man had more sense than this. What is he thinking, to fall into Alice's trap so easily?"

"She hasn't won yet, Mrs. C.," she assured her confidant.

Saturday finally arrived. The women cooked their meals and decorated their boxes with clues to their identities. Angelina dressed hers in pink and sapphire velvet ribbons and twisted the same into her curling tresses. Her full skirt repeated the same colors in stripes and flowers. She wore a white lace blouse with a short pink jacket over all.

"Sarah, which is your box?" she asked when she arrived at the church.

"The one done up in yellow and green bows. What about yours?"

"The pink and blue. Can't you tell?" Angelina swirled around for the full effect. "I've got an errand to run. See you soon."

Angelina dashed to Jedadiah as he entered the church.

"Jed, I need to speak to you."

She pulled him out into the daylight.

"Are you okay, Angie? I heard the news about you and Jonathan."

"I'll be fine, Jedadiah. It'll work out somehow. Listen, Sarah's box is yellow and green. Maybe this will help." She crushed a wad of currency into his hand. "Don't let anyone else get her box, especially Edward."

"Angel, this is twenty-five dollars. I can't accept this." Jedadiah tried to hand it back to her. "This must be your whole pay so far."

"Close, but it's worth it to me to see you both happy."

"Which box is yours, Angie?" he asked as he pocketed the cash. "Perhaps I should bid on yours instead."

"That, my friend, you'll need to guess."

Angelina turned in a swirl of pink and blue and hurried back into the building. As she reentered the building, she saw Sarah excitedly talking with Edward. She involuntarily shuddered.

The ladies' auxiliary bustled about the damp sanctuary, putting the final touches on the decorations for the box supper. Jonathan read in his study as the women worked. Jedadiah entered the study with a sharp rap on the broken door.

"Hi, Jed," greeted Jonathan cheerily. "What's up?"

"Have you lost your mind?"

"Excuse me, Jed, did I miss part of this conversation?" Jonathan asked, confused.

"Apparently you missed a lot recently. The news is all over town. When did you break your relationship with Angelina?"

"Last night, Jed. Why is that your business?"

"I'm your friend. I'm also Angelina's friend. Unfortunately, one of my friends is a fool. Don't forget what I said about Angelina being mine if you let her go. Others have their eyes on her too." Jedadiah stormed from the office without waiting for an explanation.

Jonathan bounded from the desk chair and seized Jedadiah's arm. He pulled him back into the study and vainly attempted to close the door.

"Don't I get a hearing? Am I already tried and convicted? Do you think I wanted to release Angelina? One of my friends has lost his good judgment of me, I think." Jonathan whispered so that no one in the sanctuary would hear him.

"So, explain it to me."

Jedadiah folded his arms and plopped into a chair in the corner. He listened with growing anger and resentment towards the Bardsleys. When Jonathan had finished telling the entire story, Jedadiah threw his Stetson onto the desk and stood with his hands on the desk.

"What you're telling me is that old man Bardsley has you over a barrel, so you're being a martyr by denying yourself Angelina to save the church. As a member of this church, I don't think that's necessary. God will take care of the church whether you martyr yourself or not." Jedadiah stood erect and folded his arms. "Money isn't the only thing that matters, Jon."

Jonathan's principles winced at Jed's remark.

"I haven't rejected Angelina, merely postponed a formal commitment to her. I hope she's making me a special Yankee dinner tonight, if she's not still angry at me."

Jedadiah replaced his Stetson.

"I wouldn't fix you a cup of coffee if I were her. She probably did your dinner for you, though. She's in high spirits for someone who's angry at her suitor. I hope your secret courtship doesn't explode in your face, Jon. Let me know what I can do to help, though."

---

The auctioneer was Henry Miller, the barber. Jonathan, as pastor, began all the bidding at one dollar. Most of the married men had no competition as they bid on their wives' meals at two dollars. Then Henry held up a yellow and green box.

"Here we have fried chicken and sweet potatoes from a sweet young thing. What do I hear as a bid?" he called out.

"One dollar," called Jonathan.

"Two," shouted Jedadiah.

"Three," answered Edward.

"Four," countered Jedadiah.

Edward glanced back at the pastor. Why wasn't he bidding? Sarah told him this was Angelina's box. A glance at Sarah confirmed his suspicions. She had lied to him to trick him into spending the evening with her.

"Five," answered Edward, as though he hadn't caught on to the trick.

"Six," called Jedadiah.

Edward bowed to Jedadiah, and Henry declared Jedadiah the winner. Jedadiah dropped the six dollars from his wallet into the offering plate and collected his box. A look at Sarah proclaimed her disappointment. As he passed Angelina, he winked.

"Next, we have this beautiful pink and blue box containing Yankee pot roast and Boston baked beans."

A buzz went through the crowd. The owner of the box could only be Angelina.

"One," called Jonathan coolly.

"Two," called Edward.

"Five," called Jonathan.

The buzz in the crowd grew louder.

"Ten," countered Edward.

Jonathan hesitated. All he had in his pocket was ten dollars, not enough to make a counter bid.

Jedadiah slipped him the twenty-five dollars Angelina had given him earlier.

"Thirty-five," answered Jonathan just before Henry closed the bidding.

"Fifty!" shouted Edward.

Jonathan shook his head in defeat and handed the twenty-five dollars back to Jedadiah.

"Two hundred fifty," called a voice from the rear of the church.

All eyes turned to see the identity of the surprise bidder.

"Mr. Howard," whispered the crowd.

Edward bowed to the highest bidder, Mr. Howard. Henry declared the bidding completed for the pretty pink and blue box and announced that Angelina was the gift box donor. Angelina looked at Jonathan in horror. He shrugged his shoulders in as small a way as possible.

Mr. Howard deposited the money into the church plate, accepted the box, and walked to where Angelina sat in a back pew. He doffed his hat to Angelina and handed the box to her.

"Ma'am, it's good to see you again. It was my pleasure to donate to the church fund."

Angelina accepted the box with a questioning look. "Thank you, Mr. Howard. I appreciate your generosity to the church."

"Don't worry, Miss Mercy. I have no other intentions. Choose the man you would like to share this with. My brothers expect me home for dinner with them."

"Wait! Can I ask a question?" Angelina asked him. His nod gave her permission. "Are you ... Jesse James?"

The man took her hand and kissed it gently. "Ma'am, Mr. Howard is my *nom de plume*. It allows me to be a normal citizen in St. Joe. If I tell you my real name, I'd have to kill you, if you know what I mean."

Angelina shivered. "I guess that's an answer then. Thank you again, Mr. Howard, for your donation."

Mr. Howard nodded and went over to where Jonathan stood.

"I have no time to eat just now, Pastor. Perhaps you'd enjoy Miss Mercy's Northern dish and the vittles too."

He nodded to Jonathan and strode from the church. Jedadiah returned Angelina's money unobtrusively as all eyes watched Edward stalk off into the crowd.

Next Joshua bought Alice's box and whisked her away onto the church grounds. Jonathan and Angelina found a spot under a tree and shared their Yankee pot roast and baked beans. Jedadiah and Sarah fumed and fought through the entire meal, to the amusement of the other diners.

At the end of the supper, Jonathan announced the success of collecting enough funds to repair the copper roof. He also announced the need for five hundred dollars to replace the steeple.

Jonathan walked Angelina home when almost everyone else had left. They discussed the miracle Mr. Howard, whoever he was, had created for them.

"God still controls our lives, Angel," he said as they reached Crabtree's. "The Bardsleys never will do so completely."

"Thank God," she whispered.

He kissed her gently as he left.

"See you in worship tomorrow."

---

Angelina pulled her trunk from its resting place as soon as she entered her room and unlocked it. She gathered three envelopes and cash from its hiding place. The first envelope she marked *Steeple—$500*. The second she marked *Greenes—$250*. The third she marked *Taylors—$250*.

On Sunday she placed all three with the designated amounts of cash into the collection plate as it passed.

As Angelina unlocked the door Monday morning, Jonathan awaited her. As she handed him his *Gazette*, he winked at her and handed her the coin and a small silver ring. At her look of surprise, he put his fingers to his lips and smiled.

"Jonathan, I can't accept this," she whispered. "No commitments, remember?"

She fingered the delicate ring of silver with the "T" inscribed on its flat, round surface.

"This is not a commitment, Angel. This is a promise. A promise that you can trust me to do the right thing by you. A promise that I will not humiliate you or compromise your reputation. A promise that I will return first thing every morning for my *Gazette*."

She giggled at his giddiness.

"It's our secret promise, Angel. This pinkie ring belonged to my mother, God rest her soul. She would want me to give this ring to you."

She slipped it into her pocket. "You mean it's a secret courtship we're involved in."

"Remember I told you I didn't feel any less strongly toward you." As Mr. Crabtree entered the room, Jonathan said, "Good news, Mr. Crabtree. We received a sizable donation yesterday, anonymously, that will cover the cost of the new steeple too. Work begins tomorrow. I hope the work is complete by the Fourth of July fair." To Angelina, he formally said, "Thanks for the daily, Angelina. Have a good day." He turned on his heel and strode from the store.

Angelina could barely contain the laughter that threatened to bubble up in her relief and amusement. She fingered the ring in her pocket. She had just the right silver chain to suspend it on too.

That evening, Angelina escaped to the river. She pulled off her flat shoes and stockings and hitched her skirt up to dabble her feet in the lapping water of the wide Missouri River. As she pranced along the edge of the bank, she played hide and seek with the river running into the water and running away from the gentle waves that licked her feet. She pulled the chain around her neck from its hiding place inside her bodice and fingered the tiny silver ring hanging there. She laughed as the warm water covered her toes in silt, then wiggled them in the mud. She hitched her skirts higher to protect the hem from the muddy water.

Jonathan walked along the edge of the bluff sorting the events of the past week in his mind. It was hard to believe Angelina had only been here a week. What changes she'd made in his life!

Something at the river's edge caught his attention. Long wavy, black hair flew behind the porcelain girl chasing the lapping waves. He watched her play in the water's edge, her skirt nearly to her knees.

*She's still a child at heart, despite her former life and the hardships of the week*, he thought. Only eighteen, he reminded himself, feeling so much older than his own twenty-eight years.

Watching her play, he grieved for the child in him who had died on that late April day when his parents had died.

*Captain de Angelo tried to revive that child in me, encouraging me not to be so serious*, he thought.

"Look at the clouds, Jonny," he'd say in his thick Italian accent. "Don't they look like a fire-breathing dragon?"

*I only saw the smoke rising from the house as I walked home from school that day*, he remembered.

"Listen to the waves against the hull and let them rock you to sleep, Jonny," he'd say.

*I only heard the pounding of my heart as I raced down that road and up to the blazing house*, he recalled.

"Look at the silver crests of foam, the wealth of the sea, my boy," he'd say.

*All I saw was the gleam from my mother's ring as I found her dead on the kitchen floor. The same ring I gave Angelina today*, he thought.

*God became my soul love, Angel*, he thought to her as she ran, unaware that he watched her. *It hurts too much to lose a person you love. God will never die. He will protect me, guide me, and bring me to Him when I die. I can depend on Him whenever I need Him. It's so much safer to care for His people through Him and yet be detached from them as well.*

"How can I explain to you, Angel, how hard it will be to give you my heart?" he asked aloud.

As he watched her, she slipped in the Missouri's silt and fell into the lapping water. He laughed aloud as she struggled to stand and shook the water from her sodden skirt. Instead of retreating from the edge, however, she hitched the contrary skirt higher still, revealing her lovely white curved ankles, calves, and knees. Like a beautiful heron, she stood in the water on long, slender legs with her skirts feathered up around her hips.

Though he enjoyed the sight, he feared someone else might also be enjoying the view as well. He descended the path from the bluff to the bank to go to her.

He found her lying on the grassy bank with a cloud of black hair billowing above her fair, flushed face. Her gold earrings glowed in the sunset. Her long legs stretched luxuriously in the fading warmth of the sun. Long lashes closed over her brilliant blue eyes as she drowsed in its warmth. The tiny silver ring dangled from a delicate silver chain bearing a key as well.

His heart swelled at its sight.

She didn't hear or see his approach.

"Ahem." Jonathan cleared his throat to warn her of his approach.

Angelina sat bolt upright from her prone position and yanked her skirts down over her bare legs. She pulled her long slender feet up under her still wet skirt.

"Jonathan, how long have you been here?" she accused playfully.

"Long enough to enjoy the view along the river bank from the bluffs," he hedged.

He folded his long legs and sat beside her. He caught the silver ring in his large hand and gently pulled her face closer to him.

"So you're wearing Mother's ring," he noted.

"Are you offended, Jonathan?"

"Not at all. I'm very pleased."

He resisted with difficulty the urge to kiss her as he had in the churchyard after the storm. He knew it would be too dangerous for them to kiss passionately in God's romantic sunset with her stretched out here on the bank.

*The temptation to go much further would be too risky*, he surmised. *My* Lord *would not approve. I've stretched my principles quite enough for one week.*

He released the chain reluctantly and rose from the bank. He offered his strong hand and pulled her to her feet. She collected her flat slippers, stockings, and Bible from the grass. He took her hand as they navigated the steep incline to the bluff above.

They walked silently, hand in hand, to the church yard.

"I can make it home alone, Jonathan," she finally said. "Our secret courtship wouldn't be much of a secret if the town saw you walking me home like this too often."

She stretched and kissed him playfully. He caught her in his arms and kissed her carefully. She broke from his grasp, giggling, as she skipped the final blocks home.

*Be careful not to give your heart away*, his organized mind warned. His heart knew it might already be too late.

# FOURTH OF JULY FAIR

The hot, humid July days of Missouri summer arrived with a vengeance.

Jonathan arrived promptly at nine each morning to purchase his *Gazette*. Angelina escaped to the bluffs and riverbank most evenings to read Scripture and pray, as well as to chance upon Jonathan there. Jonathan couldn't always get away from his responsibilities at the church. Whenever he could get away, though, the bluffs afforded them a private place to continue their 'secret courtship.' Each possible evening they shared their lives, their laughter, and their frustrations.

Those same two weeks were a blur of activity in St. Joseph. The first order of business involved sweeping away and repairing the storm's damage. The church roof received repair and a new steeple. With the storm all but forgotten, the town turned its attention to preparations for the Fourth of July Fair. Ladies finished their canning, gardening, handiwork, and quilts. Others planned their prize cakes and pies with which to compete. Men practiced roping skills, groomed their animals for show, and finished woodworking projects.

A flurry of last-minute preparations kept Angelina busy at Crabtree's until well after six on the day before the fair. Men and women alike hurried in to purchase confections, notions, and accessories for their fair displays. Angelina stayed up late into the night to finish recording the day's transactions. She missed her visit to the bluffs as well.

Crabtree's remained closed on Saturday, the Fourth, so all could go to the fair. St. Joe celebrated the Fourth, not in honor of independence, certainly not for the sake of the Union, but for the alleviation of the boredom of everyday life. The citizens on the edge of the frontier welcomed any social event to see friends and to change the pace of the ordinary.

Angelina could barely believe her eyes as she rode onto the fairgrounds beside Sarah in the Jones's wagon. Open plains just days before had transformed into a giant carnival. Booths of every description dotted the grounds. Ring toss, ball throw, pony rides, and a dunking booth were only a few of the varied selection. The Tower of Strength rose above it all with its gleaming gong reflecting the hot, July, Missouri sun. A gigantic pit blazed in preparation for the lunch and supper beef barbecue. Booths that displayed crafts and food stood beyond the Tower. Participants in the judging anxiously displayed their creations, hoping for the coveted blue ribbons. Rodeo grounds partitioned off the midway games and display booths from the animal show pens. Livestock paraded in their pens, groomed and coaxed by their proud owners, both young and old.

"Isn't it wonderful, Angie?" asked Sarah in amazement. "Hard to believe it will only be here for a day and then gone again tomorrow, isn't it?"

"I've never seen such a thing," replied Angelina.

"Later we'll watch the rodeo, the three-legged race, and the sharp-shooting competitions," explained Sarah breathlessly.

"Tonight's the best, though. Dancing and fireworks, Angie! Think of it! Colored, booming sparks brightening the prairie sky."

"It all sounds wonderful." Angelina sighed at the wonder of it all. *How will I ever find Jonathan in all these people?*

"Here's the quilt booth. Your fine stitches will win this quilt a blue ribbon."

Sarah hung the double wedding ring quilt from the appropriate line in the booth. A profusion of colorful patches and delicate stitching fluttered in the breeze.

"Sarah! They're all so beautiful. How will the judges ever decide on just one?" Angelina declared as she fingered the beautiful artwork.

"This is nothing. Wait until you see the rest. You should have brought something to display, Angie. One of your fashionable dresses would have won first place any day."

"No, Sarah. I have plenty of competition from Alice to keep me quite happy. There's only one prize I want to win this summer." Angelina grinned at her friend.

Sarah smiled. "Jonathan. Am I right? I still think he's too old …"

"I know, and too poor and too public. You're probably right. It really doesn't matter, though, does it?" Angelina hugged her friend impulsively.

"You're in love with him, aren't you?"

"Isn't it wonderful to be in love? You should really try it." Angelina pirouetted, setting her full skirt to full sail.

"You're disgusting. I think I'd like you better drunk. At least then I'd know you'd be better in the morning. Come on." Sarah jerked Angelina in the direction of the canning booth.

Angelina giggled as Sarah pulled her into the canning booth. There they laughed heartily over Mrs. Jones's onion relish.

"You see, Angie! I told you Mama had no need for an onion the first day we met. Mama raises prize onions for relish every year. She always wins the blue ribbon."

They continued their stroll around the grounds, admiring the work displayed for judging. They drooled over the cakes at the cake booth. Mrs. C.'s chocolate cake stood proudly among the rest.

"Mrs. C.'s cake always wins. I think she slips rum into the icing. The judges always love it!" Sarah informed Angelina.

They found Kate Bardsley proudly displaying an intricate work of embroidery in another booth.

"What do you think, Angelina? I just finished it last night with that bit of floss you sold me late yesterday," she asked.

"It's lovely, Mrs. Bardsley," Angelina replied.

"Please call me Kate. I feel so responsible for the way Alice and Charles are treating you. Don't give up on Jonathan, though. You two make such a wonderful couple. Alice is so fickle. I'm sure she'll find another man shortly."

"Thank you, Kate," Angelina replied, stifling the desire to laugh.

"What a lovely pair of ladies," came a masculine voice from behind them. "If I take one on each arm, I'll be the most hated man at the fair."

"When will you ever be serious and settle down? You can't flirt and chase women the rest of your life. Someone's bound to catch you someday," chastised Sarah.

"I'm sure you're right, Sarah, my love," he gushed expansively. "Until then, I intend to enjoy as many of them as I can."

"You were right, Joshua," said Angelina. "You are the incorrigible one."

Joshua threw his head back and laughed broadly. "So, you can finally tell brother Jed and me apart."

The threesome enjoyed a good laugh at Joshua's expense. He steered the ladies to the woodworking booth.

"I'll leave you both in the care of older, wiser, and more responsible brother," he said as he made an elegant bow.

"Say what you will about my brother, but he does know where to find the best looking ladies. Good morning." Jedadiah took Sarah's hand and kissed it gently. After a lingering gaze into Sarah's dark brown eyes, he released her hand and hugged Angelina tightly. "What do you think of my creation?"

He gestured to an intricately carved wooden chest. Flowers and hearts adorned the lid. Scrollwork repeated a pattern over the entire piece.

"What a beautiful job!" Angelina exclaimed. "I didn't know you were skilled at woodworking."

Jedadiah winked knowingly at Sarah, who grinned happily.

"My father was a cabinetmaker before he came to St. Joe. He took up ranching instead because he thought he'd make more money at it. In his spare time, he made hope chests and cabinets for friends and family. Sarah has one of my father's chests, don't you?"

"Yes. Mr. Johnson made a special chest like this one for me." Sarah lovingly rubbed her hands over the carvings.

"Tell her why yours is so special, Sarah," he prodded.

"Mr. Johnson insisted that since Jed and I were special friends as children, we would someday marry. He wanted his son's wife to have a very special hope in Jedadiah and the Johnson family." Sarah blushed, remembering Jeremiah Johnson's words when presenting it to her on her thirteenth birthday.

"So your father taught you how to make them too, Jed?" asked Angelina, breaking the embarrassing moment between Sarah and Jedadiah. "Who's this one for?"

"Someone very special, Angie, who needs hope very badly," said Jedadiah lovingly. He yelped when Sarah stomped on his foot.

"Come on, Angie," demanded Sarah as she spun a confused Angelina away from the chest and toward the midway.

"Sarah! Look at the flowers!"

Angelina exclaimed over every bud and bloom she saw in the gardening booth. Then she saw it. Alone in the back of the other entries stood a single blush rose with the edges trimmed in red.

"Look how perfect and unusual this rose is, Sarah," she gasped. "This is a prize winner for sure."

The display card had fallen face down. Angelina lifted the card to discover the name of the gardener who had grown such a special rose.

"My Angel's Rose," the card read. "Reverend Jonathan Thomson, First Church, St. Joe."

Angelina felt for the silver ring at her neck inside her bodice and whispered, "This is a promise."

"Who grew it, Angie?" asked Sarah, intrigued by Angelina's reaction.

Angelina smiled as she handed the card to her friend.

"How romantic!" Sarah sighed.

Angelina replaced the card upside-down on the table. On the back she wrote Jonathan's name to preserve their secret a little longer.

They ate popcorn and cookies, cider and candy until they both thought their corsets would pop.

"It's not fair at all. You won't gain an ounce after this feast. I'll probably gain ten pounds before it's all over," the plumper Sarah groaned. "I guess I'll just have to dance all the dances at the square dance tonight to work off the extra weight I've gained."

Angelina frowned. "Sarah, I've waltzed and reeled, but I've never squared. How do you do it?"

Sarah laughed and began to speak, when the ringing of the Tower of Strength gong caught their attention.

"No one ever hits the gong at the fair," Sarah declared. "Who could be that strong?"

The gong rang again as they dashed to the Tower.

"Do it again, Jon. Prove you can do it three times in a row," Jedadiah dared Jonathan.

Jonathan had removed his coat and tie and rolled up his clean, crisp shirt sleeves. The Tower mallet rested easily in his hands.

"I can't afford to hit it again, Jed. Ten cents is my limit."

"Here's a dollar, man," Jedadiah declared, as he laid the money on the barrel top. "Do it twenty times."

"Jed, this is unnecessary. Take your money back."

Jonathan spotted Angelina's earrings before he actually saw the rest of her. That brilliant flash in the crowd of spectators could only be her, though. Soon he saw both Sarah and Angelina on a run to the Tower.

Jonathan looked at Jedadiah hard. "Okay, take this bet. Twenty tries, ten apiece and we're even. If I get more, though, you buy me lunch. Deal?"

Jedadiah saw the ladies then too. He muttered under his breath to Jonathan, "That's a swindle, Jon. You just want to look good for Angelina."

"Here's a chance to win Sarah," he spread his arms magnanimously, muscles bulging at his shirt seams. "Beat the weakling pastor, Jed."

Jedadiah winced at Jonathan's remembrance. On Jonathan's first day pastoring in St. Joe, Jonathan had allowed Jedadiah to rant and rave over the "weakling Yankee pastor" coming from Harvard to lead the church. After Jedadiah's tirade, Jonathan had identified himself to his embarrassed soon-to-be friend. Jedadiah knew too that Jonathan's strength could best him any day.

"I knew you wouldn't forget that," Jedadiah muttered.

By now the ladies were in hearing range.

"Okay, Jonathan. You're on. Winner gets lunch."

"And wins the company of a lovely lady," whispered Jonathan. "I'm up by two already," he declared loudly. "Your turn to hit two."

Jedadiah rolled up his plaid sleeves and swung the mallet with all his might. The indicator rose to just below the gong. The second swing only raised it half the distance. He flushed in embarrassment.

"Swindle," he muttered under his breath.

Jonathan smiled. He accepted the mallet graciously and swung it down hard onto the platform. The gong sounded loudly.

"That's three, Jed," reveled Jonathan.

Sarah turned to Angelina in wonder. "Jonathan hit the gong three times!"

The rest of the crowd muttered the same sentiment as the pastor reared back for his fourth swing. The gong sounded loudly at his triumph.

"He doesn't look too old to me, Sarah," Angelina said innocently, grinning proudly.

When the match finished, Jedadiah had grazed the gong three times to Jonathan's nine solid hits. Jonathan missed the last when he caught Angelina's eye as she blew him a kiss in midswing.

Jedadiah bought lunch for all four before setting off to ride in the rodeo. He won prizes for roping and riding but got thrown off the untamed bronco while Jonathan, Angelina, and Sarah cheered him on.

After the rodeo, they circled back through the booths to see the winners of the judging. Jedadiah gloated over his blue ribbon for the carved hope chest. Sarah exulted in her blue ribbon attached to her quilt. Mrs. Jones, Mrs. C., and Mrs. Bardsley also won blue ribbons for their entries.

Jonathan guided Angelina to the gardening booth.

"I saw your rose, Jonathan. It's beautiful." Angelina burst with pride when she spied the blue ribbon attached to the vase.

"Did you also see the name I gave it?" he asked cautiously.

"Yes, Jonathan. I'm flattered and pleased."

Jonathan retrieved the vase from the back of the table and plucked the bloom from it. He placed the ribbon on his jacket and presented the rose to Angelina in a humble manner.

"Will you accept it from me?" he asked.

"I don't know if I should since we're not courting any longer," she answered coyly, for the benefit of any bystanders.

He looked crushed.

"Of course, I'll accept it. It's lovely, Jonathan."

As he affixed the rose to her bonnet, he whispered in her ear, "No more lovely than its namesake, Angel." He kissed her ear unobtrusively.

A bruised Jedadiah tied himself to Jonathan for the three-legged race. Sarah and Angelina cheered as the two strong men took an early lead. Sarah waved Jed's Stetson frantically. Two feet from the finish line, Jonathan's long stride stretched too far for Jedadiah's stability. The pair tumbled as the onlookers laughed and moaned at their loss.

Following the race, Jedadiah challenged Jonathan to the sharpshooter's competition. Jonathan cocked the rifle and shattered each bottle placed for his shots. Jedadiah missed only one.

"Maybe you should have been a marine sharpshooter after all," ribbed Jedadiah. "But I'm sure some small boys' mothers are awfully glad you didn't."

Jonathan punched Jedadiah in the shoulder to signal his mock anger with Jedadiah's remark. A giant bell called hungry fairgoers to the barbecue pit for a dinner of barbecue and fixings. It was delicious after a full day of activity.

Jonathan and Jedadiah left Sarah and Angelina on their own in order to help Phil Taylor with his livestock.

When dinner ended, fiddling began in the distance.

"C'mon, Angie, first dance is ladies' choice." Sarah pulled at her arm to run to the dance platform.

"Go ahead before me, Sarah. I'm too tired and full to run anywhere," Angelina encouraged.

Sarah took off to find Edward somewhere in the crowd, and Angelina sighed. The evening had barely begun, and she felt exhausted. She took her time strolling to the dance platform, admiring the lingering displays and watching the other couples. The men won toys for their sweethearts at the game booths; the women oohed and aahed at their men's prowess. The hot sun had cooled, so Angelina removed her bonnet to admire her rose, releasing her black curls to the summer evening breeze. The only way the evening could improve would be to have Jonathan with her, without fear of Bardsley recrimination.

As though conjured, Edward appeared at her side.

"Good evening, Angelina."

Angelina jumped, despite her best intentions, and stammered out a reply, "Edward. Shouldn't you be at the dance floor? I'm sure Sarah's looking for you."

"I have no interest in Sarah Jones," he replied coolly. "I'm interested only in you."

His arm encircled her waist as he pulled her between two game booths along the midway. The air was hot and still between the tents. Edward held her face with his hands and brought his mouth down hard onto her lips. Angelina struggled to be free, but he wrapped a leg around her lower legs. She was afraid of falling if she moved. Fear rose in her chest as one of his hands moved to her chest and began unbuttoning her blouse.

"Aah, what is this pretty little silver thing on your chain?" asked Edward darkly. "Capital T. Thought the pastor knew better than to cross my father."

She gasped for breath as his lips bruised hers. When he touched her bared breast, she bit his lip as hard as she could. As he howled in pain, Angelina extricated herself from his grasp and ran, panic-stricken, toward the fiddle music. Jonathan's rose dropped onto the walkway. Edward stomped it and twisted it into the straw.

Angelina ran blindly across the midway directly into Jedadiah.

Jedadiah took one look at her twisted hair, wild look, and gaping disheveled clothes and swept her up into his arms. He carried her purposely to a protected spot in the trees beyond the grand stand. The silver chain and pinkie ring Jonathan had told him about dangled at her exposed breast.

"What happened?" he asked with concern. "Who did this to you? Are you all right?"

It was then that she started to scream. No one but Jedadiah heard her as the music and pounding of feet on the wooden stage drowned out her horror. Jedadiah held her close as she wept.

She whispered only one word as she cowered in his arms, "Edward."

When her sobs subsided, Jedadiah gently smoothed her hair as she rearranged her clothing. She gasped as she realized Jedadiah could see Jonathan's silver ring.

"It's okay, Angelina. I know about your secret courtship. Jonathan needs to know about Edward, though."

Angelina shook her head violently. "He'd … kill … him," she stammered. "No, I've caused him enough grief. Thanks for saving me yet again, Jed. You should be wooing Sarah."

"My friends need me first. Sarah loves me; she'll wait for now." He waved away Angelina's protest. "She doesn't know that she loves me, but she'll remember soon."

He helped her to her feet. She smoothed the grass and wrinkles from her skirt.

"I'm not hurt, Jed, just frightened."

"We'll just keep him away from you then, won't we?" Jedadiah promised. "Let's find Jonathan."

He led her from the shelter of the trees to the dance floor. What they saw there sickened them both.

Alice hung around Jonathan like a limp rag doll. The slow waltz fiddle music for the ladies' choice dance prompted Alice to rub her petite body on Jonathan's. She reached to caress his face, but he dodged her gracefully. Jonathan spoke quietly to her and attempted to guide her off the dance floor. Her hysterical drunken screams of defiance drew the attention of all the dancers and the rest of the crowd.

"Aren't I good enough for you, Mr. Preacher? That little daughter of a whore is better than me? Is that what you think? I can make you love me, Jonathan. Give me a chance, Jonathan." Alice broke into slobbering sobs.

Jonathan, red-faced, finally picked her up in his strong arms and carried her off the stage to her embarrassed mother.

"I take it back," Sarah said from behind Angelina. "I like you much better sober."

Jedadiah looked ready to spit nails, when Jonathan appeared among the threesome. Jedadiah threw his Stetson into the ground and stomped off a few yards, grasping Jonathan's arm tightly.

"These are the people you sold Angelina out for?" he shouted at him angrily. "While Angelina is being accosted, you're playing with that drunken dragon lady on the dance floor."

"You don't know what you're talking about, Jed. You know it would be rude and in no one's best interest if I refused Alice the ladies' choice dance."

Their voices rose to an angry roar. Sarah comforted Angelina as they watched the men square off. Their words were indistinguishable to the rest of the crowd above the music.

"You should have been watching over Angelina so that dance could have been hers. Now all three of you are disgraced," Jed replied angrily.

"It's none of your business, Jed. Stay out of it!" Jonathan shouted back.

"No!" screamed Angelina as Jedadiah threw the first punch to Jonathan's chin.

Sarah held her back as Jedadiah swung a right punch toward Jonathan's midsection that Jonathan dodged. Jonathan grabbed Jedadiah's arm and wrestled him to the ground. The men wrestled against each other for several minutes as a crowd formed. The struggle ended in a draw as they separated from the entangled clench.

"I'm sorry, Jon. I just think you need to think of Angelina," Jedadiah gasped into Jonathan's ear.

"I'm trying to do just that," Jonathan gasped back. "I also have a responsibility to the church, Jed."

"I'm trying to understand that, Jon," Jed replied as they helped each other up from the ground.

As they stood back up, exhausted, the first of the fireworks screamed into the night air. The crowd looked upward at the brilliant display of color in the sky and clapped their approval. Sarah released Angelina so Angelina could run toward the men. Jonathan swept her up lightly into his arms and carried her off to a secluded spot.

"Is what Jedadiah told me true?" he finally asked. "Did someone really attempt to hurt you? Who?"

She nodded tenuously. "I've caused you enough hurt, Jonathan." She pulled the chain from its hiding place and began to remove the ring. "I'll not come between you and Jedadiah too."

Jonathan's hand closed on her trembling hands as she tried to release the clasp on the chain.

"No, leave it there. It would hurt me more to take it from you. Jed and I are fine. We're best friends. What's a best friend for if you can't go a few rounds with him when you're angry?"

A burst of color enlightened the night sky revealing the fear on Angelina's face.

"Who tried to hurt you, Angel?" he asked tenderly.

Angelina looked away from him into the dark. "I don't know him, Jonathan," she finally replied with the lie. LORD, *forgive me for lying to protect Edward from Jonathan.*

Another whistle and burst of fire lit the night sky.

Jonathan bent and kissed her tender lips gently in the once more dark night.

Gold earrings reflected the fiery burst of color from yet another explosion as they kissed.

# MYSTERIOUS SUSPECT

After the fireworks, Jonathan took Angelina back to Sheriff Jones's wagon.

"I'd take you back myself, but it's better if you go back with Sarah. And you need to tell the sheriff what happened tonight. In fact, it might be good if you stayed the night with Sarah."

Angelina nodded as she released his hand reluctantly.

"Smile, darling," Jonathan whispered. "Our time will come."

Angelina tried to smile at Jonathan's blue eyes, but Edward's menacing voice filled her ears. Sarah ran up to her and grabbed her shoulders.

"Guess what, Angie! Edward danced the last dance with me!"

Angelina forced a smile and flashed it at Jonathan as Sarah dragged her to the wagon. Sheriff Jones helped the girls into the wagon as Sarah jabbered about everything that had happened that day.

"Can I stay overnight tonight?" asked Angelina as Sheriff Jones helped her up.

"Mrs. Jones, do ya think we have room for another young lady in our home?" the sheriff asked.

"Angie, you are welcome anytime. Are you okay?" asked Mrs. Jones when she saw Angelina's face. "Are you afraid to go home?"

Angelina nodded and gulped. "Yes, something happened tonight, and I'm afraid it could happen again."

"Angie, what's wrong?" Sarah asked, alarmed. "Did someone try to hurt you? Who did it?"

Sheriff Jones turned on the seat and looked into her face. "Is this a matter for the law, ma'am? We'll talk when we get back to the house."

Sarah grabbed Angelina's hand and squeezed it hard. The wagon bounced back to town.

※

When they reached the house, Angelina and Sarah hurried to Sarah's bedroom. "You need to tell me right now what happened!" declared Sarah. "Who was it and what did he do to you?"

Angelina reached behind her for the bed so she wouldn't fall to the floor. She swallowed and nodded. Sarah got a nightgown out for Angelina as she took off the damaged blouse.

"What did he do? Did he hurt you?" she repeated as Angelina redressed. Sarah saw the silver ring as Angelina hid it quickly. "Who did this?"

Angelina shook her head and took a deep breath. "He scared me, Sarah. He reminds me of my nightmares. I have no other rational reason to be this afraid of him."

"What kind of nightmares do you have? It's something that happened in Boston, isn't it? It's the reason you came to St. Joe, isn't it?" Sarah asked. "Well, are you going to tell me or make me guess?"

Angelina nodded as she pulled the cool cotton gown over her head. "Remember when I told the ladies about my mother's business at the quilting bee. On my thirteenth birthday, Mama told me about what happened after the parties. And so for the next three years, I watched the well-dressed men with disdain as I saw them in church with their families in the same attire they'd worn to the party the previous night. I began to avoid the steps during the parties for fear that someone would mistake me for one of Mama's girls. Then someone did, and I had to leave."

"What happened that you had to leave?" asked Sarah.

"I was nearly raped. A man came upstairs into my bedroom. He was horrible, Sarah. He knew I was a virgin and wanted to … have me." Angelina began to cry. "After that I went to live at Mr. Martino's general store. The nightmares replay the event over and over, but I can never see his face."

"Someone threatened to hurt you tonight? In St. Joe?"

Angelina nodded as she wiped away the tears. "What should I do?"

"You need to talk to my dad. He is the sheriff, you know. Who scared you tonight?"

"I am afraid to tell you. He hasn't really done anything! Why would I want to tell the sheriff unless he'd actually done something?" Angelina passed her hand over her eyes and lay back onto the bed.

Sarah sat down next to her. She leaned against the wall and sighed.

"You need to understand that menacing someone is also a crime. Whoever it is wants to scare you, and it's working. Talk to my dad in the morning. He can keep whoever it is away legally."

"Legally is not the same as actually," Angelina groaned. "I want him totally away."

"Tell me who it is. I bet Jonathan or Jed would help with a protection detail."

Angelina sat up quickly and grabbed Sarah by the shoulders. "You cannot tell anyone anything about this whole thing. I don't need any of the men in town forming a posse to get … him. Just let me handle it my way."

Sarah pulled Angelina's hands away and held her close. "Don't be afraid. I'm your friend. Don't forget that when you are alone. The guys want to help too. There's no reason to be alone here."

Angelina nodded and hugged her friend tightly. They finished getting ready for bed and snuggled in. Sarah blew out the light.

"You can tell me who it was, Angie. It's okay."

Angelina pretended to be asleep already. *How would Sarah take the info that her intended beau attacked me?* Angelina lay awake most of the night for fear that the nightmare would return.

---

"Wake up, young ladies! Breakfast is on, and Angelina needs to get to work on time."

Angelina rolled over and laughed as Sarah sat up with her hair a jumble.

"Did you sleep well, Angelina?" asked Mrs. Jones. "I know you were shook up when we came home from the fair."

"I didn't sleep much, but that's okay, Mrs. Jones." Angelina yawned. "I'll eat a bite and be on my way. I appreciate being able to stay with Sarah last night."

"We are glad to have you," said Mrs. Jones. "I'll leave you two to dress."

Mrs. Jones closed the door as she headed back to the kitchen.

"Talk to Dad before you go, Angie. He could help, you know," Sarah said as she stretched. "You don't have to tell me if you don't want."

"Sarah, I don't want you to be upset. It was Edward," Angelina blurted out. "He tore my blouse, touched me inappropriately, and tried to take advantage of me. He must be the guy from my dream."

Sarah turned around and examined Angelina's blouse. Then she looked out the window toward the bluffs as she buttoned her own blouse.

"What if you're wrong, Angie?" Sarah finally said. "What if Edward isn't the guy you think he is? What if you misunderstood his intentions? You could ruin his life … and mine!"

"Sarah, I have no desire to hurt you or anyone else!" Angelina protested. "I never wanted any of his attention. You know that!"

Sarah whirled away from Angelina and headed to the kitchen alone. Angelina sobbed as her friend turned her back on her. She pinned the ripped blouse as best she could and slipped from the room and out the front door.

---

Angelina hid in the back room, nose to the ledgers, as much as possible the rest of the morning. She had no desire to come face-to-face with Sarah, Edward, Alice, even Jonathan or Jedadiah. The Crabtrees left her alone since the store had very little traffic just after the fair. She balanced the books and reconciled the inventory with the invoices. Eventually, she ran out of paperwork to hide behind.

"Mr. Crabtree, what else can I do for you? The books are caught up."

"Miss Mercy, kindly run the receipts over to the bank and then take the rest of the day. It appears the town partied too much at the fair yesterday."

"Thank you, sir. I may take a nap. Sarah and I stayed up too long talking last night," she said.

"So that's where you were last night. I told you she wasn't with a man!" said Mrs. Crabtree to her grumpy husband. "You take the rest of the day, Angelina. We shan't need you today."

Angelina nodded and picked up the bag with the cash for the bank. She walked to the bank and deposited the money. On the way back to the store, she ran into Sheriff Jones on the boarded sidewalk.

"You left without breakfast this morning, Angelina. What's going on?"

Angelina shook her head slowly. "If I tell, Sarah may never forgive me."

"So what did Edward Bardsley do this time? Sarah should be desiring Jed, not Edward. It would be my pleasure to remove him from the town. He gives me pause, like I'm waiting for something awful to happen. Come with me to the jail, and let's talk."

Angelina looked into the lawman's kind eyes.

"Come on, girl. Let me do my job. They didn't give me the tin star for nothing."

He offered his arm. She took it and accompanied him to the office, where she told him the story of the night before and of the last night in her mother's home. He leaned back in his chair with his boots on the desk. He nodded while she told the whole story. When she was done, through her tears and many hankie wipes, he asked one question:

"When were you attacked in Boston?"

"It was an evening in October 1866. There's a police report, but no one ever found any evidence to help find him."

Sheriff Jones nodded knowingly. He moved his boots back to the floor and stood and stretched. He grabbed his hat from a peg behind his desk next to the jail cell. He sat on the edge of the desk and cocked his hat back so he could look into Angelina's terrified, blue eyes.

"Don't worry, young lady. Let me check on a few things. I'm thinking the search committee was in Boston around that time. Edward Bardsley was on that committee. Also, don't worry about Sarah. She blows up quickly, but she'll get over it. She never holds a grudge, and maybe she'll finally get her head on straight about Edward Bardsley. Come around the house tonight for dinner. I should have a start on an answer by then. It'll be okay."

He held out his hand to help Angelina stand. He gave her a fatherly shoulder squeeze. Angelina sniffed and wiped her eyes.

"Thanks. I appreciate it, Papa Jones."

"So we'll see you later?"

Angelina nodded.

The back door swung open before Angelina could even knock on the door.

"Angie!" cried Sarah. "I'm so sorry about what I said to you this morning. I'm so sorry you were frightened. Can you forgive me?"

"Of course, Sarah. We're friends, right?"

Sarah hugged her so tightly Angelina could barely breathe.

"Sarah, let the girl breathe," declared Mrs. Jones. "We're so glad you decided to forgive Sarah's tiff this morning. We're on the side of anyone who stands up to the Bardsleys."

"But I don't know who it was. What are the odds of me moving halfway across the country to the exact same place of my attacker?" said Angelina.

Sheriff Jones clip-clopped into the kitchen, kissed his wife, and hugged his daughter. He nodded to Angelina.

"Checked on that matter we chatted about earlier. The time frame fits. This makes our man a definite suspect."

Angelina felt her head begin to pound and the room begin to spin. *Could Edward be the man who tried to rape me in Boston?*

"Hon, quit talkin' in riddles. Who is 'our man'?" scolded Mrs. Jones. "Privacy is always kept within these walls, Angie."

Angelina nodded to Mrs. Jones and felt herself growing faint. She swooned and saw the floor turning dark as it rushed to her. The last words she heard was Sarah saying, "I'll go get Jedadiah!"

When Angelina became conscious, she woke to Jedadiah and the sheriff arguing.

"Bardsley!" shouted Jedadiah. "I want to call that man out."

"Don't do it, Jed," warned the sheriff. "Let me find a way in the law to handle this. Just 'cause we know it's truth don't make it truth in a court of law! We only got opportunity and bad character."

"Don't you need to also keep Angie safe in the meantime?" asked Jedadiah heatedly.

"Don't you go starting a lynch mob, Jedadiah Johnson! No one needs to go attacking a respected family in our community."

"Respected? Respected? You are crazier than a rabid dog to say that!"

"I shoulda known better than to expect a Johnson to be rational about this. I should be talkin' to Pastor Jonathan. He should know what's going on," answered Sheriff Jones.

"No!" Angelina called out.

Angelina struggled to sit up from the divan, but the room spun again.

"Stay down, Angelina," Jedadiah said as he rushed to her side and took her hand. "I know you asked me not to tell him last night, but he deserves to know who the enemy is, whether provable in a court of law or not."

Angelina shook her head carefully. "Jonathan cannot know. He cannot serve the church and take on the Bardsley family. Jedadiah, help me keep him safe from them."

"You know, your secret courtship has almost as many people who know about it as people who don't! And Jon thinks no one knows," said Jedadiah incredulously. "What will I do with you and Jon?"

"Maybe you could help her get home safely. She was upset about what happened at the fair and didn't get enough sleep last night. She just needs to rest right now," Sarah said. "Surely this is just a misunderstanding."

Jedadiah nodded, "Okay for now, but I want to know more about this, Sheriff. Let me help if I can."

He helped Angelina to her feet. Sheriff Jones nodded slightly so Angelina did not see.

"I'm sorry about dinner, Mrs. Jones. Jed, please don't tell Jonathan," Angelina said. "Promise?"

"Only for now, Angie, only for now," said Jedadiah as he eased her toward home.

# HOPE CHEST SHOWER

Missouri summer arrived with a vengeance that next week. The stifling air begged for a breeze. Crops lacked rain. The people of St. Joe prayed for respite, knowing that none would come until the first days of September.

Angelina did not return to the bluffs during that week following the fair. The nightmare returned each night; the man in her dream remained faceless. She feared being alone by herself at dusk. She feared running into Edward and having her nightmares come true. She only hoped Jonathan would understand when he went to the bluffs and she wasn't there.

Each morning Jonathan arrived for his *Gazette* but never asked why she hadn't come. Always there were too many people for them to speak of it. His eyes asked the question she couldn't answer, though. The lie she had told him about Edward weighed on her heart.

Saturday morning after the fair, Jonathan strode into the store.

"Mr. Crabtree, I have need of Angelina at the church this morning. Is it all right if I borrow her? The church's books are in a state of confusion."

"Certainly, Preacher," answered Mr. Crabtree. "Just be sure she's back to do mine later."

"Of course, Mr. Crabtree. She'll be back later this afternoon." To Angelina, he asked, "If that's okay with you, Angelina?"

"It's fine, Pastor," she replied. Her heart jumped at the chance to spend time with Jonathan, even over the church's finances. "Let me get my things."

They set out for the church in a business-like manner. Jonathan's long legs strode just that much longer than hers that she felt she had to run to catch up.

"Jonathan! Slow down!" she begged.

"Sorry, Angelina. There's work to be done."

His cool manner puzzled her. Was he angry with her? She reached out and caught his hand. The touch radiated through her body like a lightning bolt.

"Please, Jonathan, slow down," she asked him again.

He turned to face her and saw the sun reflect against her earrings, lighting her face. His grin reassured her that he had also felt the charge in their touch.

"Keep up, little angel. The sooner we get to the church, the sooner we can talk privately." He stretched his legs to a greater gait.

Challenged, she picked up her skirts, exposing her ankles in her flat shoes and began to run. This time she rejoiced at being tall enough to ignore high-heeled fashion. As she passed him, he just missed her with a lunge.

Laughing, he started to run behind her, hoping no one else was noticing their race through the remaining blocks to the church. He passed her easily, then slowed just enough for her to catch up. As she nearly passed him again, he easily increased his speed and ran the rest of the way to the church. She raced behind him in pursuit.

He fell down on the church steps, gasping for breath as she entered the churchyard and collapsed at his feet.

"I swore I would never chase any man," she gasped. "You've made a liar out of me, Jonathan." *In more than one way.* She cringed inside at the thought.

He laughed a deep laugh and dragged her up from her repose and into the church.

The dark sanctuary coolness relieved their overheated bodies. The quiet, reverent atmosphere calmed her fears and acted as balm for her hurt. The smell of wood polish and floor soap beckoned her into the darkness. Angelina slid into a cool pew and relaxed in its wooden arms as she caught her breath. She wiped back the escaping tendrils of her chignon. Jonathan folded himself into the pew in front of her and watched her recover.

"I've missed you, Angel," he finally said, breaking the silence. His words echoed in the large open room.

Suddenly shy, she answered, "And you too, Jonathan."

His mind had imagined all the possible reasons she had avoided seeing him in the evenings. *Did I do something wrong at the fair? Did Alice's display hurt her? Did my rose offend her? Did the struggle with Jedadiah really bother her?* Finally he concluded that the stranger had hurt her in the only way he could imagine.

"Is something wrong, Angel?" he asked quietly. "Did that stranger damage you in some way you're afraid to tell?"

When she failed to answer his probing question, he asked, "Did he take improper license with you, Angelina? Did he … violate you?"

When she began to cry, he assumed he had guessed correctly.

"Sweetheart, you were not at fault for some man's improper advance. If you turn up … in a family way … Angel, we'll simply leave town and marry and raise the child like one of our own."

As he babbled on, Angelina shook her head fiercely shaking her chignon loose. Her hair tumbled to her shoulders and down her back.

"Jonathan, stop talking," Angelina forced out between sobs. "He didn't actually have relations with me."

She stood from the pew and walked to the window. The new window pane of colored glass reflected her image back. In the reflection, she saw Jonathan walk up behind her and touch her hair. He checked his touch, opening his mouth to speak and closing it.

"Then I don't understand," he finally said quietly. "Is it me?"

She whirled around and faced him, then dodged the arms he held out to her. She walked to the altar and sat down before it.

Lord, *what can I say?* she prayed quickly.

He came and sat beside her on the front row.

Finally she broke the silence. "I'm afraid to come to the bluffs alone. I'm afraid I'll not get away so easily the next time … this man … tries to rape me. I'll not come to a marriage with you like that."

He wrapped her in his arms and held her close.

"Lord, help me, I'll kill the man who did this to you with my bare hands," he intoned darkly. "No man has the right to molest my Angel."

Angelina thought of all the women in Madalaine's who gave themselves freely to a different man every night. She thought of her mother, who loved Michael but refused to allow him to marry her.

*Perhaps I belong back at Madalaine's, after all,* she thought. *I would never want Jonathan to kill any man over my virginity. The women at Madalaine's seemed to think very little of that precious commodity I still possess. Is it worth enough to ruin two men's lives?*

Unconsciously she fingered the silver ring that had worked its way out of her bodice.

"Jonathan, I'll be okay. I guess it just isn't proper for me to walk alone, though. We'll need to find some other way if we're to court secretly. Perhaps we should cool our relationship for now until we can meet publicly."

"Perhaps," he reluctantly agreed. "I would not knowingly put you in danger, Angelina. I'll try to be satisfied with a glimpse of you to begin my morning. I have no right to ask you to do any more than that." Old sailors' curses ran through his mind, unbidden. *If it's love, it will keep*, he reminded himself.

"Where are these books that need my help, Jonathan?" she asked as she wriggled free from his grasp. "Or is that a contrived story to get me alone with you?"

"Unfortunately, that story is true," he sadly remarked. "Let me show you."

They spent the rest of the morning in the study balancing the church's accounts. Angelina finally saw in black and white the stranglehold in which the Bardsleys held the church. She also saw the pittance the church paid its faithful servant.

He certainly did not stay for the money, she thought. "Too poor," echoed Sarah's words in her head.

He left her alone with the books as he collected lunch from the parsonage. When he returned, they ate at his desk and returned to work as soon as the meal ended.

As the study clock chimed two, Angelina put the last figure into the ledger and closed the books. She leaned back in Jonathan's desk chair and stretched.

"Now, this has been one fun afternoon, Jonathan, but I probably need to return to Crabtree's. Can you walk me back?"

"Of course, Angel," he replied. He hesitated and said, "I wish I could tell you that I love you. I can't give my heart away freely, though. It's been closed to human love for so long that it's afraid to hurt again."

He picked up the silver ring on the chain around her neck.

"Angel, my mother wore this ring in her death. I've carried it around the world to remind me of the hurt I felt when I found her dead and still wearing it. It's truly a promise that I've released it to your care. It represents my faith in God to restore love to my heart someday. I can't give you any more of my heart right now." He grinned his lopsided smile. "I still need time, Angel."

"I have nothing but time, Jonathan," she replied. "Walk me home now. We'll find a way to free your heart someday."

Angelina rearranged her disheveled hair and tucked the silver ring back in its secret place. They walked the few blocks back to Crabtree's along the cobbled streets. Jonathan greeted the men who passed on foot, in buggies, and on wagons. Angelina fanned herself to relieve the heat of the relentless afternoon sun. Dust rose from the street as the traffic passed.

"Where are the women, Jonathan?" she asked suddenly. "I don't think I've seen very many women all week long. Even Sarah hasn't been in to see me."

Jonathan blushed and stammered slightly, "Perhaps it's the heat."

Angelina screwed up her face at his perplexing answer.

"What are you hiding?" she asked suspiciously. "Is something happening I don't know about?"

"Here's Crabtree's," he announced, sidestepping her question. "Have a wonderful rest of the day." He looked as though he'd burst if he said another word. He turned and strolled away.

She entered an empty store. Mr. Crabtree appeared from behind a stack of hardware.

"Angelina, you're back so soon," he remarked oddly. "Why don't you take a break in your room since business is slow?"

*How odd*, she thought. "If that's what you want, Mr. Crabtree."

He nodded vigorously, a smile pulling at his normally somber face.

*What is going on around here?* she wondered.

She opened the inner door to her room.

"Surprise!"

Jedadiah's blue ribbon hope chest sat in the middle of the room, wrapped in pink and blue ribbons. Around the room stood all her friends in the ladies' auxiliary. Wrapped gifts piled around the elaborately carved wooden chest.

"It's not my birthday," she finally managed to say.

The women all laughed and talked at once as they left their places and rushed to hug and greet her. Sarah pulled the rocking chair from the corner up to the chest.

"Sit, Angie," she commanded. "I get to make a little speech, and I want you to hear every word."

She folded her soft, plump hands and waited for the room to grow silent. Women sat on the floor, on the bed, and on Angelina's traveling trunk brought from the closet. Some leaned against the wall.

"Now then," Sarah began. "No woman should go out from her mother's home without a hope chest, even if her mother is a bordello madame."

Giggles resounded around the room.

"Ladies!" she chastised sternly. "And since you have managed to miss owning one, we felt you should still have one. I'm sure you recognize Jedadiah's chest from the fair. We commissioned him to make it for us especially for you, Angie. As you saw, there's not one better in all of Buchanan county."

"Hear! Hear!" shouted Nell Johnson. "The boy takes after his pa."

A round of applause followed her pronouncement.

"Jed wanted to be here to present it himself, but we told him a proper shower includes no men!" Sarah exclaimed with delight.

The women giggled, clapped, and hooted at the very idea.

"A shower?" Angelina asked. "But I'm not engaged nor planning a wedding. Why would you give me a shower?"

"Angelina, there are some things a woman should have before she catches her man!" explained Mrs. C. "Hope is one. A hope chest filled with household goods is another. It's like a dowry."

The silver ring touched Angelina's breast under her bodice as she leaned back in the rocking chair. *Faith*, he'd called it. *A promise of faith. The chest represents hope. Now abideth faith, hope, and love, these three*, she remembered from 1 Corinthians 13, *but the greatest of these is love.*

"Are you listening to me, Angie?" Sarah broke into her reverie.

"Of course, Sarah. Please continue."

"Now then, open the chest to see your next gift."

Angelina untied the pink and blue ribbons and reverently lifted the hinged lid. It smelled of freshly sanded cedar, and its red sides glowed from the work of a patient craftsman's hand.

"No, Sarah, I can't accept this. It's your hope chest quilt."

"Angie, I got more hope where that came from. You may need it sooner than I do," Sarah replied, winking slyly. "Besides, I've still got the blue ribbon for it."

She helped Angelina unfold the now familiar double wedding ring quilt the ladies had quilted on her first Sunday in St. Joe.

"Open mine next," the ladies cried out in unison.

Angelina began unwrapping the brown paper packages tied with fanciful ribbons of satin and velvet. The paper held sheets and linen towels, tablecloths and napkins, embroidered pillowcases and tatting. The gift from Mary Taylor held a rolling pin.

"To hit the varmint with when necessary," Mary explained.

Another held an iron fry pan from Mrs. Miller, the barber's wife.

"For the same purpose as the rolling pin," Mrs. Miller explained sheepishly.

Phoebe Greene, with a squalling infant in her lap, gave her a baby bonnet and booties.

"Well," Phoebe explained defensively above the newborn's plaintive cries, "you do hope to have at least one child, don't you?"

"Not if it cries like that," Sarah whispered in Angelina's ear.

Angelina giggled as she unwrapped her gift from Mrs. Johnson. She blushed when she discovered two lovely embroidered pillowcases. The intertwined hearts contained the letters A and J.

"Do you know something I don't?" she asked Mrs. Johnson.

"Well, Angelina," she stammered. "The way I figure it, three of the eligible bachelors in town have names that begin with J. That's my two boys and the pastor. It's a pretty safe bet you'll marry one of them. I'd be proud to have you marry either of my boys."

As Angelina blushed, she noticed Sarah's sulk at Nell Johnson's proclamation.

*So she does have feelings for Jed*, Angelina thought.

Sarah and Mrs. C. served tea and chocolate cake to all the shower attendees as they surveyed the bounty of treasures. Then they placed everything into the hope chest and scooted it across the room to the foot of her bed.

"Thank you all," Angelina said as the guests departed.

"Did you like it? Were you surprised?" asked Sarah earnestly, when they were alone.

"Yes, Sarah. It was lovely. Thank you for my quilt." Angelina embraced the shorter, rounded girl. "You're the best friend I've ever had."

"And you to me," Sarah affirmed. Sarah hugged her tall friend back. "Here's to the hope of capturing Jonathan publicly," she announced. "I find it hard to believe he's not already won in his heart."

Angelina hoped she was right.

Mrs. C. returned from the store followed by Mr. Crabtree.

"We have something else to add to your hoard, Angelina, from Eb and me."

Mr. Crabtree carried in a large draped object. Angelina lifted the drape and gasped.

"A sewing machine?" she exclaimed. "But they're still so new! How did you?"

"Wholesale," answered Mr. Crabtree. He turned and walked back to the store.

Angelina hugged Mrs. C. "It's more than I could ever ask for."

"And you've been more like a daughter than I could ever ask for Ebenezer and me, dear. Enjoy creating those new fashions for St. Joe to admire. You're good business for yard goods, notions, and hats." Mrs. C. turned to leave. Then she turned back and added, "Get Jonathan before his head gets in the way of his heart, Angelina. He loves you, you know, whether he knows it or not. I can see it in his eyes." She winked and went back to help in the store.

"Now abideth faith, hope, and love," Angelina quoted aloud. "These three. But the greatest of these is love."

# FASHION CONSULTANT TO ST. JOE

July days passed into early August. The heat and dust continued.

Angelina could hardly believe she'd been in St. Joe for two months. Letters from Dr. Ben and Mama left her homesick for the Boston harbor and home. Most mornings, seeing Jonathan resolved her blues with hope and faith.

Jonathan received a note from Dr. Graves as well, inquiring about Angelina's well-being. Between the lines, Jonathan read an unasked question concerning their relationship to one another. The relationship between him and Angelina frustrated him to no end. He wanted to love her, and he needed to love her. Something besides the Bardsleys stopped him short of the courage required to release his love to her.

Each day he looked into the silver-backed shaving mirror. Each day he asked, "Is she the one, LORD? If she is, give me the courage to love her completely."

As each day passed, Angelina felt her hope slipping. What if Alice succeeded in seducing him? What if he decided her own background was too much of a liability? Her fear still kept her from the bluffs. It seemed hard to hope when she saw him so briefly. The silver ring seemed her only link to him at times.

The best news in town came from the Greenes. With an anonymous donation of cash, they had purchased the necessary supplies to build their barn.

The cowbell on the store door rung constantly one early August morning as Angelina sold yard goods to nearly every woman in St. Joe. Pink, blue, green, and yellow gingham sold with bolts upon bolts of muslin and lace. The ladies asked for Angelina's fashion advice.

"How does this color match my skin?"

"Do my eyes shine next to this blue like yours do?"

"Should the neck be round or V-shaped with the shape of my face?"

"How would this lace look on this collar?"

Mr. Crabtree smiled at the gold pieces and currency the women paid for their fabric but frowned at the untouched ledgers on the work desk.

"You're doing a fine job as fashion consultant," he remarked wryly in a momentary lull. "Perhaps you'd like to do the books sometime today too. After all, that is why I pay you."

"Yes, sir," Angelina replied and crept back to her desk.

Moments later, the bell rang again, and she heard a voice ask for her assistance. She resolutely pressed on in her record-keeping until she heard Mr. Crabtree bellow, "Miss Mercy! Come and help this customer!"

Sighing, she laid aside her pen and rose from the desk. Turning around she saw that her customer was Alice Bardsley.

"Angelina, my dear," she sweetly spoke, "I hear you're giving fashion advice to the whole town. You simply must help me choose the best fabric to dazzle a certain man."

Angelina grimaced. Beyond the meek petite figure, Angelina saw a black widow spider luring Jonathan—her Jonathan—further into the Bardsley web. Putting on her best smile, Angelina pulled the few remaining bolts from the shelf. She pushed back an escaping curl with tired hands.

"What type of dress did you have in mind, Alice?"

"Why, Angelina, I thought you'd know just the thing for me to seduce Jonathan. After all, Jonathan is a man, even if he is a pastor."

Angelina began to count to ten in Italian.

*Uno! Every fiber of my being aches to slap Alice's whiny little face.*

*Due! How dare she insinuate that I am no better than Madalaine Mercy!*

*Tre! How dare she propose to seduce my Jonathan!*

*Quattro! How dare she try to draw me into a public battle with her!*

This last thought cooled her anger quickly.

*Cinque! Of course, that's exactly what Alice wants.*

*Sei. If I lose my cool now, it will make Alice's whole week.*

*Sette. It will ruin the week for me.*

*Otto. Jonathan knows what Alice is like.*

*Nove. She has no chance with Jonathan.*

*Dieci. The best defense is a good offense.*

Angelina smiled sweetly and asked, "How far would you like him to go?"

It became Alice's turn to bristle and blush. Turning to the fabric, she described a dress with ribbons tying the back together exposing her arms and back, as well as her bosom with a deep décolleté. The crinoline she described would take up half a dance floor.

"Green is your color, Alice," Angelina pointed out the last bolt of polished cotton. *And mine too!* she thought as she recognized the depths of her jealousy. *Green, green, green! After all, Jonathan can hardly stand to be in the same room with Alice!*

Alice finally chose the green polished cotton and a profusion of laces and ribbons to match. Angelina wondered whether the fabric and ribbon would look better on Alice's crinoline or on a circus wagon.

*Forgive me, Father!* she quickly prayed.

Lunch finally arrived. Grabbing an apple, Angelina headed to the bank with the morning's receipts. Counting the money twice for the teller's benefit and then listening carefully to the teller's count, she carefully wrote the amount in the notepad she carried to record all transactions. After all, bankers made mistakes too; she knew that for a fact after working in Mr. Anderson's bank.

"Angie!"

Turning from the teller's window, Angelina spied her friend, Sarah.

"Is there a bolt of fabric left at Crabtree's?" she inquired.

"Not much remains, Sarah," Angelina replied, falling in step with her friend as they walked the dusty road back to the store. "What is going on that every woman in town needs a new dress?"

"Haven't you heard about the Greenes' barn raising on Friday?"

"I thought the Greenes were building a barn. Why would they want to tear down a barn?" Angelina replied in horror. "Why would that event precipitate every woman buying a new dress?"

Sarah laughed at her friend's ignorance. "Be calm, Angie. It's a barn raising, not a barn razing." She laughed at her friend's look of puzzlement. "They're building a barn on Friday, and the whole town will help. The women bring food and take water to the men while they work. After dinner, Jonathan will bless the structure, and we'll have a big barn dance."

"Sorry, Sarah," Angelina replied, blushing. "I'm a city girl. What do I know about barns? I know more about sailing the sea than building a barn. I suppose the reason I'm not invited is so Alice will have a clear field at Jonathan."

Angelina frowned, dejectedly brushing dust from her skirt. Despite Angelina's cool front, Alice's barbs had struck deep. The gold earrings swayed and flashed in the noon sun.

"Don't be ridiculous, Angie! No one needs an invitation! This isn't Boston, remember? Besides, what makes you think Jonathan can be fooled into Alice's arms? Aren't you the one who catches his attention these days?"

"I'd noticed that this wasn't Boston quite a while ago," Angelina answered sarcastically. "Alice seemed quite confident of stealing his attention today. Frankly, Jonathan pays very little attention to me these days."

Ignoring the sarcasm and her friend's blue mood, Sarah continued, "Everyone just comes with food and tools and dancing clothes. I'll get Daddy to pick you up in his wagon early Friday morning. Then we can spend the entire day together without you working in that dreary store. Is any of that green polished cotton left? The green brings out the color in my eyes.

She swirled and dipped and batted her big, brown doe eyes at Angelina in the middle of the road. Men at the feed store whistled and shouted. Sarah blew them a kiss.

"Sarah, control yourself!" Angelina grabbed her arm and pulled her out of the road into her back room at Crabtree's.

"I can't help it, Angie. Being with you brings out the wanton woman in me," she teased. "Besides, you forget that not one of those men dare lay a hand on me. Remember? My daddy's the sheriff."

"Sarah, you can be so exasperating! No, the polished green cotton is going to be on Alice Bardsley."

She related the incident of the morning to Sarah quickly without the emotion she had felt at the time.

"What a witch!" denounced Sarah. "You should have sold her red or black cloth. Either suits her personality better. If she wasn't Edward's sister, I'd write her off altogether." Sarah spit at the floor to emphasize her disgust.

Angelina shook her head. "Sarah, she's still loved by God, you know. We're to love her too."

"Angie, I love her just fine in the LORD. I just can't stand her here on earth!"

At this, Angelina laughed and began pulling the big trunk from its resting place behind the closet curtain. Taking care to hide the silver ring from Sarah's sharp eyes, she procured the key from the chain around her neck. She carefully unlocked each brass clasp and flung the lid open.

"Angelina Mercy! Where did you get such treasures!" exclaimed Sarah. "Don't tell me your sea captain friend gave them all to you!"

"No, Sarah. Not all of them came from Captain Michael. The trunk did, though, as did the clothing he brought me from Italy on his last voyage before I came to St. Joe."

Sarah rifled the fabrics and laces while Angelina talked. Angelina told the story that accompanied each piece Sarah held up. Finally, Sarah held up a piece of emerald watered silk.

"Now this is what I was looking for you, Sarah. Please take this if you must turn someone's head. I think I'd prefer Jedadiah, though, if I were you."

Angelina shuddered at the thought of Edward's frightening dark face and her fear of him.

Sarah's turn to be shocked had finally arrived. "Angie, I couldn't possibly take such a gift."

"Please, Sarah, green is not my color. What good is watered silk I can't wear? Take it and be alluring on Friday. You'll surely keep Alice on her toes. Just remember that Jonathan is mine."

Sarah placed the folds of fabric on the bed with respect. She turned to the trunk and held up a gauze blouse. "I've never seen such a beautiful and sheer fabric, Angie. How do you wear it?"

Angelina carefully concealed the ring and slipped into the gauze blouse and the accompanying lace camisole. She tied the neckline to a proper fit and tucked the tail into her cotton skirt.

"The style is typical of most Italian women. The style provides plenty of room for what God has given a woman by being less restrictive where it counts. No corsets to wear with this."

"Angie," Sarah gasped. "It's beautiful on you. Will it fit me if I keep my corset on?"

Angelina laughed and hugged her friend. "Of course, Sarah."

Angelina helped her with the ties. She demonstrated how, by loosening the ribbons, she could bare her shoulders. She showed her how to tighten them to make it quite prim. Glancing in the mirror, Sarah declared that this was just the style she needed for the dance. The green watered silk would drape just right for both a peasant blouse and a full skirt.

"I think I'll wear my corset just the same, Angie. You may not need a corset. My body needs all the help it can get. If only I had the earrings too," sighed Sarah.

Reaching into the trunk, Sarah pulled out a blue silk blouse, similar to the gauze one she wore. Below it was a silk skirt decorated in a kaleidoscope of blues, greens, reds, and golds. It swirled in the daylight, setting the room afire with its brilliance.

"Angelina, you must wear this to the dance. Let me see it on you!"

Angelina obliged her friend. Without the heavy barrier of corset, the smooth silk felt cool on her body. She twirled. The swirling colors reminded her of a wanton gypsy. It made her feel beautiful and desirable.

*If only Jonathan wanted me.* She sighed.

"What's this, Angie?" Sarah caught the glimmer of silver as Angelina twirled around the room, lost in her own thoughts, and fingered the chain and ring. "Whose name starts with T?"

Angelina blushed. "It's Jonathan's. You can't tell anyone I have it, Sarah. He gave it to me as a promise."

"A promise of what, Angie?"

"A promise that we could someday court publicly. A promise that he would try to give me his whole heart one day. It's faith, Sarah, between us and God for the future."

"How beautiful! How romantic!" Sarah released her grip on the chain around Angelina's neck. "How long have you had it?"

A knock shattered their friendly banter. "Miss Mercy, five women are in the store awaiting your assistance. I require your services immediately!" shouted Mr. Crabtree through the inner door.

The friends giggled as, in a flurry of fabrics, they redressed and stored away the precious pieces. Sarah carefully tucked the blue blouse and brilliant skirt into the drawer of the dresser. Angelina locked the trunk and scooted it back into its resting place.

"Remember what I said about the dance," Sarah said conspiratorially

Angelina shoved her friend out the alley door, brushed back her escaping curls, and took her place in the store.

After an exhausting day, Angelina rejoiced to lock the door to Crabtree's at six. She'd barely turned her back when a knock sounded on the door. She peeked beneath the shade to see Jonathan standing on the porch. She quickly unlocked and opened the door.

"Good evening, Jonathan," she said softly. "Is there something I can do for you? I'd just locked up, but if there's something you need …"

"Only you, Angelina. I only require you for now."

He pulled her out onto the porch with him and seated her on the bench outside Crabtree's. His blond hair glowed in the evening's sun. He was dressed impeccably as always. His blue eyes danced with delight at her perplexity.

"I don't understand, Jonathan. What's happening?"

Jonathan collapsed his frame onto the bench beside her and grinned the lopsided grin that made her heart melt.

"This isn't working out well, is it? Our arrangement, I mean. Perhaps we should dissolve this secret courtship of ours."

Angelina shoulders slumped back against the back of the bench.

*Alice doesn't even need her circus dress to catch him. She had him already. If only my fear had not paralyzed me so, he would have been mine*, she thought with increasing grief.

She closed her eyes to try to stem the rush of tears she knew would come soon.

*Don't cry in front of him*, she willed.

Despite her best intentions, the salty water slipped down her cheeks, unbidden. She felt his arm slip behind her shoulders.

"You don't understand, Angel. Please don't cry, sweetheart."

He lifted her porcelain tear-stained face.

"I mean, we should end the secret part of our courtship, not the courtship part of our secret courtship. I'm frustrated to death by being unable to see you more than a few moments each morning. I will never feel my love for you without being able to see you, touch you, kiss you, and talk with you." His smile turned serious. "I'll not allow Charles Bardsley to control whom I court any longer. May I see the ring I gave you?"

She couldn't accept all the words he said at once. Confused, she pulled the chain from beneath her bodice and unhooked the clasp. She slid the ring into his waiting hand. He took her slender hand in his massive one and placed the delicate silver ring onto her left pinkie finger.

"This ring belongs where everyone can see my intention to court you. As long as you agree, Angel, this courtship will no longer be our secret."

The tears overflowed down her face and onto his shoulder as she hugged him in plain view of the citizens of St. Joe passing by Crabtree's that night. He stood easily with her arms wrapped around his neck and his arms wrapped around her tiny waist. Her feet hung from above the earth as they clung together.

"Thank you, Jonathan," she whispered through her tears. "Thank you."

# EDWARD'S SUGGESTIONS

"Good thing the roof is fixed," said Jonathan aloud as he dressed and tied his tie. "Hope it doesn't rain on Friday for the Greenes' barn raising. He'll be needing that barn at harvest."

Sunday morning clouds hung over the river outside the parsonage window. From the look of them, a summer thunderstorm loomed nearby.

He hummed happily to himself as he finished combing his hair in the mirror. Since the day he'd declared his courtship to Angelina public, he'd felt wonderful. Flaunting the Bardsleys' influence restored his confidence and self-esteem. He enjoyed her company tremendously after a month apart, as well. He could hardly wait to see her this morning, wearing his mother's ring and sharing the news of their relationship with the good people of St. Joe.

He frowned as the first streak of lightning coursed through the sky toward the river.

"Lord, protect us today from nature's wrath. Protect those on their way to the church house, even now in their open wagons and on foot. Keep the roof you have so graciously given us safe and secure and leak-proof."

Thunder answered his petition dramatically. Drops of rain began, first here and there and then in glasslike sheets. Sharp raps at the door beckoned Jonathan across the room in two bounds.

"Edward," greeted Jonathan. "Please come in out of the weather. We'll have a small congregation today, I warrant."

Edward swept into the room, shaking rain drops from his umbrella onto the wood floor.

*Dressed in magnificent apparel as always,* thought Jonathan. *He always looks as though he is going to the opera instead of worship. A display of his wealth, no doubt.*

Jonathan smoothed the worn sleeve edge, self-conscious of the difference in quality and age of their suits.

"Jonathan, I'll get right to the point of the matter," Edward began. "I'm quite concerned with your, ah, relationship with Miss Mercy."

A blush betrayed Jonathan's cool exterior appearance at Angelina's name.

"What about it, Edward?"

"I'm concerned about your reputation, Jonathan. A pastor of the church should have a spotless reputation, as should his wife. The Scriptures make that abundantly clear." He paused dramatically. "I fear you do not realize Miss Mercy's reputation. She has duped you. Dr. Graves has made a fool of you. You have failed his test."

"I beg your pardon," Jonathan interrupted. "Under any other circumstances, I would have to call you out for words that question a lady's reputation. If you have a quarrel with me, Edward, discuss it. Leave Angelina out of it, though."

"Ah, but dear Jonathan," patronized Edward. "The problem is Miss Mercy. She is a fraud. She represents herself as an angel of light, but she is the devil's handmaid."

"Edward, I warn you that this lady is very, well, special to me."

"I know, sir, and that is just the problem. The lady, as you call her, is the daughter of a prostitute. Does she even know who her father is? Her mother brokers other women for men's sexual pleasures. She lived in her mother's home, a bordello, in the back streets of north Boston."

"Edward, I am well aware of her upbringing," Jonathan replied, shaken. "I also know her to be a fine Christian, raised by a fine man of God."

"A Christian does not frequent the devil's abode, Jonathan," answered Edward. "When I visited Boston to procure your services for this church, I heard of this Madalaine's Palace her mother runs. I also heard men drool over the madame's daughter, a pale, black-haired creature with gold earrings. They bragged and betted on who would be getting her services for the evening the night I was there. I say she's not who she represents herself to be. She is probably even unfaithful to you. Haven't you noticed the attention she receives from every man in town? Why would the elusive Mr. Howard purchase her box at the box supper to give it to you? Perhaps she also gives away her favors to him."

"Edward, get out of my home with your evil suggestions!"

"That's fine, Pastor," replied Edward slyly. "Just remember where the money comes from to pay your salary and to provide this fine home."

"Is that a threat, Edward?" The angry red flush caused his bronzed face to glow.

"Let's not grow ugly, Reverend. I know you could easily whip me in a fight, though I doubt it would be the godly way of settling this argument."

Edward drew out his cigar and lit the end with precision.

"Do this for me. Think about what I've said. But remember each time you look at those fancy earrings of hers the sordid life that produced the dirty money that bought such gold. Also consider whether she is able to resist the influence of her mother and the prostitutes who raised her as a child. How innocent and virginal could she be given those circumstances? Do you really believe she's undefiled? How open is she to you? Perhaps she's hiding something from you."

Jonathan's fists clenched at his side.

*If this event had occurred aboard the* Congress, *the* Madalaine, *or any other ship on which I've sailed, I'd spread him across the deck with a single punch*, he thought. *I could easily kill him with my bare hands between my own strength and the strength of my anger.*

"Edward, leave this house. Do it now before I forget that the LORD has called me to save life rather than to take it."

"Just think about what I said. I would hate to see you lose this pastorate, your first one. It would be bad for your career to be dismissed for inappropriate behavior such as frequenting a whore."

Lightning brightened the room, and thunder immediately shook the building. Edward left in the din before Jonathan could reply. The chiming of the mantle clock reminded Jonathan that it was time to be at the church to open the doors. Adrenaline pumped through his strong body, pounding in his veins and throbbing in his head.

"Alice no doubt put him up to this," he shouted at the clock. "LORD, bring me composure to handle this morning's worship. Give me sufficient strength to greet Edward in civility in five minutes. Cool me down in your showers."

Lightning and thunder answered his petition.

The service dragged on. Each minute seemed a lifetime. Being late into the building, he had no opportunity to speak to Angelina when she arrived drenched. Edward smiled contentedly throughout the service, as though nothing had happened.

Yet every time Jonathan looked at her, the earrings caught the flashes of lightning from the outside window. They swung in a seductive manner as she sang, smiled, and greeted the people around her. Her blouse fell open in an attractive yet nearly risque fashion.

*Could it really be true?* he thought with reluctance. *Surely she is just what she seems to be: a victim of the sin and not the sinner.*

Questions pounded at his brain. *What is she hiding from me since the day of the fair? Did a stranger really accost her at the fair? Did Jedadiah stumble upon her in a tryst? Is she really still a virgin? Where does she get her money? Ebenezer doesn't pay her much.*

A horrid thought crossed his confused mind as the last hymn finished: *Perhaps she doesn't come to the bluffs in the evenings because she has a lover. Is she someone's paid mistress? Edward's?*

His knees buckled with the emotion he felt as he rose to address the congregates. His carefully prepared sermon disappeared from his normally organized mind. What would he say next? Surely the LORD would guide him if he said whatever came into his mind.

"Good morning," he began. "Consider the rain that falls this morning. It rains on the just and the unjust. Truly both arrive at the church this morning just as wet, just as innocent seeming. But does what we see reflect each person's true nature?"

*What am I saying?* he thought with horror. *What will I say next?*

"Since the nature of a person is so well concealed by the front she puts before the world, she must be careful to give a true accounting of herself."

*She?* he thought. *Am I talking about Angelina?* LORD, *forgive me if I hurt her now.*

"So throw off the trappings of the old world and the past. Live a life full of Christ's purity and abundant life. Avoid the fancy apparel and jewelry of the worldly whore and put on chastity and simplicity of dress avoiding adornment of any kind. Scripture says a woman's beauty comes only by her spiritual nature and not by the adornment of her body or the wearing of gold earrings …"

*Did I say that?*

He shuddered as the eyes of the entire congregation turned to look at Angelina. *What have I done?* He saw the tears well up in her brilliant blue eyes. He saw her pull her wet shawl around her beautiful shoulders. She jumped from her seat and raced for the back door, skirts flying behind her. In one step, his long legs cleared the steps from the pulpit. In several more he reached the back door to the astonishment of the congregation.

Edward smiled. Alice grinned contentedly, watching the young pastor make a complete fool of himself in front of his congregation. Edward had known just the thing to bring him down hard.

"Angelina! Please stop!" he called after her. "I don't know what I was saying. Let me explain."

He reached her at the street. His strong hands pulled her shoulders around to face him. Her tear-lined face tugged at his heart as their eyes locked.

"What could you possibly say to explain away what you just said to me in front of my friends, in front of the church's people, in front of the Lord?" she asked between choked sobs.

"Nothing." Jonathan looked away, ashamed. "I can say nothing to change what I did. I'm sorry."

"Is that what you think of me?"

"Of course not, Angel," he stammered. "I care deeply for you. It's just that ..."

He thought of Edward's earlier accusations. *They are no excuse for the turmoil they caused in my mind*, he concluded. He sighed. *I fell into the trap he laid for me.*

"I'm sorry. Please let me walk you home."

"I don't think so, Reverend Thomson."

Her words cut like a knife down to his soul as he watched her walk down the street, avoiding the muddy puddles, toward Crabtree's. Jedadiah brushed past him and ran to catch up with her, taking her arm in his. Shame-faced, Jonathan ignored the stares from the townspeople as he walked resolutely to the parsonage, past the mocking grin of Edward Bardsley.

Sunday night, Angelina did not return for prayer service. Jonathan didn't really expect her.

Monday, a large bouquet of parsonage roses arrived at Crabtree's.

"What do you make of it, Ebenezer?" whispered Mrs. C. as she accepted the bouquet from the young messenger boy. "These are the pastor's best roses. For August, it must be nearly every bloom."

"He needs more than those to pull off explaining that debacle we witnessed on this past LORD's day," answered Mr. Crabtree. "Angelina! You've a delivery to take care of."

Angelina cautiously peered from the back door. Convinced that the only people in Crabtree's were the owners, she came into the main room.

"Look, Angelina," encouraged Mrs. C. "You've twenty or more of the parson's best roses. No one else keeps roses like the pastor. I bet I've got just the vase to hold them too."

*What happened?* she thought. *Just when I thought things were different here, it's the old neighborhood all over again.*

The nightmare had returned during the night and kept her awake most of it. Mercifully the man was still Edward in her dream. She feared the face would be Jonathan's when she saw the man who nearly raped her. The feeling she had now was not much different.

The cowbell erased her reverie.

"Angie!" Sarah greeted her friend. "What beautiful roses! They have guilt written all over them. They must be from your Jonathan."

"My Jonathan? I think he disowned me yesterday."

Mrs. C. took the flowers from her hands and arranged them in the vase as the younger ladies looked on.

"What should I do, Mrs. C.?" Angelina asked.

The older woman smiled and shrugged. "Forgive him, of course," she replied.

"Forgive public humiliation in front of the church?" Sarah shook her head with amazement.

"Of course," she continued. "Unless you want to lose him to Alice, Angelina, you forgive him. Your virtue is not nearly as questionable as hers. She's waiting for you to spurn his apology. I vow she probably had something to do with yesterday too. You and the pastor are perfect for one another, regardless of the Bardsleys' opinion. The pastor has been so relaxed and happy since you've arrived. No one has ever beaten Ebenezer and me at whist the way you two do. You're natural partners."

"Cards and life are not the same thing," replied Angelina, bordering on tears. "I want nothing I do to harm Jonathan."

"Then do not be bullied by Edward. Jonathan can care for himself quite well." Mrs. C. smiled, imagining Edward in a fight with the reverend. "No contest."

Angelina grinned through her tears at a similar thought. She wiped her eyes and nose with her lace-edged hankie. "I'm sure you're right, Mrs. C."

Mrs. C. handed the vase of roses to Angelina.

"So do you accept them or not? If you do, put them in the window that looks out toward the street so everyone can see that you have them. There's nothing else to do if you want him still. Public humiliation, public apology, public acceptance. The problem is over."

Mrs. C. brushed her hands, as though wiping away the previous day's events.

Resolutely, Angelina took the vase and set it in the window sill. She pulled the lace curtains as far back as possible to be sure the parsonage roses were on public display.

Jonathan watched the roses bloom and wilt in the window of Crabtree's. His shame kept him from entering each morning. His face carried the battle scars from the nicks and cuts borne of trying to shave without seeing his guilty eyes in the shaving mirror. He spent the week visiting church members to apologize for his Sunday behavior.

With his apologies completed, the question still nagged at his mind. *Could Edward be right about Angelina after all?*

# THE BARN RAISING

Friday finally arrived.

Mr. Crabtree consented to give Angelina the entire day off for the barn raising. Mrs. C. would come around lunch time. Angelina rose before dawn to prepare her Italian specialty to take to the Greenes'. She'd prepared her own pasta and simmered her meat sauce nearly all night. The challenge had been finding all the herbs and enough tomatoes to feed an entire town.

Jonathan had not been in Crabtree's all week. Angelina had sent him a note thanking him for the roses. She wondered if he knew she forgave him. Angelina wondered too whether the day held more heartache. Could she and Jonathan return to their courtship? Did he still think those horrid things about her?

She dressed carefully in her loose gauze blouse and a sturdy cotton skirt. After all, a barn raising surely was quite informal. She pulled her thick, long hair into a long ponytail and braided it so it hung down her back. It would be easier to tame as the day got long and the sun hot. Finally she placed her bonnet on to shield her fair skin from the prairie sun. She stepped outside into the dawn light just as the Joneses' wagon appeared down the dusty road. She hoped she'd made the right choice for the dance in her clothes' bag.

"What is that delicious smell?" called Sarah from the wagon back.

"Just Italian food like Mama used to make," answered Angelina with a cheerful smile.

"Your Mama could cook too?" queried Sarah in disbelief. "I'd think running a bordello would be time-consuming!"

"Sarah!" rebuked Mrs. Jones. "It is not polite to discuss the sin of others' relatives in their presence!"

"I guess it's okay to talk about them in private instead." Sarah giggled behind her mama's back.

Angelina laughed and threw her thick braid over her shoulder. It was going to be a good day with her best friend. She reached over and hugged Sarah briefly. Both ladies smiled at one another in easy camaraderie.

Sarah helped Angelina place her pot and bag into the wagon. Sheriff Jones helped Angelina into the wagon.

As the wagon pulled up to the Greenes' farm house, Angelina could hear hammers pounding nails into barn lumber. Though the sun was barely up, the framing already rose above the plain. Women bustled about, setting up tables groaning with homemade bread, biscuits, sausage, hot cakes, and jam. The smell of coffee wafted over the breeze. The sounds of voices, hammers, and banging pots accentuated the urgency of the day's agenda. One by one, wagons arrived with additional workmen and women. The men ate quickly and returned to their task.

As the morning wore on, Angelina carried a water bucket and dipper to quench the men's thirst.

"Good morning, Reverend Thomson," she timidly remarked as she came upon him. Instead of his normally formal attire, his shirt was red and black plaid cotton, like so many of the other men, and his pants were sturdy cotton. "I almost didn't recognize you, Pastor. You could have been Joshua or Jedadiah from a distance. Would you take a dipper of water from me?"

Jonathan blushed at her reference to the sermon and his subsequent shunning.

"Of course, I could use a cool drink," he replied sheepishly. "Please forgive me, Angelina. I really meant no harm."

"I accepted your apology on Monday, Jonathan. Why haven't you come for your *Gazette* all week?"

She smiled at him. Her gold earrings caught the golden mid-morning sun. He winced as the light caught his eyes.

*Must she wear those earrings?* he thought.

"I find we still have a problem, Angel. Your earrings have become a constant reminder to me of the life you led before coming here," he remarked quietly.

"No, Reverend. They remind you of the life my mother led. May I remind you that I am not my mother?" shot back Angelina.

"Truce for the day, Angelina!" exclaimed Jonathan as the men quit hammering to better hear their discussion.

He took the dipper from her and took a long drink until the hammering began again in earnest.

"Please forgive me. I fall short of the Lord's plan occasionally too. I'm afraid that your earrings present a poor picture of you to the world. They announce to some that you are a prostitute."

"I beg your pardon, Jonathan! They say no such thing. All beautiful women in Italy wear earrings. Earrings represent their material wealth and complement their natural beauty!" exclaimed Angelina as her voice began to rise. "How dare you judge me on outward appearances!"

"Angelina, the Scriptures say that a woman should be adorned with her virtue and not with jewelry or braiding of the hair. A beautiful woman is one who loves the Lord and cares for her family," retorted Jonathan in his best preacher's voice.

"So what you are saying is that because I wear these earrings and braid my hair that I am not beautiful nor godly?"

"I said no such thing, Angelina. I'm merely pointing out that Christians should do nothing to interfere with their witness to the world. If your earrings present a false image, then you shouldn't wear them!"

"What do you mean 'if they present a false image'? Are you saying you think I am a prostitute? I thought you of all people knew me better than that!"

"That's not what I said, Angelina. I said that your witness depends on your appearance to the world. The earrings are not as important as your image to the world!"

"Remember, Jonathan Thomson, that the LORD looks on the heart. Perhaps you should study your theology a little closer! Maybe it's your heart that needs changing instead."

The laughter and applause brought them out of their private debate to discover that their conversation had become public.

"Angelina, I think you're beautiful!" called Joshua from the scaffold.

"I like your earrings, Angie. They add sparkle to the prairie sun," announced Jedadiah from the lower wall.

"Here, here," shouted Edward Bardsley from the lumber pile.

Blushing and angry, Angelina grabbed the dipper from Jonathan and slung it into the water bucket. The splash soaked them both to the skin. The men roared with laughter at the sight of the big, strong pastor bested by an angry young woman. Some whistled at Angelina's thin, soaked gauze blouse that had turned transparent in the deluge. Angelina took the bucket, dumped the rest of the water bucket onto Jonathan's blond head, and marched away, satisfied for now. Sputtering in the drowning, Jonathan's red face was not from sunburn.

"I can't believe you did that!" Sarah greeted Angelina with a shawl to wrap around her exposed bosom. "And he had it coming, too! Don't apologize. You were right, and everyone knows it."

A glance at the food tables showed an irate Alice angrily talking to anyone who'd listen. Angelina winced.

"Oh, Sarah," moaned Angelina in embarrassment. "I've lost him for sure. Alice will have him now."

"I hardly think so," answered Mrs. C. from behind them. "First of all, he loves you. Second, eventually the pastor will settle on the most Christian woman he can find to be the pastor's wife he desires. Alice will never be the one. She's mean-spirited and immoral. Even Reverend Thomson knows that. Earrings or no, you've got Alice bested, and she knows it. Why else would he care that you wear the earrings? You just don't fit the mold he's formed for the pastor's wife."

"I think he'd better break his mold," agreed Mrs. Jones. "For someone who's always preaching about being godly and God's plan toward his children, it's amazing he doesn't recognize a godly woman and God's plan when she's right in front of his nose. He's so much in love he can hardly think straight; that's his problem. He's befuddled and confused."

"Angelina, what do you want him for anyway?" asked Mrs. Johnson. "He's arrogant and self-righteous. For a pastor that's okay; for a husband, it's a nightmare. I should know." The women laughed, remembering Jeremiah Johnson before his death. "Jed or Josh, either one, would treat you real special if you've a mind to find a man who loves you without hindrances. You'd be more than welcome in our family."

Angelina found herself surrounded by sympathetic, advice-giving mothers and friends.

*What a day this is turning into!* thought Angelina wryly. *Not only have I offended the man I love and embarrassed him in front of his congregation, but I've divided the town between those who think I should be through with him, those who think I should fight for him, and those who think I should leave him to Alice.* L ORD, *what should I do now?* she prayed to the brilliant blue sky.

Silence seemed the only answer for now. As she began to feel disconsolate, Sarah took her into the house.

Sarah, unusually serious and quiet, picked up Angelina's left hand and pointed out the ring on her finger.

"I know he's too old, too poor, and too public. Angie, he's also afraid to give away his love. That's what this ring is about, isn't it? He's afraid to love you, for fear of being hurt."

Sarah lifted her seated friend's face to look her in the eye.

"Is he worth the hurt it will take to finally capture his heart, my friend?"

Angelina nodded as her tears flowed.

✻

Angelina's words hammered in Jonathan's ears the rest of the morning with the sound of the hammers and saws. Occasional laughter would send a blush of red to his face that burned his ears.

*Dr. Graves was right when he counseled me to reconsider marrying Alice,* he thought as he worked. *Then he sent me a bride. What a sly old theologian Dr. Graves had turned out to be. This love he advised, though, hurt mightily! How can I set things right without another scene? This must be love,* he thought. *Otherwise my chest wouldn't ache so badly.*

The barn rose to completion as the sun rose across the sky. At noon, women laid out the food they'd prepared for the hungry workmen. Angelina's pasta quickly disappeared. Alice shot Angelina a look of hatred as her fried chicken languished on the table.

After all the men served their plates, Angelina found a quiet place under a shade tree to eat the little she had gleaned from the remaining dishes. She nearly turned the whole plate over when strong arms grabbed her shoulders from behind.

"Jonathan! Please don't frighten me so!" Tears ran down her face as the nightmare replayed briefly in her mind.

"I'm sorry, Angel," he said as he wiped her tears.

He held her hands until her tears stopped.

"I'm so sorry for embarrassing you on Sunday and this morning. The issue is between you and me. Let's set it aside for today. If the LORD wants us together, He'll help us resolve our conflict. Truce?"

"Truce," she answered.

"Why are you always so frightened when I touch you without you knowing it's me?" asked Jonathan carefully as he finished the last of her pasta. "You know all of these people well. Surely you don't expect anyone here to harm you, do you?"

*Only Edward*, she thought. "I've been attacked before," she began. "A man came into my bedroom at *Madalaine's*. He tore my gown and threatened to take my virginity. I've had nightmares ever since. The man is always faceless. Sheriff Jones told me that this happened when the committee was in Boston to meet you."

Sitting under the spreading oak, Jonathan held her in his arms as she wept. He felt anger rising in him.

"Are you saying the man in the nightmare is someone from the committee? Is it the same man who attacked you at the fair?"

Angelina nodded carefully.

"Angel," he said quietly in her ear as her earring brushed his chin. "I swear that no one will ever harm you as long as you are under my care." *No*, he thought, *she is not her mother*. LORD, *help me remember that despite the gold earrings.*

Jedadiah walked up to where Jonathan cuddled her under the tree.

"We need you, Jon, to help raise the roof into place. No one else has your strong arms. I'll gladly take over for you here, if the lady doesn't mind."

Angelina jumped up from the ground with embarrassment. "I'm fine now, Jed."

She wiped the remaining tears from her face with the back of her hand.

*Jonathan cannot know about Edward at the fair*, she thought. *Only Jed and the Joneses know that.*

She watched Jonathan and Jedadiah go to put the roof in place. Then Angelina stumbled back to the Greenes' house to help the women clean up from lunch.

As sunset approached and the last of the roofing was hammered into place, the men poured buckets of water over their now shirtless backs to rinse away the sweat and grime. The women laid out bread and slices of ham and cheese for sandwiches. Potato salad overflowed the board buffet. Hungry workers ate their fill. All anticipated the barn dance to come.

As everyone ate, Phoebe Greene wondered aloud, "I wonder what's happened to the Taylors. I've not seen any of them since Sunday a week ago."

Everyone agreed with Phoebe's observation and wondered about their whereabouts. Jonathan made a mental note to check with the Taylors in the morning.

Fiddles played as the new yard goods whirled around in a wild variety of fashions and colors. Angelina watched in awe at the array she had sold only one week before at Crabtree's. She nearly laughed when Alice showed up. What a strange dress she had concocted with the ribbon and polished green cotton. Circus wagon music played in her head as she watched Alice's arrival, curtsies, and flagrant flirting.

"What could any man see in that woman?"

Angelina startled. At first, she thought it was her own voice stating her thoughts aloud. Her brilliant silk skirt floated colorfully as she whirled around to see Sarah behind her.

"Sarah!" exclaimed Angelina. "Green does wonderful things for your eyes and your complexion. I'm glad you took it. And the style is beautiful for you."

"And for you, my friend. I only wish I didn't need my corset to look as thin as you do without it," replied Sarah warmly. "If Jonathan doesn't notice you this evening over that circus clown, I'll eat his hat."

"Sarah," replied Angelina wryly. "I think he noticed me quite well this morning. Perhaps it's not a good thing to be noticed."

"Angie," petitioned a masculine voice. "Would you dance with me?"

Jedadiah whisked her away into an energetic square dance, despite her protests that she didn't know how to square dance. They laughed together as she and he twisted and knotted together during the dos-si-dos. Jedadiah handed her a cup of cider at the close of the song and propelled her out the door of the newly built barn.

The stars shimmered in the black prairie night. The cider was sweet and cool, fresh from the Greenes' cellar.

"You know, you've captivated the pastor." Jedadiah spoke first, breaking the silence. "And that's a good thing for Jon. He needs someone to help him bear the burden of the church and its work."

Angelina's look of surprise spurred him on.

"Angie, you know I love Sarah, always have and always will, but I love you like a sister. I will always be there to protect you, even if it's from Jon himself." He laughed congenially and held out his hand to her. She accepted it carefully.

Angelina leaned on Jed's strong shoulder. How she wished she loved him differently! He would make a wonderful husband for Sarah and father for their children, if she ever realized it. He was handsome and strong yet sensitive and tender as well.

"You're really special, Jed, like the older brother I always wanted," she whispered tenderly.

"Big brothers take care of their sisters," said Jedadiah, "but you seemed to handle Jon all by yourself this morning."

Angelina blushed at the remembrance of the morning's fight with Jonathan. "I still need to apologize for the way I treated him this morning."

"Looked like you did an adequate job during lunch. I never saw such an invigorated worker as Jon this afternoon." Jedadiah turned serious. "Be careful of Edward, though. Don't be alone with him, okay?"

A chill went down Angelina's spine. That information she already knew. The fair was only part of the reason, though. She was afraid to guess at the rest.

"Jed, why are you keeping Angie from the party?" jibed Joshua. "After that delicious lunch, she deserves to dance 'til dawn."

Angelina smiled warmly at them both and took an arm from each man. Like bookends, she thought to herself with a chuckle.

As they entered the barn, she caught Jonathan's eye as he whirled Alice around on the dos-i-do. Her heart sank at Alice's triumphant sneer. Near them, Sarah and Edward danced together. Jed sulked at Sarah's dancing partner.

"Jed, Josh, I'd like to sit for a spell. Would that be okay?"

Jed looked worried as he led her to a chair in the corner. Joshua kissed her hand flamboyantly, winked at his twin, and whisked Sarah away from Edward on the dance floor.

"Are you all right, Angie?" Jed inquired worriedly.

"I'm fine, Jed. It's just been a long day."

Jedadiah followed her line of vision to Alice in Jonathan's arms. After kissing Angelina's cheek, he strode purposely across the dance floor. To Angelina's surprise and delight, Jedadiah cut in on Jonathan and Alice. On his first turn, he winked back at her conspiratorially while she laughed.

"Alone at last," whispered Jonathan seriously when he found his way to Angelina's corner. "Can we dance now that Jed has freed me from the spider's clutches?"

Angelina giggled, remembering the same vision she'd had only a few days ago. *Perhaps Alice can't win after all*, she mused.

They took up a slow waltz as the music slowed for an intimate dance. Jonathan held Angelina in his arms carefully, as though holding a porcelain doll. She closed her eyes as his strong arms gracefully propelled her across the dance floor.

"I tried to apologize this morning for what I said in the pulpit Sunday morning. I was unkind and certainly not inspired by the Lord. I'm afraid I was influenced by a different source."

"Alice," Angelina stated.

"No," he replied, annoyed and blushing again. *Why did he blush every time he was near this woman? Surely his professional training should keep him from blustering like a fool! Surely the Lord could help him keep himself under control!* "Edward. I'm afraid Edward was the one who reminded me about your mother's professional concerns."

"How would Edward know except by Alice?" asked Angelina. Her eyes reflected her sudden fright. *Could Edward really be the missing face in my dream?*

"Edward went to Boston a little over a year ago with the pastor search committee to interview me for this pastorate. Apparently he found out about your mother then."

Jonathan cleared his throat, wondering how Edward had found out about Boston's famous bordello so quickly and intimately.

Then he added, "After all, all the Harvard men know of Miss Mercy's establishment. Even the divinity school is not untouched by the world. I'd even heard about Madalaine's beautiful black-haired daughter with the rings of gold in her ears. I'd just never realized it could be you until Edward pointed it out. After what you told me this afternoon, I'm concerned about you and Edward. Could he be the face in your dream?"

"I don't know, Jonathan," answered Angelina hesitantly.

"Don't be afraid. I'll do my best to protect you from Edward, if necessary," he said. "Angelina, remove your earrings and put the past aside. Then we can continue courting publicly."

"Why do I need to remove the earrings, Jonathan?"

"Edward was right about one thing," he began. "It wouldn't be right for the pastor of St. Joe Church to wed a prostitute's daughter. The earrings merely announce your past."

"You're saying that if I get rid of my earrings you can forget that my mother is a madame in a bordello? That somehow we can fool the world into believing a lie?" Her voice trembled as it rose. "My mother has not been a prostitute since my conception. She's a broker and protector for others who work in the business. No doubt that it's wrong. But at least she doesn't try to live a lie!"

Her voice had reached a crescendo just as the music stopped on the dance. The barn resounded from the slap of her hand on his cheek. All eyes watched her blue eyes flash in anger, the gold earrings sparkle in the lamp light, and the brilliant whirl of color as she stormed from the barn into the night, alone.

Jonathan stood stunned, with one hand on his stinging cheek. The weight he felt on his chest threatened to crush his pounding heart.

# THE NIGHTMARE RETURNS

"Thanks, Brother," Alice said victoriously. "They'll never patch that one up."

"Well, the rest is up to you, sis," he replied. His smile was cold as he pointed out the red-faced pastor. "Console the heartbroken lover," he hissed. "Angelina is mine."

Edward and Alice watched from the barn entrance as Jedadiah and Sarah followed Angelina into the black night. Jedadiah lifted Angelina into his arms and placed her sobbing form into the Johnson wagon. Sarah climbed up next to her and placed her arm around her as the wagon headed off to town.

The Johnson wagon pulled up in back of a dark Crabtree's. Jedadiah fumbled with the key Angelina had handed him and helped Sarah bring the distraught woman into her one-room home.

"Angie," he inquired cautiously. "How can I help you? What did he say? What did he do? Should I call him out?"

"No," she murmured. "I just need to sleep. I'm so tired." A sob escaped from her hurting chest. "I just really want to be alone now."

Jedadiah took both her hands.

"Don't forget I'm your friend. I'll do whatever you need. Let me knock some sense into my best friend. I think he's lost his mind to treat you this way."

Angelina shook her head.

"No, Jed. It's between him and me. You can't make him love me just the way I am."

"But, Angelina, I know he loves you. If only ... "

She put her finger to his lips and shook her head. Jedadiah's shoulders slumped in frustration.

Sarah helped Angelina to the bed as Jedadiah returned to the wagon.

"I'll be out in just a few minutes, Jed," Sarah called as he left. "What can I do, Angie?"

"Just go back to the dance with Jedadiah," she replied tiredly. "And don't be alone with Edward. Stay with Jedadiah. He's a good man, Sarah, and he loves you so much. If not Jed, look for someone else."

"I'm afraid to leave you alone, Angie," replied Sarah.

"I'll be fine, Sarah. What else could possibly happen today?"

Sarah helped her off with her blue silk clothing and helped her on with her cotton gown.

"Bolt the door after I go," Sarah said as she closed the door behind her.

Angelina never heard Sarah's last words. In her small bed, she drifted into sleep on top of the covers.

The dream returned, unbidden as always. In the dark of the night, the door creaked open. She heard the footsteps on the wooden floor. She opened her eyes and the faceless man had a face. To her horror, the face was Edward Bardsley! Screaming, she struggled from the reaches of sleep to consciousness to erase the rest of the replay. Even in the depths of unconsciousness, she now remembered that night clearly. Edward was the one who had nearly raped her in her mother's home. What seemed impossible before was clearly the truth.

Her eyes flew open. She still felt the hands on her shoulders.

"Ah, Angelina, you're awake." It was the deep voice from her dream.

She struggled to wake the rest of the way by attempting to sit up, but strong arms restrained her.

"Don't struggle so, princess. I've waited a year and a half for tonight."

Edward's face was clear to her now. *This nightmare is reality*, Angelina realized with horror. *Everyone else is at the Greenes', including Jonathan and Jedadiah.*

"Edward! Unhand me!" she proclaimed. Her voice sounded braver than she felt.

"You act like some virgin princess, but I know who you are." His voice trembled with anger. "You're just like your mother, a slut just like her."

"Not true, Edward, and you know it."

"They wouldn't let me have you in Boston, acting like you were special, not to be soiled. I sought you out anyway. Then I found you; they still wouldn't let me have you. I'm Edward Bardsley. I get whatever I want, Angelina. And I want you."

Angelina struggled to free her legs as he tried to pull her gown up. When the gown went past her knees, she bent them and pulled them straight up into him. As he shrieked in pain, she jumped from the bed and ran for the inner door of Crabtree's. As she struggled with the bolt, he grabbed her hair and pulled her back to him. His face contorted in anger and pain.

"I know the truth," he breathed, "God brought you all the way to St. Joe from Boston to be my own pet, my mistress. Submit, woman."

At this, he grabbed the front of her nightgown and tore it as she broke from his grasp again.

"You're insane, Edward!" she shouted, hoping someone would hear her. *Where are you, Jonathan?* she thought ruefully. *Maybe you're right. I've brought this on myself.*

"Am I?" Edward produced the double-barreled derringer from his handsome waistcoat. "I have wanted you for a year and a half, and I will have you, Angelina."

"Kill me if you like." Angelina leaned against the alley door, holding her gown up to cover her heaving chest. "I'll never prostitute myself. I'd rather die than have you violate my virginity."

"Don't be a fool, Angelina," spat Edward. "You can live very well as my mistress. Jonathan will never want you now. No one else can have you either if I can't. Don't make me kill you."

Angelina heard the wagons on the stones in the alley as she leaned against the door, but she dared not take her eyes off Edward. She heard the voices of Sarah, Jedadiah, and Sheriff Jones outside the door. She felt rather than heard the sharp raps on the door. She reached for the bolt behind her and found it already unlocked.

"Angie! Are you all right?" Sarah called from the other side of the door. "Angelina?"

"Don't move, Angelina. Don't scream, or you are a dead virgin," cautioned Edward.

In a flash, Angelina dived for the floor to free the door. The derringer went off as the door flew open. The cartridge grazed Angelina's arm as she rolled under the bed away from the shot.

"Hands over your head, Edward. I've a six-shooter aimed at your head, sir." The voice belonged to Sheriff Jones. "Drop the gun, son."

Edward aimed the second shot at the sheriff. Before he could get off the shot, Sheriff Jones fired.

Sarah rushed to the side of the bed as the derringer hit the floor.

"Angie, are you all right?" Sarah saw the blood on the floor before she saw Angelina under the bed. "Jed! Come quickly! Angie's hurt."

Under the bed Angelina wept and held her arm as the blood streamed onto the floor. She saw lights and Jedadiah's boots as he rushed to the side of the bed.

"Angie, trust me to pull you out safely" were the last words she heard as she passed out under the bed.

Jedadiah could only guess what had occurred in this room. His anger burned against Edward and Alice, who had obviously plotted the whole thing.

Angelina roused as Jedadiah and Sarah gently pulled her from her safety spot. As she stood, the front of her gown gaped open. With a cry, Sarah grabbed the quilt from the bed and wrapped her friend in it and held her tightly. Blood stained the quilt. Jedadiah stroked Angelina's long hair and held both ladies tightly as they cried. Mrs. Jones hurried to get the doctor to bandage Angelina's arm.

Men finally hauled away Edward's lifeless form.

"Angelina, Edward is dead. Tell me what happened." Sheriff Jones gently pried the threesome apart and settled Angelina in the rocking chair in the corner. Sarah found Angelina's robe in the wardrobe and wrapped her in it.

Angelina told the events of the night, as well as the night one and a half years ago. The Crabtrees pulled up to the store and heard the story at the same time as Sheriff Jones and the *Gazette* reporter.

Doc Smith treated her wound and prescribed rest and a sedative. Sarah took her back to the Joneses' home to sleep, away from the bloodied room.

Mr. Crabtree unlocked the door at nine the next morning to find Jonathan on the porch.

"Good morning, Mr. Crabtree. I've come for my *Gazette*."

"Pastor, you should ask Richard, the newsboy, to hand deliver one to the parsonage. It'd save you walking down here every morning."

"It doesn't hurt me to walk. And it gives me a chance to check on Angelina."

"Well, the *Gazette*'s not arrived yet today. I suspect it'll be late since a late-breaking story will no doubt be on the front page."

Mr. Crabtree looked at Jonathan hard.

"Where's Angelina this morning?" Jonathan inquired. "Surely she's up by now."

"Surely you know what happened here last night," Mr. Crabtree accused. "You don't have a clue, do you?"

Jonathan unconsciously rubbed the raw cut on his chin from his shaving that morning. "What happened?"

"She's in bed at the Joneses' like the doctor ordered."

"*Gazette*'s here!" called the newsboy as Jonathan opened his mouth to ask why Angelina had seen a doctor last night and why she was at the Joneses'.

Mr. Crabtree paid the boy and unwrapped the bundle. "Here, read about it yourself."

### EDWARD BARDSLEY KILLED DURING ASSAULT
#### Miss Mercy Shot In Attempted Rape

As Jonathan scanned the account, his worst fears came true.

*Edward was the faceless man*, he realized in horror. "Is she all right, Mr. Crabtree?" he asked with concern.

"I'm going to be fine, Jonathan."

All eyes turned in Angelina's direction as she entered the store. Her dress was impeccable and her hair gleaming. Except for the bandage protruding under her sleeve and the dark circles under her eyes, she looked no different from the night before. The earrings caught the sunlight streaming through the window.

"Angel," Jonathan spoke softly, for fear she'd disappear from his sight like a flesh and blood apparition. He took her carefully in his arms and held her. "I feel like this is my fault, somehow."

"Ridiculous. Last night, you said it was my fault," she answered stiffly. She wriggled free from his embrace.

"That's ridiculous too, and you know it. You had no control over Edward's sick mind," affirmed Mrs. C. "Just get that thought out of your head. Why don't you and Jonathan take a picnic lunch to the bluffs and patch up your differences? You can avoid the curiosity seekers today. It'll be bad enough in church tomorrow."

Angelina eyed Jonathan cautiously.

"Give me another chance, Angelina," Jonathan pleaded.

Angelina looked to Mrs. C. for advice. Mrs. C. smiled and nodded.

"Okay." Angelina nodded and smiled a weak smile.

As they prepared to leave, Philip Taylor burst through the door.

"Pastor, you've got to come to the ranch with the doctor. Mary and the kids have measles. Stephen's real bad. I don't know what else to do."

"Phil, come into the street."

Angelina propelled the distraught man into the street with Jonathan trailing behind. "You must be careful, or you'll infect the entire town. Jonathan, have you had measles?"

"No, Angelina, but I must go to their aid."

"Poppycock," she said softly. "You cannot afford to be infected with measles. The church depends on its pastor. Besides, Kate Bardsley will need you today to console her over Edward's death."

She shuddered at the remembrance of last night's events. Turning to Philip Taylor, she spoke in reassuring tones. "I'll come with the doctor. I can nurse your little ones and take care of the house for Mary while she's sick. I've already had measles."

Doc Smith heard her announcement.

"Young lady, you are supposed to be in bed this morning. I'll have no more talk of nursing anyone with measles. She's right, Pastor. You shouldn't take the chance, either."

"I'm going anyway, Doc," Jonathan said firmly. "It's my calling, and the Lord will protect me if it's in his providence to do so. I'll see Kate and the rest of the Bardsleys this evening."

"But Doc," Angelina pleaded, "I really need to get away for a while. Physical labor will help me forget last night. And there's no risk that I'll get the disease."

Doc Smith thought for a moment. "Phil's gonna need help if what I just heard is true."

Angelina retired to her room to pack her traveling bag with essentials for a week's stay. Mr. Crabtree grudgingly approved her leave for as long as necessary. Angelina, Jonathan, and Doc Smith left with Phil Taylor for the Taylor's ranch in northwest Missouri.

# MEASLES

The Taylor wagon lurched and jerked along the dirt path across the Missouri plain.

Angelina and Jonathan rode with Phil, while Doc Smith followed in his buggy. Silence punctuated the angry words that hung between them. Angelina's gunshot wound ached less than her heart. Jonathan searched for words to describe his horror and his feelings that somehow he could have prevented it. He was glad for the delay in seeing the Bardsleys. He wondered how he could effectively minister to the Bardsleys' grief over Edward, given the situation of his death. He trusted that God would find a way to help the Taylors and give him words to say to console the bereaved later when he returned to town.

The wagon pulled into the fencing of the ranch. The small house sat in the middle of a large tract of land. Fences held back cattle and horses in one field. Another field grew hay to feed the livestock during the cold Missouri winter.

What the foursome discovered inside the Taylor house was chaos. In the main room, each of the five children were in various stages of the measles. Pallets lay against the walls for each child. Mary languished in the bed in the big bedroom.

The oldest, Ethan, seemed nearest recovery. He cradled the youngest, Stephen, in his arms. Stephen's arms were listless. His eyes were glassy and droopy. His baby body radiated heat from his high fever. Angry red splotches splashed over his dry skin. His congested cough interrupted his mournful cries.

Angelina gently lifted the baby from Ethan's lap. She cradled him and sang softly in his ear.

When his eyes closed, she whispered, "Ethan, draw cool water from the spring and bring it back here immediately."

Ethan ran from the house with a bucket, relieved at the arrival of a sensible adult.

Angelina held the baby while Doc Smith examined him. Phil looked on anxiously.

"Pneumonia," the doctor finally said. "It's really bad, Phil. He may not have much longer."

Phil crumpled as Jonathan caught him on his way to the floor. Ethan returned with the water. Angelina sponged the tiny body as she rocked him and sang him a lullaby. Her earrings rocked in time to her song.

Doc Smith examined the other children as Phil and Jonathan broke the news of Stephen's condition to Mary.

"No!" Mary cried out, coughing. "Not my baby! I want my baby!"

Angelina quickly brought the child to his distressed mother. Jonathan and Doc Smith attended to Stephen, Phil, and Mary.

Angelina set to work in the main room. As Angelina rolled up her sleeves and wrapped a towel around her waist, she noticed Ethan watching her with round eyes.

"Aren't you the preacher's girlfriend?" he finally asked.

Angelina twisted the silver ring on her finger.

"I guess so, Ethan."

"You gonna marry him?" he asked.

"If he wants me," she answered. "I'm Angelina. How old are you, Ethan?"

"Nine next month. Is Stephen gonna die?"

"I don't know, Ethan. Can you help me gather all these dirty dishes and clothes into piles so we can clean up this place?"

"Yes, ma'am, Angelina. That's a strange name. It sounds like an angel's name."

"Some people call me that. Others call me Angie. Which do you prefer?"

"Angie sounds okay to me. You talk different. Like the pastor. Are you from Boston, like him?"

Angelina smiled. "Yes, Ethan. You're really smart."

They worked side by side while the three other children slept restlessly. Ethan fetched more water from the spring, which Angelina boiled for dishwater. She washed while Ethan dried. Ethan asked question after question concerning Boston, the sea, ships, trains, and the pastor.

With the dishes clean, Angelina began preparing food for lunch from the meager supplies in the cupboard. Ethan ran to the spring house to find butter and cheese. From the smokehouse, he also brought some bacon.

The smell of sizzling bacon awakened a golden-haired girl in one corner.

"Ethan, is an angel helping clean our house? Is that bacon I smell?" asked the sleepy child. "I never saw a black-haired angel with gold earrings before."

Angelina brought cool water over to the wakened child's pallet.

"What's your name, sweetheart?" she asked.

"Amy," she replied. "Are you an angel?"

Angelina laughed. "My name is Angelina. No, I'm not an angel, Amy. How are you feeling?"

"A little better. Where's my mommy?"

"She's resting in the bed, Amy. How old are you?"

"Six. How old are you?"

"Eighteen."

Angelina washed the golden-haired girl's face and arms. She removed the sleep shirt and washed her. Ethan found fresh clothes to slip over her clean body.

"Amy, I think you're nearly over the measles. Your spots are all gone, and you seem to feel better."

"Can I go out and play now?"

"Soon, Amy. Would you like to help me with the other children?"

"Yes, Angel."

Amy and Ethan named the other children for her. The four-year-old was Joel. He still seemed feverish but eager to move around. The two-year-old was Ellen. Ellen cried and whined and rubbed at the angry red splotches to make them go away. Together they washed and cleaned the children and found fresh clothes for them all.

Jonathan watched these proceedings from the bedroom doorway. He smiled at the way she took command of the situation and loved on the four children in her responsibility.

*She'd make a great mother for someone's children*, he thought. *Will they be my children?*

"Pastor, Mary and Phil will need you soon," Doc Smith whispered into his ear.

Phil comforted his wife as the doctor tended to little Stephen. Jonathan went back into the sickroom to comfort the grief-stricken parents.

Angelina served the four children a lunch of bacon, cheese, and tomato on bread at the wooden plank table. She prepared a tray for the adults in the bedroom as well. When the children had finished eating, she washed their dirty dishes and faces.

Angelina led the four children out into the yard to wash clothes at the stream. Joel and Ellen mostly splashed water on everyone else while Angelina, Amy, and Ethan attempted to wash and hang the clothes.

Angelina's dress clung to her curves, sodden with soapy water. Her hair curled loose from her braid and dripped water from the drenching the four children gave her. Angelina removed her bandage, now soaked, exposing the raw wound. Jonathan caught a face full of spray as he walked to the stream to speak to Angelina as she splashed Ellen back.

"I'm sorry." She laughed. "You're not as wet as I am, but I'm also not very sorry, either."

Jonathan smiled his lop-sided grin.

*She is like a child*, he thought. *Pure, holy, innocent. A very beautiful, grown-up child.*

"Angelina, may I speak with you?"

"I bet he's gonna kiss her since she's his girlfriend," called Ethan from the stream. "Ooh, yuck!"

The smaller children made faces.

Angelina made a face back at them and laughed with them. Jonathan led her away to a spot close enough to observe the children at play in the soapy water at the creek yet far enough away to be private.

"What is it ... Pastor?" she asked hesitantly.

"Please call me Jonathan. When you call me 'pastor,' I know you're mad at me. You probably have every right to be mad. Please set that aside for now."

He paused, seeking her approval. She nodded.

"Stephen's passed on to be with the Lord, Angel. Mary needs help dressing the baby for burial. Phil and I will dig the grave and hammer together a simple coffin. Doc's going to check the others more closely and prepare them for the service."

Tears streamed down her face as she nodded her assent. Jonathan flicked a soap bubble from her hair.

Angelina felt a tug on her wet skirt.

"Angel?" a small voice petitioned. The golden-haired Amy looked up into her face. "Is Stephen dead?"

Angelina knelt swiftly to Amy's tearful face and hugged her tightly. Together they wept. Jonathan helped her up with the child in her arms. The other children ran to her side and clung to her as they cried.

---

"Lord, bless this family who lack this little one today. Thank you, Lord, for allowing Stephen to live among us these six months. Thank you for the joy he gave his mother and father, brothers and sisters. Comfort them in his passing, Lord. Give us the strength to remember that you gave us life and you take us on to life with you. Amen."

Jonathan closed the Bible, picked up a handful of dirt, and tossed it into the newly dug grave. It thudded on the hastily made wood box in the bottom that held its precious load. Mary sobbed from the chair Phil had brought from the house so she could attend the burial. Phil held her close as he squatted beside her. The children cried and clung to the dry skirt Angelina had changed into for the funeral.

As the family turned and headed back to the house with Angelina, Jonathan removed his suit coat in the afternoon August sun. He picked up the spade beside the grave and began shoveling the dirt into the hole. Tears coursed his face as he slung the dirt in anger into the hole.

"Why does death come to those we love?" he said in prayer. "God, why do we have to hurt when we love someone? Is it worth the pain, God?"

As he worked, the Taylors, Doc, and Angelina took the children back to the house. Alone with his anger, he felt empty inside. His anger mellowed to sorrow, not just for the Taylor family, but for his own loneliness.

"Lord, help me remove the bitterness I've carried for so long. You've taken my parents, my war friends, and this small child. They didn't deserve to die. I should have found a way to bring Edward to you. Then his horrible death and Angelina's fear could have been avoided. Let me give my heart to Angelina without reservation. Help me not to be alone anymore."

His aching heart didn't notice the aching in his arms and shoulders as he furiously shoveled the loose dirt into the lonely grave.

---

The late afternoon sun blazed through the tiny bedroom window. Mary mercifully slept.

"Pastor, we best be getting back if you're to aid Kate this evening. The rest of the Bardsleys will take a pound of flesh from you if you're not there soon," Doc Smith observed. "From me too, I suspect."

"You're probably right, Doc."

While the doctor gathered his equipment into his black bag, Jonathan tapped Phil awake from his nap.

"Phil, I need to go back to town now. I'm sorry I can't stay longer. Doc says the other kids are nearly well. Mary will be ill for perhaps as much as a week, but she'll recover."

Phil nodded and added, "Thanks, Reverend, for being here, for digging the grave, and burying our baby."

Phil began to weep as he shook Jonathan's hand.

"I don't have anything to repay you for your time and trouble, though."

"Don't need to, Phil. That's what the church pays me to do," assured Jonathan. *Shame that Bardsley controls those purse strings*, he thought ruefully.

Jonathan left Phil with the doctor to discuss Mary's care. Upon entering the main room, he saw Angelina comforting the four children and reading a Bible story from the big family Bible about Zacchaeus. She made a comic picture as she pantomimed the motions of the short little man climbing the sycamore tree. She pretended to look into the distance to find Jesus.

As Jesus arrived at the tree in her storytelling, she looked up to the wooden beams of the house and called out, "Zacchaeus, you come down. I want to have supper with you!"

The children laughed through their tears.

"Why would Jesus want to have supper with that old sinner?" asked Ethan with disdain.

"Perhaps," Angelina began, "because he knew that sinners need Him and His salvation even more than good people do. Sinners appreciate his gift of forgiveness even more, because they see their need for it so much more, Ethan. Remember, Ethan, Jesus loves us all and wants to save us all, no matter how bad the sin in our lives."

The light glimmered on her earrings as she bent to hear Joel's question. Jonathan felt his heart jump at her simple reply. The earrings stood for that life of sin. Could he forget and forgive that as easily?

"Do you know what happened next, Ellen?" she asked.

The other three children raised their hands and shouted, "I know!"

Angelina pointed to Joel. "Tell us, Joel."

"He fell out of the tree, and Jesus caught him. Mama never lets me climb a tree because she's afraid I'll fall out."

The children laughed, and Angelina smiled.

"You know what? Joel's right, in a way. Jesus did catch Zacchaeus," she affirmed. "When Zacchaeus came down out of the tree, Jesus went to his house for lunch—"

"Like bacon and tomato sandwiches, Angel?" interrupted Amy.

"Something like that," Angelina agreed. "And then Zacchaeus realized how sinful he was and agreed to be a new person. He decided to be the person God wanted him to be: truthful, honest, and generous."

The children clapped their hands in delight. Angelina startled to realize Jonathan stood at the bedroom door, clapping as well.

"Well done, Angelina," he said. "Can you leave your rapt audience to discuss our traveling plans?"

The children clung to her and begged her not to leave. She hugged each one hard and followed Jonathan out of the house to the front step.

"Jonathan, I can't leave these children now. Their mama is in no condition to care for them right now. Phil has enough on his hands and ..."

Jonathan held up his hands to stem the flood of words flowing from her lips.

"I think you should stay until Mary's well enough to care for the children. You're doing an exceptional job. The children love you."

"Children give their love easily, Jonathan," she answered quietly. "So do I."

The unasked question hung between them.

Jonathan broke the uncomfortable silence first.

"I need to get back to comfort the Bardsleys. Kate will need me."

"Alice and Charles will eat you alive." She frowned. "Please tell Kate for me that I'm so sorry that it all came out the way it did."

"I will. Doc will bring you back after his last visit with Mary next week."

"Fine. Take care of yourself, Jonathan. I'd hate for you to get sick too." She took his hand. "Think of me while I'm here."

The lowering sun caught her earrings as she searched his face for a sign of his feelings for her. Even Ethan saw a sign of love from him. Surely she could see it too. What she saw instead was confusion.

"Of course I'll think of you. Nearly every minute, Angel. I only wish I knew how to conclude my thoughts."

"I love you, Jonathan."

She spoke so quietly he could barely hear her.

"I'm ... not ready, Angel." He hung his head. "I'm sorry."

Doc Smith interrupted their time together as he stepped onto the porch.

"Let's go, Pastor," he said as he breezed past the two of them. "Angelina, will you stay and help out for the next week or so?"

"Of course, Doc. Tell Mr. Crabtree."

He nodded as he placed his things into the buggy and hitched the horses.

"Good-bye, Angel," Jonathan said. He tenderly kissed her lips and left in Doc Smith's buggy.

"I'll be praying for your ministry to the Bardsleys, Jonathan," she called as she waved.

Jonathan and Doc Smith arrived at the Bardsleys' by six. Townspeople gathered in each room to pay their respects to the family and repeat the scandal surrounding Edward's death. The *Gazette* story had been detailed about what had happened in Boston as well as in Crabtree's store.

Jonathan rapped at Edward's bedroom door where Kate and Charles kept vigil over the body.

"How dare you show your face here?" Charles demanded as he opened the door. "Your sleazy Yankee girlfriend caused my son's death!"

"Let the pastor in, Charles," Kate's soft voice requested. "I'm so glad you came, Pastor."

Jonathan sat beside her in the second of twin emerald velvet chairs. Charles fumed in the candlelit darkness. Jonathan took Kate's hand.

"I'm so sorry, Kate."

"How is Angelina? I heard she was hurt."

"She's nursing the Taylors' measles tonight. She asked me to give you her regrets over this unfortunate incident. She's strong, Kate. The wound will heal."

"Jonathan, Edward tried to rape and kill her. Will that wound heal so easily? I think not!" Anger tinged her sweet voice.

Kate wiped her eyes with her lace-edged handkerchief.

"If only Edward had turned out differently." She sighed.

"It was that woman who caused all this!" bellowed Bardsley from the darkened corner.

"Angelina was the victim, Charles. Edward received swift justice. For that I am thankful. I couldn't have borne the grief of justifying his actions to the world."

Charles Bardsley stormed from the room. Kate and Jonathan discussed funeral arrangements. A simple burial service would follow on Sunday afternoon.

The week went by quickly. Mary grew stronger as the week wore on. Angelina cleaned and loved children all week in their mother's absence. She told stories and washed clothes and dishes. She swept floors and fixed meals. She comforted Phil in the evenings after the children and Mary had fallen asleep. She wept after he turned in for bed at her tiredness, homesickness, and the situation with Jonathan. She was heartbroken that he was unable to tell her that he loved her too.

Doc Smith came several times during the week to check on Mary's progress. The children healed quickly. At the end of the week, Doc suggested Angelina could leave with him since Mary was nearly well.

"No, Doc. I need to stay until she's able to care for four children."

The children cheered their approval.

Angelina stayed an extra week caring for the Taylors. Doc Smith brought her home late the following Friday afternoon.

# ANGEL OF MERCY

Mrs. C. waved a tired and thinner Angelina to her room when she checked in with the Crabtrees. Angelina procured a glass of cool water, an apple, and a slice of bread and relaxed in her rocking chair. After spending two weeks at the Taylors' nursing Mary and caring for four children, it felt good to sit back and close her eyes.

A sharp knock at the alley door roused her from her dream. She picked the glass and plate up from their resting place on the floor and hurried to the door, expecting to see Jonathan.

Her visitor was Alice Bardsley instead.

"So glad you're finally back, Angelina." She bustled in, hurriedly carrying an elaborate gown. "I need help with this gown for my wedding tomorrow. I knew I could trust you with my little secret."

With that, Alice began stripping off her clothes to reveal an ill-fitting corset.

"You see the problem, don't you?"

Angelina looked in horror at Alice's misshapen body as she turned in the lamp light. Her breasts spilled over the confines of the corset. Her waist swelled at the waist-ties pulling the corset up in the front. The laces nearly burst in the back.

"Perhaps you don't understand, after all. I thought with your experience you'd know right away." Alice began unlacing her corset setting free her expanded petite body. Her breasts hung like twin pendulums. Her belly expanded with new freedom. She turned again in the light to expose the whole scenario.

"You're pregnant?" Angelina guessed reluctantly.

"Right. Jonathan's marrying me in the morning, so I need this gown fitted tonight."

Angelina's dropped glass shattered into a million pieces. She dropped into the rocking chair for support.

"Jonathan is the father?" she asked weakly.

"Of course not. Jonathan's too high and mighty to bed any woman. There's probably something wrong with him. No, I guess I said that poorly. What I planned to say was that Jonathan's marrying me to Joshua Johnson. Jonathan's merely performing the ceremony."

Alice pulled on a robe from her pile of clothing and laughed.

"Serves you right to be frightened, though. That would be the best revenge. After all, I've already lost Edward due to you. Now I've lost Jonathan forever too. Yes, Angelina, you have finally won." Alice turned serious. "I'll not lose this baby or Joshua, though. Help me fit into this gown so I don't disgrace my parents further."

Angelina slowly rose from the chair, swept the glass from the floor, and set to work squeezing Alice's swollen body into the petite ivory satin gown. Late in the night, with every seam let out and the corset as snug as possible without injury to Alice or the baby, the gown finally fit.

"Will you come to the church tomorrow for the ceremony? You know our little secret. I know you'll not spread the gossip around town. You're not that way."

"I don't think that would be appropriate, Alice," Angelina finally answered. "Of course, I would never share your secret with anyone."

Alice struggled into her other clothing and whisked away into the night.

*How confusing this whole evening has been*, Angelina puzzled. *Perhaps Jonathan and I can ...* An overwhelming desire to sleep consumed the rest of her thought.

The ringing of the church bell in the new steeple awakened her that August Saturday morning.

"So the deed is done," she said aloud from her rocking chair, where she had spent the night. "Poor Joshua! I hope he's able to handle the mess he's gotten himself into. And the dragon lady is now Jedadiah's new sister-in-law." She laughed aloud as she stretched the kinks from her long legs and back.

She dressed hurriedly. She discarded her corset since it merely hung around her thin, tall frame. She clipped the belt on her dress with a brooch, pulling her waistband tighter. The bodice drooped around her still full breasts.

*Sarah will die when she sees me*, she thought, as she gazed in the mirror on the wardrobe. *I look as if I'm the one who's been ill. At least no one can accuse me of being pregnant.*

She checked in at the store to see if she needed to work on the books. After one look at her droopy clothing and pale skin, Mrs. C. shooed her away for rest and relaxation until Monday.

Without fear of Edward's advances, Angelina walked to the bluffs with her Bible to spend time alone with the Lord. The breeze caught her hair. She laughed as the wind blew her hat away. She chased and caught it just as she got to her favorite tree. Sitting beneath it was Jonathan.

"I've missed you, Angel," he said quietly. "Are the Taylors finally well?"

"Yes," she said shyly. "Phil should be over the last of it by Monday or so, barring complications. Doc Smith brought me home yesterday afternoon."

Jonathan sniffled and wiped his nose. His breathing was uneven.

Angelina knelt beside him and touched his forehead.

"Jonathan, you're burning up! How long have you been ill?"

"It's only a summer cold, Angel. It just began yesterday. Nothing to worry about, dear." He smiled at her with glazed eyes and sneezed. "Alice told you about the wedding this morning."

"Yes, Jonathan," she replied.

Her earrings flashed the morning light as always.

Jonathan sneezed again and began to cough.

"Jonathan, you belong in bed. Do I need to fetch Jedadiah to put you there?" asked Angelina with concern.

"You're probably right. If I'm going to preach tomorrow, I'd best get some rest."

Angelina helped him up from his spot on the ground and felt his weakness as he leaned against her heavily.

*Measles,* she thought. *I knew he shouldn't have gone!*

"I know what you're thinking, Angel. It's not measles. It's just a summer cold. Either way, it'll run its course in a week."

Angelina walked him home. At the parsonage gate, he paused as though to kiss her. A sneeze interrupted the moment.

"We still have things to discuss, Angelina."

"I'll send Jedadiah to check on you later," she promised as she turned him toward his front door.

After seeing him stumble over the threshold into the parsonage, Angelina set out for the sheriff's office.

"Sarah!" she called as she entered the jail.

"'Morning, Angelina," the sheriff greeted her. "Haven't seen you in a long time. I know Sarah will be glad to see you. She's around back with Jedadiah Johnson."

Angelina walked through the back door, toward the sheriff's home. Jedadiah and Sarah sat on the bench outside the small white home, kissing. She smiled in satisfaction at the sight.

"Good afternoon, Sarah," she said.

The blush on Sarah's face welcomed her more than the timid hello she expressed. Sarah jumped up from Jedadiah's embrace and ran to hug her friend.

"Angie, what diet have you been on?" she asked, concerned. "Starvation is not in vogue. In fact, I hear some girls are eating more just to achieve this nice rounded look of mine."

Angelina shrugged and hugged her back.

Jedadiah took her in his arms after Sarah finished hugging her.

"I've been so worried about you," he said. "After … what happened … you just disappeared to the Taylors' for the last two weeks. I was afraid he had actually raped you."

At the remembrance of that night, Angelina sat down on the bench.

"No, Jedadiah. He never succeeded. I can successfully die an old maid virgin."

"Unlike Alice. " Sarah giggled.

Ignoring Sarah, Angelina addressed Jedadiah instead.

"Jed, Jonathan needs watching out for today. I can't go and care for him. I'm afraid he has measles too. Could you go and check on him? Perhaps you can get Doc Smith to go over and check him out?"

"I'd be delighted, Angie," he said. "You know I'd do anything for you. Checking on my best friend is no hardship. I'll go now so you and Sarah can catch up on the gossip."

Turning to Sarah, he said, "See you later, sweetheart."

They kissed briefly but with much emotion. Angelina giggled to see her two best friends in all the world so much in love.

The next morning dawned hot and humid as the congregation of St. Joe Church arrived. Angelina anxiously awaited Jonathan's arrival.

"Jedadiah, how is Jonathan?"

"He was really ill yesterday. He refused to let me call Doc Smith, though."

"Stubborn man," whispered Angelina. "Tell me about your a new sister-in-law."

Jedadiah laughed and related the events since her departure to the Taylors'.

Jonathan appeared moments before the time for service to begin, ragged and bleary-eyed. He struggled to the podium, directed the hymns, and began his sermon. His throat was scratchy and sore. His eyes blurred. Bouts of dizziness overwhelmed him at times. The last things he saw as he finally passed out were Angelina's gold earrings.

Angelina reached him first. Jedadiah was right behind her. Doc Smith elbowed his way through the concerned crowd.

"Measles," said the doctor as he loosened Jonathan's tie and collar to reveal the angry red rash. Many in the crowd stood back at his diagnosis. "If you've not had it, leave the building now."

Angelina, Jedadiah, Mrs. Johnson, Mrs. C., and Mrs. Bardsley remained with the doctor as the others left.

"I'll need someone to stay with him around the clock since he's got no family here," Doc began his orders. "Martha, could you take the first shift and get him in bed? Jedadiah can help move him to the parsonage. Angelina, I know you want to help, but it may not be, well, appropriate."

Angelina nodded through moist eyes

"Kate, stay with Martha. Help her make any arrangements and help her until nightfall. Sue, could you come at nightfall with Nell and watch over him?"

All nodded agreement and swung into the task of moving the semiconscious pastor to the parsonage. Angelina hung back from the crowd and twisted the silver ring on her finger. When they had gone, she fell on her knees at the front of the church and began praying for his recovery. One death was one too many claimed by the measles.

It was Nell and Jedadiah Johnson who found her there on her knees, long after putting the pastor to bed.

"Angie," Jedadiah interrupted quietly. "You need to eat. I suspect you didn't eat right during the last two weeks at the Taylors' either."

"You need to be fattened up when Jonathan is well so he's got something to squeeze in his hugs, Angelina," declared Mrs. Johnson.

At that, Angelina began to cry hot tears. Jedadiah gathered her frail frame into his arms and cradled her.

"I don't even think he wants me, Jed. He hates my earrings. Edward convinced him I'm hiding an immoral past. He can't love me because of his mother," she burst out.

"Whoa, Angelina. That man loves you regardless of what he says. That's no reason to shrivel up and starve yourself to death," encouraged Nell Johnson. "He's just confused by the likes of Edward, God save his black soul, and Alice, the immoral—"

"Mother, she's your daughter-in-law now. Watch your tongue," Jedadiah reminded her.

"Family or not, that's no reason I have to like her, after she seduced Joshua into a conception."

Jedadiah began to laugh.

"I suspect it wasn't a hardship for Joshua, Mom," he choked out.

A smile played at Mrs. Johnson's hard look until she couldn't continue to suppress it. She began to giggle at her youngest son's exploits. Angelina giggled a little too.

"Let's go to the hotel for a bite."

Jedadiah put Angelina down and offered his arm.

"Sarah's waiting outside for us, and I'm sure she's starved. We like our women plump in this family," he declared, poking his mother in a fold of fat while she laughed.

---

As they ate, Kate Bardsley rushed up to the table dressed in her mourning black.

"Angelina, you must come, appropriate or not," she said breathlessly.

"Is he worse?" Angelina asked fearfully.

"He's delirious with fever, Angelina. He's calling for you. He won't take a drop of water or soup from either Martha or me. He just keeps calling for 'Angel.'"

Angelina stood hurriedly from her meal and shook off the dizziness from emotional strain and tiredness. She and Kate hurried from the hotel restaurant toward the parsonage with Jedadiah close behind.

When they arrived at the parsonage, they could hear the ragged cries from the bedroom.

"Angel," Jonathan called feverishly. "Find Angel."

He thrashed in the bed while Mrs. C. held him down. Jedadiah took over for Mrs. C. while Angelina took his hot hand and stroked it slowly to calm him. Immediately his frantic actions ceased.

"Angel," he called to her with unseeing eyes.

"Yes, Jonathan, I'm here for you. I'll stay as long as you need me here."

He gripped her hand and fell into a deep sleep.

Jedadiah released his grip on Jonathan's strong shoulders as Jonathan relaxed. He sat down on the side of the bed.

"Are you up to caring for Jonathan too? You don't look so well yourself," he inquired.

"If Jonathan wants me here, how can I leave, Jed?" she asked him in return.

One look into Angelina's sapphire eyes told him it was so.

The older ladies took turns chaperoning Angelina's care for Jonathan. They washed him while Angelina ate or took care of her own needs. They changed his bed while Angelina slept on the parlor couch. They sat in a chair in the corner while Angelina sat beside him in the chair by the bed to read Scripture to him or to wipe his fevered brow.

At times he raved incoherently. Other times he called her name until she spoke to him and held his hand. The rest of the time he slept restlessly in the too-small bed. For five nights and four days, Angelina kept a constant vigil beside Jonathan's bed.

Just before dawn on the fifth day, Angelina fell asleep in the chair beside the bed as Kate Bardsley slept in the corner.

Jonathan stirred in the bed, unbeknownst to his exhausted nurses. As he opened his eyes, he saw the lovely young woman with hair the color of the midnight sky, asleep by his bed. Her earrings intertwined with the curling strands and reflected the first rays of the new dawn sun.

*This must be heaven*, he thought, as he wiped the crust from his dry eyes.

Never had he felt so helpless or weak in his entire life. All he remembered was that Angelina had returned from the Taylors' and that they still had not resolved the conflict between them. He stretched to relieve the aching muscles in his back and neck from spending so much time in a too-short bed. His head banged the headboard in his attempt to stretch.

Angelina awakened with a start at the clang and the cry of pain.

"Jonathan," she said softly. "Are you all right?"

"Angelina, is that really you?"

"Yes, Jonathan, I'm here. I've been here since Sunday afternoon."

Angelina pushed the tangled hair back from her face and retied the ribbon that had slipped from the curly mass during the night. She felt his sweaty forehead.

"The fever's broken, Jon. You'll be much better soon."

"I'm better just knowing you're here, my Angel of mercy."

Angelina blushed at his play on words with her name. She brought him a cool washcloth from the washstand and wiped his unshaven face. Lack of sleep showed on her thin face. Her hand trembled as she wrung the washcloth out.

"What day is this? Monday?" he asked hopefully.

"No, Jonathan. This is Friday. Perhaps Henry can come and shave you today, if you feel up to it."

She combed his damp, curling blonde hair with her long fingers. No red splotches marred his bronzed skin. His cough seemed less congested and less frequent.

Mrs. Bardsley awakened and saw that Jonathan was awake.

"Praise God, Pastor. We've all been so concerned."

Jonathan swallowed hard to wet his parched throat. "Thank you, Kate."

Angelina poured a cup of water and held it up to his dry lips. He drank it eagerly.

"When's breakfast, sweetheart?" he asked Angelina lightly. "I should wake to this many beautiful women every morning," he joked.

He tried to grin and broke open his chapped lips. He wiped the blood from his lips. His eyelids became heavy, and he fell into a peaceful, deep sleep.

When Mrs. C. arrived for her turn as chaperone, Kate informed her of the patient's progress. Angelina slept peacefully in the chair by the bed in her rumpled dress and tangled hair.

"I think it's time someone relieved this nurse of her duty and sent her home to a bed and bath," Mrs. C. decided.

With Kate and Mrs. C.'s prodding, Angelina finally agreed to leave for home to sleep.

She returned that evening. Jonathan greeted her from the bed as she entered the room.

"Seems I have a harem, Angel. You're the fourth woman to enter my bedchamber with barely a knock at the door today."

She blushed at her boldness.

"Would you prefer me to leave?"

"I should think not!" Nell Johnson exclaimed. "All he's done since I got here is complain that you weren't here."

"I thought maybe you'd given up on me when I was finally better and needing company," he explained.

"What did the doctor say, Nell?" Angelina asked, ignoring Jonathan's blustery remarks.

"He should be up and around in a day or two. No services on Sunday, though."

Angelina nodded her agreement.

"You seem very alert, Jonathan," she said. "Perhaps I should let you sleep without a guard tonight."

"I suppose that I would survive," he pouted playfully. Seriously, he added, "We still need to talk, Angelina."

"That can wait until you're well, Pastor," she replied. Angelina didn't like his serious tone, though.

Nell Johnson smiled knowingly.

Mrs. Johnson and Angelina decided Jonathan was well enough to recuperate alone, with Doc Smith visiting daily to check on his progress. Mrs. Johnson promised to send Jedadiah in the morning with breakfast and soup for lunch. Kate Bardsley and Sue Jones would arrive in the morning as well. That decided, they bade him good night.

As she closed the door behind her, Angelina saw Jonathan motion for her to return. She reopened the door and stepped into the room.

"What is it, Jonathan?"

"Thank you," he said gratefully. "No one but my mother ever cared for me the way you did. Good night."

"Good night, Jonathan," she said.

She swiftly stepped outside and closed the door. Her step was light as she hurried home to Crabtree's.

*Perhaps there's hope after all*, she thought, *and love to match the faith.*

# FAREWELL

Hours after Crabtree's closed, Angelina placed her pen down in the ledger. Only adding and balancing the columns remained. Angelina had worked all week to rectify the bookkeeping mess Ebenezer Crabtree had made during her three-week absence. Inventory went uncounted. Boxes of receipts constituted unrecorded journal entries. More boxes held cash and unentered bank receipts. Mr. Crabtree required a complete set of books for his morning departure to Kansas City. She stood and stretched to her full height, recognizing the room had darkened since she last looked up from her work. Her stomach growled in protest at lack of supper. She chose a cracker from the barrel and sliced a wedge from the wheel of cheese. Looking toward the river, she saw the sun preparing to set. She glanced back at the ledgers.

"No more for now," she said. "It's time for a break."

Pulling her dark hair loose from its constricting braid, Angelina approached the river. Loneliness and homesickness seemed to get the better of her. She'd not seen Jonathan for a week while he finished recovering. It didn't seem appropriate for her to visit him until they could discuss their differences.

*If only I could talk to Dr. Ben or Captain Michael*, she thought.

She nearly stumbled over Jonathan before she finally saw him. "Jonathan!" she said, startled. "I'm so sorry to disturb you."

He laid his Bible down on the bank and patted a place beside him. "Please don't be sorry. I'm having a very unsuccessful quiet time. I don't seem to be hearing the Lord's voice at all these days."

"How are you feeling?" she asked. Carefully she sat down next to him, being careful to keep a decent distance after such an intimate relationship of the past month. "How did you cut yourself on the chin?" she asked, pointing to the raw wound.

"Shaving. I'm still a little weak, I'm afraid," he replied. "I'm glad to see you, though. It's been lonely at the parsonage without your presence."

"Mostly you never knew I was there when I was."

"I've missed you since then as well. Thank you for caring for me when no one else could. You were my Angel of mercy," he said with a grin.

"You're welcome. "

*His grin is so hard to resist,* she thought, her heart moving into her throat. *Maybe there is hope after all.*

"Tell me, Angel," asked Jonathan carefully. "How did you come to be such a fine Christian woman when your mother was …"

"Not a fine Christian woman," finished Angelina.

"Well, yes," stammered Jonathan.

He could feel the blood creeping into his face and willed it back down. *Why was he so awkward with her? Normally he was at ease talking to people about sensitive issues. She was a different story.*

"Mama had Dr. Graves declared my godfather and legal guardian and requested that he be responsible for my religious upbringing. He taught me scripture and doctrine. He showed me the Lord Jesus Christ and invited me to accept Him as my Savior. I did, and Dr. Ben baptized me. He continued to grow me in the Lord. Dr. Ben taught me to have a daily quiet time with the Lord, to read my Bible diligently, and to pray continually. The

Holy Spirit prompts me to serve Him in all circumstances. I try always to hear His call and obey."

Angelina became quiet, thinking of the man who was her religious father.

*What a profound influence he had on my life,* she thought. *He sent me to St. Joe too. Thank you,* Lord, *for Dr. Benjamin Graves.*

"I wish all Christians were so well founded in their Christian lifestyle," commented Jonathan quietly.

One by one the stars began to twinkle in the black prairie sky. The river splashed gently against the bank. Far away, a dog howled. The cool dampness of evening settled on their skin as they sat on the bank together.

"How old are you, Jonathan?"

"Twenty-eight."

"Why haven't you married?"

"I hadn't found the woman God chose for me."

"Why not?" came the quiet answer in the black night air. "Surely many women have been interested. Alice seemed to think she was the right one."

"I didn't love her," he answered angrily. Standing up abruptly at the edge of the water, he tossed his coat over his shoulder and threw a rock into the river. "She's a gossip and sexually impure. God help Joshua contend with her. At one time, I thought she could be transformed into the right one for me, whether I loved her or not. I was wrong."

"Don't be angry," pleaded Angelina. She struggled to her feet to stand beside him. "It's not my business, really."

"It's not your fault. I just hate to be wrong." He reached down to retrieve his Bible. He rose to face her. "Why are you here? Isn't there a young man who claims you in Boston? Certainly you had many suitors. Most women marry earlier than eighteen."

"I had to get away from Boston. Mama's activities overshadowed my entire life. Mr. Martino took me in and taught me bookkeeping because he feared that his one fling at Mama's establishment had birthed me. The same with Mr. Anderson, the banker, who taught me about handling money. I could never be just me." Angelina sighed. "Apparently it doesn't matter how far you run. You can't escape who you are."

She turned to leave. Jonathan caught her hand and pulled her to him.

"I know something about running away, Angel. Remember? I'm one of the entries in the Jonah category myself. Settle the past and find what God wants for you. Then you can stop running."

He paused and caressed the back of her neck. He pulled her to his gentle kiss. He ran his fingers into her long tresses, catching a finger in a gold earring.

The mood shattered for Jonathan.

"If you'd remove your gold earrings, Angel, the past wouldn't follow you so closely. They're a constant reminder of the kind of woman your mother is," he whispered.

"Appearances again, is it?" Angelina could feel the anger rising in her.

*We're so close to love yet so far away,* she thought. *My earrings are not the one thing in our way. It's finally clear. He'll never forget Mama's past.*

Anger subsided to deep hurt.

"I suppose you thought you could love a gossip who is unfaithful, but you cannot love someone who wears gold earrings and comes from a questionable family background."

"Be fair, Angel. That's not what I said." His voice strained with emotion. "This isn't at all what I wanted to say. As God's representative, I must show His expectations to the church. And I am not marrying Alice, you'll recall. Your earrings are inconsequential to me. They keep you from being all the Lord can make you. They stand between you and God."

"I don't think so," replied Angelina. "They only stand between you and me. I need to get back to Crabtree's. I'll walk back on my own if you prefer not to be seen with me."

"Don't be like this, Angel," pleaded Jonathan. "Of course I'll walk you home."

Silence was louder than the night bird calls as they walked back to town. She placed her hand out to open the door, but Jonathan caught it in one of his own. Gold earrings caught the light as Angelina turned and faced him squarely. Her blue eyes glistened with unshed tears in the lamp glow from Crabtree's.

"Think about what I said, Angel. I really care deeply about you."

"Read the last chapter of Proverbs, then find another Alice, Jonathan," she retorted. "Find someone with money, a powerful family, and a host of lovers."

She snatched her hand back and slipped inside Crabtree's swiftly, slamming the door as she went. The bell rang furiously as she leaned against the back of the door. Part of her wished he'd just leave. The other part hoped he'd stay and change his mind.

*I hate to be wrong*, she recalled his angry words.

Sobs surprised her as the tears coursed down her face. She slid down the length of the door into a crumpled mass on the floor.

Jonathan reached out to open the door, to try to reason with her. He'd seen her cry, and he'd seen her angry. He had never seen her hurt as badly as she hurt now. He knew he had caused her hurt. His heart ached as it had never ached before, even after his parents' deaths.

He finally decided to give himself time to justify his comments to her, time to allow her to forgive him. He walked home to the parsonage.

The Reverend Jonathan Thomson awoke just before dawn, in the midst of a dream. He expected to see Angelina sleeping in the chair beside the bed.

*She's the one, Jonathan*, a voice called to him from the dream.

As the mist of the dream cleared and the night lifted, he saw only his clothes from last night dumped without care in the chair. Stretching, he clanged his head on the headboard. A strong urge to curse propelled him from the bed.

Restless and tired, he looked out the window. The sky was rosy-hued as the sun hung just below the horizon. He stumbled to the wash stand and splashed tepid water on his whiskered face. He reached into the drawer to find the pouch that held his shaving mirror. He slid the polished glass out of its pouch and felt its cool surface.

"No," he said. He replaced the treasured mirror, shoving thoughts of Dr. Graves to the back of his mind. "Things are not right. Henry will have to shave me today."

He dressed quickly and walked through his rose garden. Each remaining bloom wilted from lack of rain and the August sun.

"I need to water the roses today," he noted aloud.

Opting not to walk, he rode his horse into town.

"Here are the books and the statements you need for your trip, sir," Angelina said. She handed them up to Mr. Crabtree in the wagon seat. "And here's your credit letter from the bank. I hope you find the contract as you expect in Kansas City. I'll keep the store until Friday for you. Then I need to find other employment in a different town."

"Angelina," replied Mr. Crabtree, "you look awfully tired. Were the books that bad?"

"No, sir," she half lied. Her earrings reflected the dawn's first brilliant ray. "I took too long to finish them last night. I just need sleep and a change of scenery."

"I'm sorry to lose you," he replied gruffly. "I understand being homesick, though. I'll be back on Thursday as promised. Maybe you can help me in Kansas City."

She waved good-bye to him with Mrs. C.

"I'll be back in a couple of hours, Mrs. C.," she said.

Pulling the bonnet strings tightly around her chin to protect her fair face, she strode toward the sheriff's office.

"Morning, Angelina," said the sheriff. "Sarah, Angelina's here."

"Angie, you look dreadful!" remarked Sarah after hugging her friend.

"I need a shoulder to cry on and then some moral support for a task I need to accomplish, Sarah."

Angelina told the whole story of the previous night's encounter.

"You see how it is? I love him, but he can never see beyond my mother's past," sobbed Angelina.

"Then why remove the earrings?" Sarah felt confused and grieved.

"Maybe he's right after all." She paused. "If so, I need to be rid of them anyway. It won't make a difference to Jonathan, even if they are gone."

"You could be wrong, you know," suggested her friend.

*I hate to be wrong*, echoed Jonathan's angry words in Angelina's mind and heart.

"No, Sarah, I don't think so. Get your bonnet and let's visit your beau, Jedadiah."

Sarah and Angelina took the Joneses' wagon out to the Johnson ranch. When they arrived at the home, Jedadiah sat on the porch working on an intricate wood carving for a hope chest or another piece of fine workmanship. He was surprised to look up and find his two favorite women jumping down from the wagon.

Angelina explained her decision about the earrings to Jedadiah.

"Are you sure you want me to cut them off?" asked Jedadiah. His look was incredulous. "The wire cutters don't leave a clean cut. Normally, it doesn't matter on chicken coops and fencing. You still may not be able to remove them without tearing your earlobes. The ends will be sharp; I'd surely hate to hurt you, Angie."

"They need to be out no matter what, Jed. Please do your best."

"Yes, ma'am," he answered hesitantly.

The trio walked out to the tool shed. Jedadiah a pulled large pair of the wire cutters from his tool box. He tried to clean the cutting edge carefully before he performed the necessary cuts. A careful snip to each hoop completed the deed. Slowly she rotated the rings to the separation and her freedom from the past.

"Angie, be careful! The ends are sharp and mangled!" cried Sarah.

Jedadiah held Angelina while she wept. Sarah ran to dip a towel in cool water from the spring to staunch the blood that ran from Angelina's bare earlobes. The gold earrings, shiny yet broken, lay still and discarded in Angelina's lap.

Jonathan could not find Angelina anywhere. When he'd gone to Crabtree's for his *Gazette*, Mrs. C. said Angelina was out.

Later in the day, he returned to Crabtree's. But Mrs. C. coolly said Angelina was unavailable. He thought he'd heard a sob from the back room. When he moved to see if Angelina had returned, Mrs. C. angrily blocked the door.

"She's unavailable, Reverend," she'd repeated.

Confused and hurt, he returned to the river bank.

*Angel comes to the water to think and pray. If I'm here, I can prepare my sermon for tomorrow and chance meeting her*, he thought.

He turned to the last chapter of Proverbs and read the passage aloud:

"Who can find a virtuous woman? for her price is far above rubies. The heart of her husband doth safely trust in her, so that he shall have no need of spoil. She will do him good and not evil all the days of her life …"

He paused. *Certainly Angelina had taken good care of him in his illness.* He continued reading.

"She seeketh wool and flax, and worketh willingly with her hands. She is like the merchants' ships; she bringeth food from afar."

The multitude of sights and scents of Crabtree's filled his mind. The scent of the sea in Boston harbor and the smells of North Boston—her pasta and sauce at the barn raising—filled his nostrils. He pictured Angelina bending over the books at Crabtree's, inspecting the newly delivered fabric from Kansas City. He remembered her black hair blowing in the breeze on the *Madalaine* in Boston harbor long ago.

"She riseth also while it is night, and giveth meat to her household, and a portion to her maidens."

*Angelina selflessly took care of the Taylor family during their bout with measles. She cleaned and cooked. She bathed little children. She sat up with the sick and cried with the bereaved.*

"She considered a field, and buyeth it; with the fruit of her hands she planteth a vineyard. She girdeth her loins with strength, and strengthened her arms. She perceived that her merchandise is good; her candle goeth not out by night. She layeth her hands to the spindle, and her hands hold the distaff."

*Angelina was wise about money and resources. She was talented in handwork and quilting. She dedicated herself to her task and saw it to completion.*

"She stretched out her hand to the poor; yea, she reacheth forth her hands to the needy."

*Certainly Angel had offered herself in love to those in need. She offered more than that.* He was sure it was her money that had repaired the roof and fed the poor during the last three months.

"She is not afraid of the snow for her household are clothed in scarlet. She maketh herself coverings of tapestry; her clothing is silk and purple."

He thought of the barn dance. The blue silk blouse Angelina had worn showed her sapphire eyes to perfection. The vibrant colors of the skirt she'd worn swirled in his mind. He remembered all the women who had asked for her help in selecting just the right fabric and style to wear to that dance.

"Her husband is known in the gates, when he sitteth among the elders of the land. She maketh fine linen, and selleth it; and delivereth girdles to the merchant. Strength and honour are her clothing; and she shall rejoice in time to come. She openeth her mouth with wisdom; and in her tongue is the law of kindness. She looketh well to the ways of her household, and eateth not the bread of idleness."

*When did I fall in love with her?* he asked himself. *The day she arrived, I felt a jolt when I touched her hand.*

*No,* he recalled. *The day I lifted the Captain's young daughter onto the* Madalaine *was the day I fell in love with her.* He realized then in sudden clarity that he had looked for a dark-haired beauty with gold earrings ever since.

"Her children arise and call her blessed; her husband also, and he praiseth her. Many daughters have done virtuously, but thou excellest them all. Favour is deceitful, and beauty is vain; but a woman that feareth the Lord, she shall be praised. Give her of the fruit of her hands; and let her own works praise her in the gates."

*She is the one, Jonathan,* the voice from the dream repeated the truth in his mind.

But she never came. When the evening breeze began to blow a chilly hint of fall, he decided to return home for a long night of sleep in order to be fresh in the morning. Then he'd see her before the Sunday service began.

*I'll tell her then that I love her just as she is, even with her beautiful gold earrings,* he decided.

Entering the small country church, the beauty of the last rays of sunlight streaming in the westward windows of the sanctuary struck Jonathan. As he turned to go, he saw a glimmer on the altar. He strode quickly down the aisle to discover its source.

In the middle of the wooden offering dish lay two broken gold earrings on top of a folded sheet. The earrings fell to the floor in his haste to read the note. A delicate silver ring dropped from the folded note into his hand.

> Accept your ring back. I can no longer wear it since such a deep rift remains between us. My mother pierced my ears, but you have pierced my heart. Sell these and use the proceeds to serve God's kingdom. Christ's sacrifice was much greater. I leave for Boston on Friday. Farewell, Jonathan.
> Angelina

He stooped to retrieve the earrings, catching sight of the cross engraved on the pulpit. He fell to his knees instead of standing.

"Lord God Almighty, what have I done?"

# GOING AWAY

"No service today?"

An astounded congregation gathered on Sunday morning at First Church, St. Joe.

"Business to attend to in Kansas City," read Reverend Thomson's note on the door.

Even more astounding was the failure of Angelina to appear at the church to question the note.

"Why isn't she here too?"

"Perhaps they've eloped. " A romantic Mrs. Johnson sighed. "Though I still had hopes she'd marry Jed."

"Perhaps they've gotten in trouble," stated Alice firmly. "I said they shouldn't be allowed to live together like that while he had the measles. He can't face the congregation because she's in the 'family way.'"

Alice jutted out her growing belly for emphasis. Joshua swatted her spreading rear end.

Sarah began to sputter and fume. Jedadiah took her arm and propelled her away from the standing crowd as she protested vehemently.

"Shut up, Alice!" shouted Mrs. C. as she stepped into the sanctuary. "You know nothing of the situation between Angelina and Jonathan. I'm certain she knows nothing of Jonathan's whereabouts. Angelina is at home packing. She's leaving us Friday for Boston."

A buzz went through the congregation at this news.

"Well, there's something going on with the pastor," retorted Alice, ignoring Joshua's menacing stare. "And I'll bet Angelina has something to do with it."

After singing hymns, the curious congregation dispersed. Sarah and Jed hurried to Crabtree's to beat the crowd.

"Angie," shouted Jedadiah through the door. "Come to the ranch for lunch today before you're lunch for the vultures."

Angelina opened the door slowly. "What are you talking about?"

Sarah was the first to speak. "Jonathan's gone to Kansas City. He wasn't even there for morning service. They're saying horrible things. Alice even said you were pregnant."

Angelina opened her mouth to speak. One look at Jedadiah told her what Sarah said was true. She ran her long fingers through her dark hair, throwing it back over her shoulders, revealing her swollen, raw earlobes.

"Thank you for the luncheon invitation, Jed," she began slowly, "but I think I need to stop running now. Let them come and poke and pry and stare. They couldn't be more disappointed than I am." She wiped away a lone tear and smiled. "Will you help me pack, Sarah?"

The week passed quickly as she said good-bye to all her friends. Nearly every one of them came to Crabtree's that week. Angelina wore her slimmest skirts and blouses and yet they hung loosely on her from a month of hard work nursing others and neglecting her own needs. All returned from the store certain that Alice had been wrong. Perhaps Angelina is very ill herself, some said.

"Won't you come to the river with us today, Angie?" asked Sarah on Wednesday. "I've got a great picnic lunch. You need a break and, no offense, but a little weight would look good on you. You're positively wraith-like, even more pale than ever."

"I'm really not hungry, Sarah," replied Angelina.

"She's pining for her true love," stated Jedadiah matter-of-factly. At Sarah's look of horror, he said, "But, darling Angel, you know Sarah is the only one for me after you broke my heart."

The women began to laugh.

"Go on and picnic with your friends, Angelina," said Mrs. C. "You've only a day before you leave. I can manage just fine for the afternoon as long as you do the books this evening."

"You win," she acquiesced. "But not by the river, okay?"

---

Fifteen minutes after the threesome left, the store bell rang. A straggly bearded blond man stepped into the store.

"Mrs. C.," called the man cheerfully. "Is Angelina here?"

The voice was familiar, even though the beard was not.

"No sir," replied Mrs. C. tentatively. "Can I help you?"

He laughed at her confusion.

"It's Jonathan Thomson, ma'am. Like my beard? It's part of my new look."

Mrs. C. eyed him suspiciously.

"No, I certainly do not like it. You look like one of those outlaws, like Jesse James. What was so important that you couldn't preach on Sunday or at least tell Angelina where you were going?"

"Has Angelina left earlier?" A look of panic flashed in his blue eyes. "She said Friday. She didn't go sooner, did she?"

"No, Preacher, she's not left for good yet. But you've a lot of explaining to do to that young lady. She's hurting over whatever you did to her," chastised Mrs. C. "Alice is telling anyone who'll listen that Angelina's pregnant."

"Alice needs a muzzle." He sighed. "Mrs. C., I've been to Kansas City, like I said in the note. I've had a little trouble shaving while trying to get back before Angelina departs. Start praying she'll give me another chance. Where is she?"

"She's gone on an afternoon picnic with Jedadiah and Sarah, Preacher. You'd best shave and tidy up a bit, or she'll not have you at all."

Mrs. C. brushed the dust from his rumpled jacket. Impulsively, she hugged him close.

"I'm glad you're back. Maybe you can convince her not to leave us."

"I'm sure gonna try," he assured her.

Jonathan rode his horse back to the parsonage and the endless needs of his congregation.

*I'll catch her later this evening*, he thought.

He picked up the shaving mirror and promised it, "I know it's not fixed yet, but I'm trying to make it right. You'll see."

For the first time in a month, he looked at the man in the mirror closely. What he saw was a lonely, disheveled man, badly in need of a shave. He laughed and set about discarding his wiry blond whiskers.

Clean and neat at last, he opened the door to the parsonage to start out again for Crabtree's in the setting sun. The billowing dust in the east caught his attention as the rider came into view.

"Todd Valentine," greeted Jonathan. "What's the hurry?"

"Pastor," Todd began breathlessly. "You've got to come! Mama's dying, and she's calling for you. Doc Smith's already there. She's not going to last long. Will you come?"

Jonathan fingered the package in his pocket that he'd brought all the way from Kansas City and thought a long moment.

"Of course, I'll come," he said finally. "Let me get my horse."

L̲o̲r̲d̲, *it's in your hands*, he prayed silently. *If this is your will, let me get back in time.*

Friday dawned a crisp September morning. Jedadiah loaded Angelina's trunk, sewing machine, and hope chest onto the Johnson wagon.

"Can't I change your mind?" asked Mrs. C. "Won't you stay? Ebenezer will raise your pay, I'm sure, if that will help. He had a wonderful business trip in Kansas City. He'll need someone here if he opens a new store there. I'm no help at all with numbers."

"She's right; she's not much help," stated Mr. Crabtree gruffly. "You could stay a month longer anyhow, until the deal's settled."

"No, sir, I've made up my mind," replied Angelina as she shook his hand firmly. "Thanks for all you've given me while I've been here."

Mrs. C. wept as they embraced. "He came for you, you know. On Wednesday during your picnic. They say he's at Todd Valentine's burying old Miz Valentine. Can't you wait a little longer?" she whispered in Angelina's ear.

Angelina shook her head, for fear her voice would tremble if she spoke.

*If I don't leave now, I'll have no dignity left,* she thought.

Sarah and Sheriff Jones rode up in his wagon. Sarah jumped from the wagon. Ignoring Jedadiah's arms, she raced straight to Angelina and wept as they embraced.

"Change your mind," Sarah sobbed. "I've never had such a true and interesting friend. You can't leave now. I'll need a bridesmaid soon."

Angelina laughed through her tears. "Does Jed know this yet?"

"Shush, you'll spoil the surprise."

"I'll have to come back when he finds out, I guess."

Both ladies laughed through their tears.

Confused, Jedadiah lifted both ladies into the wagon and took the reins in hand to drive them all to the depot.

The train pulled in, late as always.

"Change your mind, Angie," Sarah cried again.

"Say you'll stay, my friend," pleaded Jedadiah.

Angelina took a hand from each into hers.

"I love you both so much, but try to understand. I can't stay like this; it hurts too badly. Go ahead and leave now. I'll be fine. Jed, thanks for transporting my things here."

Sarah could no longer speak.

"Angie, say you'll come back soon," said Jedadiah quietly.

"Of course. I'll come back whenever you need me, Jedadiah."

"We need you now," whispered Jed. "Jon needs you now."

Angelina choked back tears. "I can't do it anymore. He has to want me the way I am."

Jedadiah and Sarah both nodded and each gave her a last hug. Jedadiah walked Sarah back to the wagon, leaving Angelina alone on the platform. The arriving locomotive released a cloud of steam.

"We'll be ready to go in fifteen minutes, ma'am," the conductor said.

Angelina nodded and sat on the bench, watching the baggage man hoist her trunk onto his back.

"Set that right back down!" called a booming voice.

Angelina started at the familiar voice and saw a familiar blond head above the crowd and steam. The tall, bronzed man rushing toward her carried the biggest bouquet of roses she had ever seen.

"Forgive me, Angel," Jonathan said when he reached her. Jonathan tenderly caressed her scabbed earlobe. "I never intended to hurt you. Don't leave."

Angelina struggled to fight back the tears. "I can't stay."

"Well, I need to return your earrings. They're too precious for me to cash in for the church." Jonathan pulled a box from his pocket. "I can't accept them."

"Very well," sighed Angelina.

She opened the box and gasped at the shimmering filigreed gold band on top the velvet-cushioned lining.

"I found a talented jeweler in Kansas City ..." he started to explain.

"All aboard!" called the conductor. "Ma'am, are these things going or not?"

"Don't go, Angelina," Jonathan insisted. "Please marry me instead."

The train whistle screamed in urgency as Angelina hesitated, trying to think clearly.

"I love you, Angelina Mercy. I've loved you since the day I brought you aboard the *Madalaine*. I knew it the day you arrived the first of June. Please stay and be my wife."

"Yes," cried Angelina, embracing Jonathan. "I mean, no! Conductor! Please bring my things back!" Angelina called after the swiftly disappearing trunk.

In two strides, Jonathan overtook the baggage man and removed the trunk from his back. Hoisting the trunk onto his broad back, Jonathan brought it back where Angelina stood and deposited it at her feet. The baggage man retrieved the hope chest and sewing machine from the baggage car and set them onto the platform.

The train pulled out for Hannibal. A cloud of steam enveloped them as they kissed. People hung from the windows cheering and clapping as the train disappeared.

"I love you, Angel. My heart belongs to you, my love," Jonathan repeated above the din. "Be my wife and partner in ministry."

"Yes, Jonathan, I would like nothing better," she said.

Jonathan slipped the tiny silver ring back onto her left pinkie. He then slipped the gold band onto her right ring finger to announce their engagement until the wedding. She accepted the huge bouquet and hugged him fiercely.

---

Sharp raps drew Dr. Graves to his Cambridge front door.

"Telegraph message for Dr. Benjamin Graves," the messenger announced.

"I'm Ben Graves."

He accepted the envelope and tipped the messenger.

"Is it bad news, dear?" inquired Agatha from the hall.

"We'll see together, sweetheart."

Dr. and Mrs. Graves walked to the study, arm in arm. Dr. Graves slit the envelope open and removed the telegraph paper.

> "WEDDING OCTOBER 24 STOP HOPE YOU
> WILL OFFICIATE STOP ANSWER SOON STOP
> ANGELINA AND JONATHAN END"

"Good news, love," he said. "We're invited to a wedding in St. Joseph, Missouri."

# RESIGNATION

"I can't believe that Yankee would deliberately jeopardize his career and position to marry that ... that ... woman!" Charles shouted, as he banged on the table with his fist.

"But, dear, they're in love. This is wonderful news," Kate tried to soothe her angry husband.

"I'll not support the illegitimate daughter of a prostitute as the wife of my pastor. I'll not give a dime to the church as long as they are there."

News always spread like a prairie wildfire all over St. Joseph. The pastor's engagement was no exception. At most homes, the news was the delight of Saturday breakfast. At the Bardsleys', however, the news was met with scorn and disgust.

With trembling hands and red face, Charles lit his cigar.

"Please, Father," Alice begged. "Smoke makes me nauseous in the morning."

"Everything makes you nauseous in the morning, Alice. And we all know why, so don't feign innocence with me. That Mercy woman has more morals than you do, but at least you come from good stock," berated Charles.

"Sir, please do not browbeat my wife," Joshua said, rising angrily from the table. "Alice and I will have a beautiful child, regardless of the circumstances of its birth."

"And when will you have a home of your own so we can be rid of your poor rancher's face at my table?" he remarked snidely.

Joshua stood upright and looked his father-in-law in the face.

"I don't need your charity. I am in your home as a concession to my wife's condition and her desire to live in town. If it grieves you so to have us in your home, we will move today to the Johnson ranch, where my mother and brother will welcome us."

Joshua stormed from the room, dragging Alice from the table with him.

"Charles," began Kate, "I think you are overreacting to Joshua and Alice, as well as the pastor's choice of bride."

"That woman you so gladly defend caused the death of our only son. How do you forget that?"

"That woman was nearly raped by our only son. She is not at fault for his actions nor his death," she replied. "You are out of line, Charles."

"No one talks to me that way, Kate!" he bellowed.

"Perhaps it's high time they did," she answered calmly.

Kate rose gracefully from the table, collected the dishes from the table, and left Charles puffing his cigar in rage.

Jedadiah found Jonathan shirtless in the stable, pumping his iron cannonballs. Sweat glistened on his back as he worked his weakened muscles, forcing them to expand and contract with the weight of the balls. Jedadiah watched the grimace on Jonathan's face for a few moments before he finally spoke.

"What now, Jon? You've got your girl. You finally admit that you love her, and she adores you. The wedding is set. What's eating you today?"

Jonathan set the cannonballs down at his feet and wiped perspiration from his face. He wiped back his damp blond hair and caught his breath.

"Jedadiah, I'm getting a visit from Bardsley soon."

"Now you're clairvoyant? Love doesn't do that for me. Perhaps it's because Sarah isn't the daughter of an Italian bordello queen," Jed teased.

"I'm serious, Jed. Bardsley threatened me after the tornado concerning Angelina and his support for the church. That's why the secret courtship existed for a time. He will not be happy with our engagement."

"But, Jon, Alice is married to dear brother Josh, and Edward is dead. What possible consequence is it to Bardsley who you marry?"

"Power and money. Bardsley needs an excuse to hate me, as though being a Yankee isn't reason enough." Jonathan rose from his stool and rubbed his horse's mane. "He needs me to impress the Radical Republicans in Jeff City, but he wants me harnessed and under his control."

"What will you do? I never thought of you as someone who compromised his principles to please any man, Jon."

Jonathan winced at his friend's assessment.

"I've compromised far too many this summer already, Jed. I think I'll need to find a new church to prevent destroying the church and what's left of my principles."

"I'd hate to see you leave St. Joe, my friend," Jedadiah said as he clapped his hand on Jonathan's broad, scarred shoulder.

"I'll not give up Angelina now, no matter Bardsley's price, Jed."

Jedadiah nodded. "Do what you feel the Lord needs you to do, Jon. I'll miss you if you leave."

"And me, you," Jonathan said, as they embraced.

Sunday morning dawned clear and crisp, a typical late September morning. Worshippers gathered earlier than usual to congratulate Angelina and Jonathan and discuss the upcoming wedding. As the service drew to a close, Jonathan motioned to Angelina to come to the front.

Angelina rose from her seat, trembling with nervousness. Just one week before, she had hoped to be in or nearing Boston this Sunday morning. Just one week before, Jonathan had disappeared and abandoned services to go to Kansas City to have the filigreed band fashioned from her gold earrings. She wore the band on her right hand now until Jonathan would place it on her left on October 24. Just one month from now, they would be man and wife. It seemed an eternity from today.

Angelina stood at Jonathan's side. His blond head towered above her as he looked out over the congregation. She looked out in the crowd and saw her friends. She also saw a very red-faced and angry Charles Bardsley seated by an icy Kate Bardsley.

"Members of First Church, St. Joseph, Missouri, I have two very important announcements. The first is to remind you of our church business meeting this coming Saturday. I hope you will all be here to transact the business of the church."

"The second is of a more personal nature. I am pleased to announce my engagement to this lovely woman, Miss Angelina Mercy. We plan to be married here at the church on October 24. We hope to see you all here on that special day to celebrate our …" He paused and looked at Angelina and smiled. "To celebrate our love for one another and the beginning of our lives together."

The whoop from the back of the church came from Jedadiah. Sarah squealed in delight as the rest of the congregation clapped their approval. Bardsley stormed from the church building as his wife stood and encouraged the congregation to give the couple a standing ovation.

After the benediction, Jonathan led Angelina to the front door of the church to shake the hands of the well-wishers as they left. As delighted as Jonathan was over the congregation's response to his announcement, he knew the storm was far from over.

Later that afternoon, Jonathan read in the church's study. Charles Bardsley entered the study without knocking and slammed the study door.

"Who do you think you are?" he asked angrily. "You have divided my wife from me, killed my son, and alienated my daughter and son-in-law from my home."

"I find it hard to believe, sir, that I have accomplished all that in one day's time," replied Jonathan evenly.

He marked his place with the blue and pink velvet ribbons saved from the box supper Angelina had made him. He felt their smooth texture and prayed for the strength, God's strength, to handle this crisis appropriately and without compromise.

"You defied a direct order from me concerning Miss Mercy," Bardsley blustered.

"Sir, my private affairs are mine to direct. I'm sorry I led you to believe otherwise earlier this summer."

Jonathan leaned back in the desk chair and willed his tense muscles to relax.

"I will no longer pay for your support, as I promised you previously."

"That is your choice in the Lord's will for you, Charles. If the church cannot afford to pay me, and they feel the same way, I will find a new church. All I ask from you is that we be allowed to marry in this church house on the twenty-fourth of next month. My mentor has wired his agreement to perform said ceremony with no cost to you or the church."

"Resign, Jonathan, on Saturday."

"I will, Bardsley. The church body must approve that action, though. I will stay, however, if the LORD impresses on the majority of the congregation to reject my resignation. God will provide the cash to keep the church doors open if that is His will."

"Fine!" shouted Bardsley.

Bardsley stormed from the office, slamming the door. A book fell from the top shelf at the force of the slam. Jonathan walked over to the book and picked it up. The title of the book brought a smile to his face. The title read *Ministerial Ethics*.

Saturday morning arrived. Jonathan steered Angelina into the study as she entered for the business meeting.

"My lovely Angel, I think you should go back to Crabtree's while this meeting is in progress. I don't want you hurt by the things Bardsley is bound to say to persuade the other members to accept my resignation."

"What could he possibly say that I've not heard before, Jonathan? The only thing that hurts me is that he intends to put a blot on your record and reputation because of me."

Angelina sat down hard in the desk chair. Jonathan knelt down beside her and lifted her chin to look him squarely in the eye.

"Do you see these broad shoulders? The LORD built them through the endurance of many trials. They can support this trial too," he assured her. "I love you, Angelina. I'll not let you go due to Bardsley's selfish blustering. The LORD brought us together, and he'll keep us together."

He fingered her scabbed earlobes. A lump formed in his throat.

*If only she hadn't cut away her earrings*, he thought with regret.

"Jonathan, I will not leave this church while you are presenting your resignation. I will stand beside you here and anywhere else the Lord leads you. Don't ask me to leave. Whether I have the right to speak in the church is immaterial. I am a member of this church whether I am engaged to you or not."

Jonathan recognized the stubborn will of the woman he loved behind the brilliant sapphire eyes. He stroked her black hair. His kiss held a hint of the passion he felt for her.

"Very well, Angel. Please leave if it gets to be too hard to bear, though. I'll understand if you must."

She smiled and nodded her agreement.

"They won't let you leave, Jon. I know they won't."

"Then I'll work for free until the money to pay me is given by the Lord."

"Don't be concerned about money, sweetheart. Money is not the most important thing. Only faith, hope and love. And the greatest of these is love," she reminded him.

"That you have from me, my Angel."

They entered the crowded sanctuary. Jonathan reached in his immaculate, though frayed, suit pocket and fingered the paper in it. Angelina sat between Sarah and Jedadiah.

"Don't forget, Jedadiah," Jonathan warned quietly, "I'll not have you make the recommendation to reject my resignation. It must come from someone else. Someone else must have the Lord's courage to defy Bardsley besides you and me."

"I understand, but I don't like it one bit, Jon," answered Jedadiah tensely. "I'm sure they'll all stand behind us in a fight."

"But I don't want a fight, Jed."

Jonathan greeted members warmly as he moved down the aisle to the pulpit. From the pulpit, Jonathan counted the attendees.

*Getting a quorum is no problem today. Looks as if not one member is missing*, thought Jonathan. *Good. What they need to decide must include them all.*

His eyes caught Angelina's bright blue eyes at the back of the sanctuary.

L*ORD, how I miss those earrings*, he thought. *Could I have been wrong about them,* L*ORD?*

The meeting began at ten sharp. Jonathan, as moderator, invited Sheriff Jones to read the minutes Sue Jones had taken at the last meeting. After their approval, Mr. Harris, the banker, presented the finances. With old business conducted and completed, Jonathan opened the floor for new business.

Angelina took a deep breath as Jonathan withdrew the paper from his pocket. He ran his massive hands through his hair. Muscles strained the seams of the worn coat.

"With your permission, I will take personal privilege to present a piece of new business for your consideration."

He paused to allow anyone the opportunity to contradict his authority as moderator.

"Hearing no dissent, I take that as agreement."

He cleared his throat as he unfolded the paper. "To the members of First Church of St. Joseph, Missouri: Given the financial concerns of the church, given the pressure placed upon me to conform to man's ways rather than God's, given the threats placed upon me in light of my recent engagement, I hereby submit my resignation as your pastor. I take this action regretfully and at great emotional cost due to my compassion, and yes, love, I hold for all of you.

"This resignation will become effective as of 24 October, after my marriage to Miss Angelina Mercy in this sanctuary, unless the church chooses to reject said resignation by a considerable majority.

"In the LORD's service, The Reverend Jonathan Thomson."

Silence greeted his pronouncement. Jonathan looked up from the paper to a sea of stunned faces. Jedadiah jumped to his feet, twisting the brim of his Stetson.

Jonathan gave him a hard look and shook his head, nearly imperceptibly, warning Jed from his desired action. Jedadiah gritted his teeth and remained standing. The contorted Stetson brim matched the contortion of Jedadiah's face as he restrained himself.

The women looked from one to another. But what could they do? They were not allowed to speak in the church.

Each man squirmed in his seat, remembering the visits they had received from Bardsley during the week. He'd threatened to foreclose on their mortgages if they moved to reject the resignation.

"What is your pleasure?" asked Jonathan, muscles tensing.

Angelina felt the tears sliding down her cheeks as not one man, save Jedadiah, moved to reject the resignation.

"I take that as a general consensus then to accept my resignation as of 24 October. Any dissenter should speak now or forever hold his peace," Jonathan informed the members.

As he picked up the gavel to rap the end of the matter, Kate Bardsley stood.

"Reverend Thomson," she began timidly.

"Sit down, Kate. It's a disgrace for a woman to speak in the church," hissed her husband.

"No, I will not sit down. It's a disgrace for Christians to do nothing at the threats of a powerful man too, Charles!" she stated firmly. "Reverend, I'd like to speak to the matter on the floor, if you will give me permission."

"Far be it from me to silence any woman, Mrs. Bardsley," Jonathan replied. "Please speak."

"Isn't there one of you with the gumption to defy Charles Bardsley?" she asked as she scanned the crowd of bowed male heads.

Jedadiah slung the Stetson into the aisle in his frustration.

"Jed, I'm sure Jonathan has tied your tongue," she acknowledged.

Josh returned Jed's Stetson. Brother looked at brother with a hard look. Josh looked away first in shame. Still no one spoke.

"Very well, Reverend," Kate decided. "I move to reject your resignation and to support you and Angelina in any way imaginable, financially or otherwise."

Jedadiah yelled, "Second!" startling Angelina, who sat beside him.

Jonathan kept his poker face, revealing no emotion.

"The motion on the floor has been brought by a member of our congregation and seconded to reject my resignation as pastor and to financially support and encourage me and my future wife as your ministers. Those who agree with the motion and pledge that support, please stand."

Angelina jumped to her feet with Sarah right behind her. Joshua stood beside his twin as they embraced. Alice, overcoming her growing belly, stood with Joshua's help. One by one each of the congregates rose from their seats.

Jonathan choked back the emotions that threatened to overcome him as he saw every attendee stand except Charles Bardsley. He recognized each member he had served over the nearly two years he served the church. Todd Valentine, Phil and Mary Taylor and their four children, Alice and Josh, Ebenezer and Martha Crabtree, Henry Miller and his wife, David and Phoebe Greene with their infant, Sheriff and Sue Jones, and so many more stood as a pledge to his ministry. Love flooded his heart as he realized he was no longer alone.

Jedadiah threw his Stetson into the air and whooped. He grabbed Angelina and whirled her around. Sarah grabbed her and hugged her tightly.

Jonathan rapped the gavel for attention.

"Please be seated," he rasped with emotion. "If you are not in favor of the motion on the floor, please stand."

Charles Bardsley stood alone. His anger and embarrassment shone red on his face. He stalked out of the church.

Jonathan fought the smile that threatened to reveal his pleasure at the courage shown by the church members. He rapped the gavel to signal the close of the matter.

"The chair rules that the resignation has been duly rejected."

At that, he tore the paper down the middle. He handed the pieces to Sue Jones for the minutes of the meeting.

"Thank you. I hope I'm deserving of your support."

The church erupted in cheers and celebration. Jedadiah pulled Jonathan from the pulpit and pushed him out to the congregation who hugged and kissed him until all began to leave.

"I assume this means the meeting adjourned?" asked Sue Jones with pen in hand.

Jonathan smiled at her and said, "I'd say so, Mrs. Jones."

Kate Bardsley tapped Jonathan on the shoulder. Jonathan turned and hugged her tightly.

"Thank you," he said. "I hope your stand doesn't cost you your marriage, Kate."

"Nonsense," she replied. "Charles will do what I ask him to do. I've just never demanded anything before. You and Angelina are worth standing up for, Jonathan. With your permission, I'll send my tailor around to take measurements for a new suit of clothes on my account. I realize the church and Charles have not paid you enough to replace your things, and you should really have at least one new suit. Make that two new suits, so you'll have a new one for the wedding too."

"That's not necessary, Kate. "

"Yes, it is necessary. It's part of supporting you, which I pledged to do just moments ago. Please give your permission for this service."

"Thank you, Kate. I'm most appreciative."

"Pastor," Ebenezer Crabtree called. "Monday morning I'm sending in an order for an extra long brass bed for the parsonage. You and Angelina will need it. Just call it a donation."

Jonathan nodded, too overwhelmed to speak. As the congregants filed out, each promised to bring by some token of their appreciation during the next week. After all had gone, he looked for Angelina in the sanctuary, but she wasn't there. When he looked in the study, he found her standing at the window, gazing out at the river below.

"Angel," he spoke gently.

She turned and smiled with tears in her eyes.

"You said if it got too hard to come here. I couldn't help but cry at the love and affection God's people gave you today. I didn't want to embarrass you."

Jonathan picked her up in his arms and hugged her gladly.

"You will never embarrass me because I know who you are, Angelina Mercy, soon-to-be Thomson."

He whirled her around until they both laughed and the room spun dizzily.

"I love you, Angel," he announced. "How about lunch? I'm starved. We're invited to the Johnsons' for fried chicken."

"Before lunch, I have something for you, Jonathan," she said shyly.

She handed him three bank books wrapped in sapphire-colored velvet ribbon. He gasped as he read the totals in each.

"I told you, darling, not to be concerned with the money," she reminded him.

"You are the anonymous contributor, aren't you?" He handed the books back to her. "I'll not take these from you, Angel. They're yours to use at your discretion."

"But as we have need—," she protested.

"Then we'll use what we need," he interrupted her. "The Lord provides all we truly need, whether by the church or other sources."

"I've offended you, haven't I?" she asked quietly.

"No, Angel." He tilted her head so he could look into her sapphire eyes. "You just always amaze me at how truly generous and loving you are."

He wrapped his arms around her and kissed her passionately. Jedadiah found them wrapped together as he entered the study. He knocked loudly on the open door.

"You two coming to lunch or not?"

# WEDDING DAY

Saturday, October 24 dawned cold and clear.

Jonathan stretched in the large bed the Crabtrees had provided. As he stretched, he thought how glad he would be to share that bed with his bride that night. With that thought, he bounded from the bed, made it with fresh sheets, and smoothed the wrinkles from the spread.

As he shaved using the prized shaving mirror, he thought of Dr. Graves and his wife, who had arrived the week before to complete the wedding details. How exhilarating to be in the presence of the man who had played surrogate father and matchmaker for him! They would arrive soon from the hotel to celebrate his wedding.

He also looked forward to being reacquainted with the man who had sheltered him as an orphan, taught him the ways of the sea, and taken him on many great adventures.

*How ironic that he is also my beautiful bride's father!* he thought. *God does work in mysterious ways!*

He dressed carefully in the newest suit of clothes Kate Bardsley had provided him. The suit was of the latest fashion. The straight cut, tight trousers actually reached his newly made leather ankle boots instead of being too short on his lengthy legs. He adjusted the new silk tie under the turn down collar of the white linen shirt. He pulled on the high-buttoned vest. The bound-edged jacket slipped on with ease. The suit fit perfectly. He looked at himself in the long mirror on the wardrobe door. He'd never owned a finer suit of clothes.

"How glad I am I can look good for my bride," he said aloud. "Thank you, Lord, for the gifts you provide. Thank you, Lord, for Angelina. Thank you for never giving up on me, even when I'm stubborn and short sighted."

The small clock on the dresser chimed. He picked up a small oak box from beside the clock and slipped it into his pocket. With thanksgiving, he remembered the congregation who had given enough over the last month to make up for Charles's lack of contribution. Regular pay made it possible to give his bride such a special gift on their wedding day.

He opened the gold pocketwatch that dangled from a fine gold chain. The inscription read, "All my love forever, Angelina." He snapped the lid closed, deposited the watch in another pocket, and clipped the chain to a loop.

*In two hours, I'll be a happily married man*, he thought with a silly grin on his face.

"Stand still, Angie," rebuked Sarah. "How can I get these combs in your hair if you keep fidgeting?"

"But Mama said she'd be here in her telegram. She said she was bringing a surprise!" exclaimed Angelina. "What if the train is late? What if she doesn't make it?"

"Don't worry!" soothed Sarah. "If your Captain Michael is with her, I'm sure she'll be here on time."

"What if Jonathan hates Mama?" worried Angelina as she pulled at her naked, scarred ear lobes. "After all, he didn't exactly take to me right away because of her past."

"Angie, I wish you'd consented to wear Mama's gown," replied Sarah, ignoring Angelina's concern.

"Sarah, she saved it for you. I'd feel wrong to wear it first. Besides Captain Michael brought this white lace blouse and silk skirt from Italy for me before I left Boston. This veil we made from the Venetian lace in my trunk is just fine. These ivory combs from Kate will be fine too."

She swirled in the beam of sunlight illuminating the tiny church ante room that served as her dressing room. The light glistened on the exquisite lace of the veil and the ivory combs in her black hair.

"Angie, you look beautiful always! But it's your wedding day!" protested Sarah. "It should be more special."

"As long as Jonathan wants me, it will be special."

Sarah sighed. "I hope I'm not this sentimental on my wedding day to Jedadiah," she said in exasperation. "No wonder the bride needs a maid of honor. She needs someone to keep her from going crazy!"

"What time is it, Sarah?" asked Angelina for the tenth time.

"I'll go check Jonathan's clock in the study, *again*!"

Angelina sighed in relief as Sarah left her alone in the room just off the foyer and the sanctuary. She opened and closed her Bible. She discovered she couldn't concentrate. She glanced out the window for a sign of Mama and perhaps even Captain Michael.

"No," she said aloud, "they're not going to make it. The train is always late. Why should today be any different?"

Dejectedly she turned and sat in the corner on the little stool provided and leaned back against the wall, upsetting the homemade veil and pulling the combs askew again. She yanked it from her hair the rest of the way and tossed it into the opposite corner.

"Lord," she prayed, "you know how I hate waiting! Let them make it soon. Let Jonathan see them as people you love and not the sinners they also are in your sight. Continue to woo them to repentance and salvation before you. And Lord, please let Jonathan and me serve you together for a very long time."

Angelina startled as she heard new voices in the foyer. Could that be the familiar mix of Italian and Bostonian accents she heard?

She raced to the door and flung it open.

"Captain Michael!" she exclaimed as she leapt into his strong waiting arms.

"Angelina, more beautiful you look than ever. But come, you must dress. Your groom is anxious no doubt as the hour approaches," he replied with a wink. "Surely he won't have to wait twenty years for his bride as I did."

"You mean …" Angelina gasped. "You and Mama finally …"

"Yes, bambina," said a womanly voice. "I finally gave up the business to be a lonely woman waiting for her captain to come home from the sea."

"Mama," Angelina whispered as she hugged them both.

"Now, now. Come and dress. An Italian bride does not wear peasant clothing," urged Captain Michael.

He presented her with a long, battered box.

"The best dressed Italian bride of a sea merchant father wears China silk with Venetian lace handmade by the best seamstresses in Florence. This gown was your grandmother de Angelo's, Angelina."

Captain Michael directed the women to the ante room to dress the bride appropriately.

"I must meet the groom once again. Eight years is a long time between meetings, Angelina," the captain said.

Angelina giggled and hugged him once more before hurrying off to change.

The knock at the study door surprised Jonathan, Jedadiah, Sarah, and Dr. Graves.

Jedadiah opened the door to admit the tall handsome black-haired man in seaman's dress uniform. Sarah gasped at the man's obvious relationship to her friend.

"You must be Captain de Angelo," she cried out.

Jonathan stood a little straighter and saluted his old friend. The captain returned his salute and stretched out his hand to shake it. After their handshake, he pulled Jonathan into a bear hug.

"So my little cabin boy has grown into a man," the captain said at last. "And whisking my daughter away from me. Jonny, you've grown up fine, and a preacher, no less."

He slapped Jonathan on the back and extended his hand to Jedadiah and Dr. Graves as Jonathan introduced them all.

"And whose young lady are you, beautiful one?" he asked as he kissed Sarah's hand.

Sarah blushed as Jedadiah moved closer to her side.

"Mine, sir," he said.

"Good choice, son," he remarked with a sea captain's authority. "Hopefully, the bride is dressed soon."

Sarah realized she'd left Angelina alone too long and hurried off to attend her.

When Sarah returned to the ante room, she gasped at the change in the bride. "Angie, what a beautiful dress!"

"Only the best for my bambina," said a voice from the corner.

Sarah whirled around to gaze into a beautiful woman's face. It was a face that every woman would want. Her eyes were dark and mysterious. Her lips were full and reddened with color. Her olive-toned complexion blushed with a natural radiance. Her black hair waved around her face and down her back. Her earlobes held fabulous gold hoops, reminiscent of the gypsies that traveled through St. Joe on occasion. On first glance, she could have been Angelina's sister. Closer inspection revealed the lines of a hard life longer than twenty years.

"I'm Sarah," she stammered. "You must be Angie's mother."

Her smile dazzled as she pulled Sarah into her arms for a motherly hug.

"I'm glad to meet my Angelina's best friend," she replied warmly. "I am Madalaine de Angelo."

At Sarah's look of confusion, she displayed a huge chunk of diamond and gold on her left hand.

"I married Michael last week. The dress is a gift from Michael to his daughter."

"Oh, Angie, here's another gift," she remembered as she presented her with a small oak jewelry box.

"How beautiful, Sarah," replied Angelina as she lifted the lid.

"Not from me …" began Sarah.

"Oh, from Captain Michael then," assumed Angelina. "Oh no, I can't accept these from him! Jonathan would be livid!"

Inside the box, nestled in folds of velvet, lay two gold hoops with clasps for her pierced ears.

"But Angie," protested Sarah at Angelina's look of horror, "they're from Jonathan!"

"That can't be!" exclaimed Angelina. "Jonathan hated my earrings. My wedding band is made from those earrings. Why would he buy me more? This must be Charles Bardsley's sick joke to ruin my wedding day!"

Her face flushed with anger and embarrassment.

*What can I do now?* she thought frantically.

"Look, there's a note in the lid," Sarah pointed out.

Carefully Angelina unfolded the single sheet and read the words penned there in Jonathan's bold strokes:

> My Angel,
> 
> I was wrong, and you were right about the earrings. I was self-righteous, arrogant, and self-centered. The Lord has straightened me out about this matter. Please accept this gift, my love. Wear them today. My Angel wears gold earrings. At least you can remove these whenever you choose to do so without injury.
> 
> All my love, Jonathan

"Angelina, are you ready?" called Dr. Benjamin Graves through the door.

"Yes, sir," answered the bride.

Madalaine turned to her daughter and handed her a handful of rice tied up in fine lace with blue and pink satin ribbons.

"This is an old Italian custom," she explained. "To bless you with fertility and strength to bear your Jonathan many children, Angelina."

Angelina blushed and hugged her mother.

Jedadiah opened the door and escorted Madalaine de Angelo to her seat of honor. On his return, he hugged Angelina tightly.

"Just remember who the best man is, Angelina," Jedadiah announced as he turned to escort Sarah down the aisle. Sarah punched him in the arm. "For Sarah, of course, for Sarah only."

Jedadiah and Sarah left Angelina with her beloved father.

Captain Michael de Angelo escorted the bride down the short aisle of First Church, St. Joe to her waiting groom. The full church stood at her entrance. Angelina's long black hair flowed under the silk and lace of her veil and spilled down the back of the silk gown. Her fair skin rivaled the lace for delicacy and beauty. Tears glistened in her bright, sapphire eyes. The sunlight that glinted through the small windows of the church flashed brightly on her new gold earrings.

"Who gives this woman to be married to this man?" bellowed the strong voice of Dr. Graves.

Captain Michael glanced to the front row, where Madalaine wept silently. Catching his glance, she smiled and nodded. Captain Michael winked back.

"Her mother and I," answered Captain Michael in his strong, accented voice.

He kissed his daughter gently and murmured, "Be happy, my little Angel. Return to the sea with me someday, my child."

"Yes, Papa," she replied through her tears.

She returned his kiss and hugged him tightly.

As she turned, she blew a kiss to her mother. She then hugged her best friend, Sarah. Next, she smiled at Dr. Graves, who winked conspiratorially. When she finally faced Jonathan, he took her trembling hands into his. He grinned his lopsided smile to assure her of his love for her.

"Reverend Jonathan Thomson, do you take this woman to be your wife, to love her forever, to always be faithful to her, holding only God above her in your affections?" asked Dr. Graves in a stern yet emotional voice.

"I do!" Jonathan replied strongly, squeezing her hands tighter.

"Don't forget she's my goddaughter, even if you're my favorite protege," Dr. Graves whispered to Jonathan. "Watch your step, son!"

Jonathan nodded solemnly

"Angelina Mercy de Angelo, do you take Jonathan to be your husband, to love him forever, to be always faithful to him, holding only God above him in your affections?"

Dr. Graves smiled at Angelina, and she smiled back.

"I do," replied Angelina as she gazed into Jonathan's eyes.

"Remember, my children, what Paul wrote in 1 Corinthians 13," Dr. Graves remarked. "'Now abideth faith, hope, and love, these three. But the greatest of these is love.' Never replace love with an imitation. Love one another, love the people you serve before God, and love the children your union will produce. When you love, Jonathan and Angelina, you show God to the world, for God is love. I now pronounce you man and wife. You may kiss your bride, Jonathan."

As they kissed, the sun reflected off her swaying gold earrings.

"I now present to you the Reverend and Mrs. Jonathan Thomson," boomed Dr. Graves.

The people of First Church, St. Joe stood and applauded. Then they filed out into the bright, cool sunlight to congratulate the bride and groom.

# BIBLIOGRAPHY

Akehurst, Richard. *Antique Weapons for Pleasure and Investment.* New York: Arco Publishing Company, Inc., 1969.

Workers of the Writers' Program of the Work Projects, Administration in the State of Missouri. *Missouri: A Guide to the Show-Me State.* (1941, Missouri State Highway Department) New York: Hastings House, Publishers, Inc., 1954.

Ault, Phil *"All Aboard!": The Story of Passenger Trains in America.* New York: Dodd, Mead, and Co.,1976.

Dary, David. *True Tales Of the Old-time Plains.* New York: Crown Publishers, 1979.

Nagel, Paul C. *Missouri: A History.* New York: W.W. Norton And Co.for American Assoc. for State and Local History of Nashville, 1977.

Additional information acquired from travel brochures and *Funk and Wagnalls Encyclopedias.*